LAW OF THE GUN

Coffin eased out his Remington and scanned the outlaw's camp. Then he stepped out of the brush.

"Evenin'," he said quietly.

Swafford looked like he would jump right out of his skin. "You!" he hissed angrily.

Coffin's instincts told him to put a bullet into Swafford right now. But his head told him the duties of a United States marshal did not include killing people in cold blood. Especially if you wanted to get information from them.

"Who helped you break loose back at Busted Shovel?"

Swafford grinned without humor. "I ain't gonna tell you. You're gonna shoot me, go on and get it over with."

Coffin shot Swafford in the right leg.

"Holy God!" Swafford screeched in shock and surprise.

"Now," Coffin said, voice unchanged, "this leaves you with a choice. Tell me who helped you and take your chances. Keep your mouth shut and die!"

VIGILANTE COFFIN

John Legg

ZEBRA BOOKS
KENSINGTON PUBLISHING CORP.

ZEBRA BOOKS are published by

Kensington Publishing Corp.
475 Park Avenue South
New York, NY 10016

First Printing: July, 1993

Printed in the United States of America

For Ben Wiseman:
For sticking around
through thick and thin.
Thanks.

Chapter One

Joe Coffin's finger began tightening on the trigger just moments before something hard clobbered him good on the back of the head. Spots dotted the curtain of blackness that was growing swiftly before his eyes, and the saloon's sawdust floor was rising rapidly. He thought that was very strange. Then the lights went out on him.

He awoke later—how much later he was not sure. He figured it was the deluge that woke him, since it was raining to beat all hell. He was soaked through, which, with the wind, chilled him to the bone. His head thumped with a steady, almost incapacitating pounding.

He was lying facedown in the muck behind a rambunctious riverfront saloon in St. Louis, and he was more than a little amazed that he had not drowned while he was out. He pushed himself up onto his hands and knees, and hung there, rain pounding on his back, trying to control the sharp stabs of pain in his head. He managed only a little, but it allowed him to push himself around and plop his rear end into the small but growing puddle. He tried to ignore the blistering pain in his head while taking stock of his situation. It was instantly apparent that he was in poor straits.

He realized that his pistols were gone, taken by the men with whom he had been fighting in the saloon. Taking them was bad enough in and of itself, but Coffin felt their loss more keenly since he had had them for a long time. The two .44-caliber Remington cap-and-ball revolvers had come with him throughout the war, and beyond.

He still had his horse over in the livery stable, as well as the saddle and bridle. They and a single change of clothes over at the boardinghouse were pretty much all he had, though. He shifted a little and dug a hand into his pant's pocket. "Damn," he snapped as he dropped his buttocks back into the water. They had even taken the few dollars he had had in his pockets. It hadn't been much, but now that it was gone, there was none left.

"Damn, if you ain't in some pickle," he muttered. It almost brought a smile to his lips.

He rose until he was standing at his full five-foot-four. He wobbled more than a little. Though he was short, he was a stocky, powerful-looking man, with dark, almost black eyes. Despite his short stature and his young age, he was rather cocky. He had a crooked, handsome little smile when he used it, which was often enough. He was fierce, proud and strong, and cared little what others thought of him—unless they were so crude as to make fun of his height. Then he got really touchy, and was prone to taking on all comers at such times. That's how he had wound up lying in the mud with the rain trying to smash him down into the ground. He was usually clean-shaven, though he often let his dark hair get rather long and shaggy.

Right now he figured he needed to get his guns back, and then get even with the five men who had taunted him. Coffin took a step and almost fell. He managed to catch himself and then stood stock still, waiting until the newest burst of pain had simmered down. "Go easy, boy," he mumbled to himself as he prepared to try walking again. He had a little more success this time.

He hobbled along, his whole body seeming to ache,

heading for the boardinghouse. His luck these past three years had been dismal. Or worse. He wondered now, as he had numerous times during that time, where he had gone wrong. Born in a rough-and-tumble mining camp in the Sierra Nevada, he was still just a child when his mother had died, and then he was dragged around from one mining claim to another by his father, a hard-luck miner who never had hit even a small lode, let alone the mother lode. He had died when Coffin was only fourteen.

Old Jake Coffin hadn't been much of a father, but he tried to do the best he could with what he had. But once he was gone, young Joe Coffin could see no reason to linger. He headed east to find relatives he had in Pennsylvania. When he did, he learned straight off that he was not welcome. So he had gone off and joined a unit of Pennsylvania Volunteers and marched off to war.

When he was mustered out, a few months after the war ended, he had no place to go. His only family, as far as he knew, were the folks in Pennsylvania who so graciously had told him to move on two years before. He did not expect he would be any better received this time simply because he was a veteran, and a wounded one.

Not knowing where to go, he headed for Sandy Hollow, a small town where one of his army pals was from. He didn't want to sponge off the friend, but he figured Nate Greenwood would help him get a job.

He arrived in Sandy Hollow in late summer. Greenwood was glad enough to see him, and even invited Coffin to come live with his family until he could get situated. The next morning, Greenwood took Coffin to the Langfeld Brothers' Iron Works.

Old Jules Langfeld looked Coffin up and down. "You're mighty young, boy, ain't you? And kind of small."

"I didn't know you had to be tall to chuck coal into the

furnace," Coffin snapped. He was always pricklish when it came to his small stature. "And if I was old enough to fight the Rebs, I figure I'm old enough to do whatever's required here."

"Touchy little bastard, aren't you, boy?" Langfeld said without rancor.

Coffin shrugged. "Does it make any difference in working here?"

"Nope. Just commenting on the facts."

Coffin nodded. "So? Do I get a job?"

"Don't see why not," Langfeld said. "You can start in the morning. Pay's a buck and a half a day, twelve hours a day, six days a week." Langfeld looked smug, since he considered himself something of an enlightened employer, what with such high pay and short hours.

"I'll be here."

The job lasted four months. It could've lasted a lot longer, Jules Langfeld told him, if he hadn't beaten three other workers within an inch of their lives.

"Damn fools shouldn't have started something, if they didn't want to get their asses whupped," Coffin said angrily.

"Bah," Langfeld snapped. "You're nothing but a goddamn troublemaker. Go draw what pay's due you and get the hell out of my plant."

"Sorry, Nate," Coffin said when they were eating supper that night. He didn't sound very contrite.

Greenwood shrugged. He was not happy at this turn of events. He was afraid that Langfeld would somehow hold him responsible for bringing Coffin to the iron works in the first place. Still, he was not the type of man to throw a friend out. "Why'd you have to go causin' trouble just before Christmas anyway?" Greenwood asked.

Coffin shrugged. "Christmas ain't much but another day," he said sourly.

They finished their supper in silence. Coffin brooded for the short while before going to bed. He was up well before his friend. Mama Greenwood, a short, rotund, exuberant woman was surprised to see Coffin up so early.

"Some coffee, Joe?" she asked.

"Please." He sat.

Once Mama Greenwood had poured him some coffee and stuck a stack of pancakes in front of him, she asked, "So, what will you do now?"

Coffin shrugged. "Ain't rightly sure."

"We'll miss you."

Coffin looked up at her in surprise, his forkful of pancake hanging in midair. "How'd you know?" he asked.

"In four months, I've come to know you more than a little. You are a good friend to my Nate, and you don't want him to get caught in your troubles."

"Most of which I cause for myself," Coffin said regretfully. He stuck the forkful of pancake into his mouth and chewed slowly.

"That's neither here nor there. What's important is that you care for my Nate. And he for you. He wrote me many letters during the war, and many mentioned you. He would not want to ask you to leave. But I can see in your eyes, too, that because Nate is your friend, you don't want to do anything that might jeopardize his work or his life here." Mama Greenwood sat on a chair near Coffin and patted his arm. "And so, being the kind of man you are, you will leave, so that Nate does not have to make such a choice."

"I didn't realize I was bein' so obvious," Coffin said with a touch of regret.

"It's obvious only to those who are looking for it." She stood, wiping her hands absently on her apron. "You eat well. I will pack you a bag of things."

"That's not necessary."

"It's Christmas."

"I still couldn't ask you to do that, Mama Greenwood," Coffin protested.

"And, so, who is doing the asking and who is doing the telling?" she countered.

There was a certain logic to the statement, and he was not about to wrestle more meaning into it. Within half an hour, he was ready to go. With sadness, Coffin belted his two Remington pistols around his middle. Then he saddled his horse. Taking the bag of grub Mama Greenwood had given him, he pulled himself into the saddle. He looked over at Mama Greenwood, figuring he ought to say something, give a proper speech to this fine woman who had cared for him as she did her own son. But there were no words, he knew, except, "Thank you, ma'am." He said the words and rode off into the snow and cold.

It was the same way wherever he went. He would pull into a town, take whatever job he could find, and work. Within a few weeks, he would get tired of being taunted or being set on, as he saw it, and he would start a fight. Then he would either pull out of town on his own accord after being roundly pummeled, or, if victorious, he was often asked to leave town.

There was some benefit to him being in Eastern towns and cities. Such places were quite gun-shy, and would look askance at anyone other than a constable carrying a pistol. Knowing that, he would generally leave his pistols behind when he went walking around, lest he stir up trouble. He could get into enough trouble without asking for it.

That changed, though, as he followed the Ohio River west and south and began hitting some of the tougher riverfront towns. There he would openly carry his pistols since nearabout everyone else seemed to.

His touchiness had not lessened a whit, though he began meeting a rougher element. As such, he even more frequently got into fights. Once in a while, they would escalate beyond a barroom brawl into gunplay. And that, in turn, would bring a cool request to leave town right then and there.

Those short, hot, furious little battles had slowly made him realize that he was mighty handy with his six-guns. He supposed that it had something to do with his coolness under fire. He had noted that in himself—and others—during the war. He was only a little surprised at that. He was a little more startled with the knowledge that he handled the weapons so easily. It was almost scary when he thought about it. So he thought about it as little as possible.

What he could not see in himself was his arrogance and his touchiness. These were as often as not the reasons for the fights. But he was completely unaware of it, and so could not figure out why men constantly harassed him over his height. All he wanted was for people to leave him alone.

Another thing he did not notice was his continual movement westward. He just simply rode, with no direction or purpose, but always west, as if being pulled.

Coffin was, he could admit to himself, a man who had little future. He didn't have much of a past either when he thought about it. Not a real, live past like other folks had, one with kin and home places and a line of ancestors he could look back upon. His past was all blood and violence and hate; anger and spite and fear. There were no pleasant remembrances, no crooning mother at hearth side. There were no dalliances with pretty girls who would be awaiting his return.

Still, he kept on going, hoping all the while that the next place would be the one where he could put down roots, meet a young woman, maybe get married and have a few kids. That was a hoot, Coffin had thought more than once. That would require him to have some kind of job, and all he knew was hard-rock mining and soldiering. Neither appealed to him. Nor did they afford much of a future either. Not a future that would involve a wife and children, safety and ease of living. Just more blood and death and hardships.

When he came to Cincinnati, he was feeling rather gloomy, but he thought that perhaps he could find a small measure of solace. The city was plenty big enough for a small man like himself to get lost in. He wondered if that would ease his mind, at least for a time.

Then he decided it didn't matter. He shrugged, and rode on into town, gravitating as if guided toward the riverfront with its festering saloons, coarse people and overpowering stench. He thought it was a sad thing that a man would feel comfortable in such foul surroundings.

Chapter Two

Cincinnati turned out to be not such a bad place for Coffin to hang his hat, at least for a while. He took a job in a slaughterhouse. It was, he thought wryly, an apt job for a man with his limited talents and his lack of concern over the sight of blood and hacked up flesh.

He left the industrial area of the city down near the waterfront every once in a while, heading up to the more respectable parts of Cincinnati after a quick wash-up and with clean clothes, of course. It helped him accept his lot in life, as he saw it. By those visits, he could keep alive a faint, flickering ember of a dream to be a respected, even wealthy man. Of course, the dream did not take into account his lack of skills at anything that would bring him a fortune. On the other hand, there had been plenty of men back in the Sierra Nevada who had no skills, no learning, and no talent but had still gotten rich.

Though the constabulary of Cincinnati frowned on the carrying of firearms, Coffin was not about to wander through the city unarmed. He took to carrying a .36-caliber Navy Colt in a holster at the small of his back under his shirt. He had taken the Colt—and another—from a dead Confederate during the battle of High Bridge just days before the war officially ended. Moments after he had picked up the two weapons, he was hit with a bullet.

He had spent quite a while in a military hospital and then on light duty. As soon as he was able to do so, he had mustered out.

He felt a lot safer carrying the pistol, especially when he was in one of the fetid places called saloons. It was unusual that he was seldom, if ever, bothered in the saloons. It took him a few days to realize why—he almost always went to a saloon straight from work. There were few men who wanted to tangle with a man already soaked with blood and reeking of cattle entrails.

Of course, there was always some idiot who downed enough rum or cheap rotgut to think himself king of his own little world. That happened once, and Coffin had pounded the man senseless. After that, most of the men went back to leaving him alone, which suited him just fine.

By the time he had been there three months, Coffin was feeling a little more comfortable. He began spending more time up in the city rather than down on the waterfront—when he could. Working twelve to fourteen hours a day in a slaughterhouse did not leave much free time.

The work was sporadic, though, many times. Occasionally a shipment of hogs or cattle did not come through when it was expected. At such times, Coffin was told not to come in. While he got a day off, it also meant that he would not be paid for the day. Almost subconsciously he was looking for better work. He had no desire to spend the rest of his life in an abattoir, not if he was to make anything of himself.

He was unsure of himself in such pursuit, though. He somehow felt unworthy of even being in this part of town, let alone deluding himself into thinking he could one day live and work here. Then he would growl angrily at himself for having such negative thoughts. He had never had them before, and he figured he should not have them now.

So he continued to go into the better part of the city, hoping to lose the unusual self-doubt through sheer determination.

Coffin wandered up into the heart of town one sunny summer day when he had no work. He had himself a good meal—pork chops with apple, candied yams and corn, followed by peach cobbler and coffee—at Franklin's Chop House. Full and satisfied, he strolled to Gabler's Tobacco Shop and picked up cigarette fixings. Just outside Gabler's, Coffin rolled himself a smoke. He had just lit it when he heard gunshots and screams.

He stepped to the end of the sidewalk and looked up and down the street. Gunshots weren't unknown here, but Coffin felt that there was something different about this.

Moments later, five men came riding hard up the street. Several men on foot—townsmen by the look of them—ran after the fleeing horsemen, firing guns as they did. Their words finally floated to him: "The bank's been robbed!"

A young woman gasped just behind Coffin. He turned his head and hissed, "Get inside, miss. Now!"

Ashen-faced, the young woman nodded and entered the tobacco shop. It was not a proper place for a woman to be, but under the circumstances she felt justified.

Coffin calmly shoved the back of his shirt up and yanked out the Colt. He gave it a swift glance to make sure it was set. The horsemen were abreast of him as he stepped off the sidewalk and calmly fired all five shots that he kept in the six-shooter.

One man fell with a thud, and two others jerked, and Coffin knew he had hit them, too. He shoved his pistol away and ran toward the dead man. Kneeling, he grabbed the man's pistol, cocked it, and, still kneeling, swung toward the horsemen again. But they had disappeared around a corner.

Two middle-aged men stopped next to Coffin. Both

were wheezing. “Good shooting, mister,” one gasped.

Coffin shrugged. “You know this thing?” he asked, lightly kicking the corpse.

The man who had spoken shook his head. “Not for sure. But I figure he’s kin of the Toomeys.” He had almost caught his breath back, and he held out his hand. “Thanks, Mr. . . . ?”

“Joe Coffin.” He shook the hand.

“Mortimer Benchley. I’m president of The First Cincinnati Bank.”

Coffin didn’t think that called for an answer, but he was saved by the arrival of Dave Worthington, chief constable—or, as he liked to think of himself, police chief.

“What’s gone on here?” he asked officiously.

Benchley explained in a few sentences, including Coffin’s role. When he had finished, Worthington asked, “How much you lose, Mort?”

“Five thousand, give or take a few hundred, I guess. I’d have to make a count to be sure.”

Worthington nodded and rubbed his square jaw a few times. “And you shot down this here one, did you, son?” Worthington asked, looking at Coffin and tapping a boot toe on the corpse’s side.

Coffin nodded.

“What’s your name, son?” Worthington asked. When Coffin told him, the constable said, “You know it’s against the law to carry firearms here in the city, don’t you, son.” It was not really a question.

Coffin nodded, trying to put a lid on his growing anger. He didn’t like being treated like he had done something wrong. He disliked even more being called “son.”

“I’m of a mind to run you in, son.”

Coffin shrugged. “Wouldn’t be wise,” he said calmly.

Worthington glared at him. But before the police chief could say anything, Benchley said, “Mr. Coffin was a big help, Dave. I don't believe any judge'd find him at fault in this instance."

Worthington nodded. "I expect so."

Coffin looked at him, thinking that the lawman was mighty dopey for a police chief. Then he took a closer look and saw the light of genius in Worthington's eyes.

"A couple of you boys come remove this trash here," Worthington ordered. He looked at Coffin again. "I'd be obliged if you was to come with me to my office for a chat."

"You're not arresting him, are you, Dave?" Benchley asked.

Worthington shook his head. "Nope. No, sir. Just want to chat with him some."

Benchley turned to Coffin. "He does arrest you, Mr. Coffin, you get word to me. I'll pay your bail. Lawyer, too, if it comes to that." He looked at Worthington. "Don't test me on this one, Dave," he said quietly.

Worthington shrugged, unimpressed by the banker's warning. "Come on, Mr. Coffin," he said, turning and walking away.

Coffin was a little surprised that the police chief had turned his back on him. He looked at Benchley, who said, "Remember what I said." Coffin nodded and followed the sheriff, his pistol now back in the holster under his shirt.

Worthington's office was about what Coffin had expected. It was a bit more bustling than others Coffin had seen, but the beat-up furnishings and equipment could have come from any marshal's office anywhere.

"Take a seat, Mr. Coffin," Worthington said. "You want some coffee?"

"That'd be nice." Moments later Worthington handed him a tin mug. Coffin took a sip and managed to keep the grimace off his face.

He wasn't entirely successful, since Worthington asked

with a smile, "Something wrong with the coffee, Mr. Coffin?"

"Other than the fact that it tastes like it came out the back end of a mule, who'd gotten it from a sick cow, no."

Worthington laughed. "It is pretty rancid, ain't it?" he asked rhetorically.

"Mind if I smoke?" When Worthington shook his head, Coffin put his cup on the desk and pulled out his fixings. With a cigarette going, Coffin leaned back "So, what's on your mind, Constable?"

"*Chief* Constable," Worthington emphasized. He sighed. "If I were you, Mr. Coffin, I'd take leave of these parts. And damn soon."

Coffin blew out a stream of smoke and then risked another swallow of coffee. "You runnin' me out, Chief Constable?" he asked.

"Nope, no, not running you out." He, too, sipped coffee and made a face. He put the cup down and pushed it across the desk away from him.

"Then what're you sayin'?"

"That you should get out of town. You're foolish enough to stay here, that's your business."

"Why?"

"That man you killed is a notorious one—Earl Toomey."

Coffin shrugged. "That doesn't mean anything to me."

"You're not from these parts, I take it?"

Coffin shook his head. "Been here only a couple of months."

"I see." Worthington paused, leaning forward with his elbows on the desk. He looked and felt tired. "The Toomey brothers—Carl, Tice, Randall, and Warren—along with several of their cousins—are the worst renegades these places have seen since before the war."

"So?"

"So . . . they're clannish buggers, them boys, always were. They've gotten worse since the late unpleasantness."

Coffin thought he could see where this was going, but he wanted it out in the open, just to be sure. "And what's that got to do with me?"

"The Toomeys aren't the kind to forget the killing—and wounding—of kinfolk, Mr. Coffin."

"So you think they'll come back through here lookin' for me, that right?"

"Yes, Mr. Coffin, I do."

Coffin nodded. He dropped his cigarette butt on the floor and squashed it under a boot heel. "And what concern of yours is that, Chief?"

"None, really."

"Then why bother me with it? They come gunnin' for me, I can handle myself."

"I'm sure you can, Mr. Coffin," Worthington said flatly. "But can you take care of the women and children who might get caught in the crossfire? That's my concern in this matter, Mr. Coffin. Not you and your safety. Theirs."

Coffin sat frozen. No matter how angry he was at the world, no matter how poorly he might think of himself, he could not endanger women and children. Not when there was an easy way out. He finally nodded. "Hadn't thought of it that way," he admitted. "I'll be gone come mornin'." He paused. "I might need your help, though."

"How can I help?" Worthington asked. He was surprised that he had gotten no resistance from this small, hard-eyed man.

"Old Hefflemeyer might be some resistant to givin' me the eight days' pay I got comin' nearly a week early."

"I doubt there'd be some resistance," Worthington said with a small smile. "That's simply a fact. That old buzzard'd cheat his ma and pa out of a day's salary if he thought he could get away with it."

"Anything you can do to weaken his stiff back?"

"I'll talk to him this afternoon. Come on by here this evening."

Coffin nodded and stood. "Obliged, Cons . . . Chief." He headed for the door, turning back when Worthington called to him.

"I'm obliged to you, too, Mr. Coffin. Not only for killing one of those sons of bitches, and wounding a couple more. But also for being so reasonable in this matter."

Coffin nodded. "I might've done some things I ain't too proud of, Chief, but I ain't ever been responsible for the deaths of women and kids. I ain't about to start now."

He opened the door and headed out.

Chapter Three

Once he got out of Cincinnati, Coffin rode slowly. He had no place to be; no place where he wanted to be. So he took his own sweet time, trying to find some purpose in his life. He would stop in a town for a day or a week, picking up whatever kind of job he could find to raise enough of a stake to get to the next town. In none of them did he find anything to keep him, and so he would move on.

By late fall, he found himself in St. Louis. It was a big enough city for him to lose himself in for a while, so Coffin found himself a job in another meat market. The only difference between this one and the one in Cincinnati was that this one had a far larger supply of game animals, from buffalo to elk, from antelope to turkey. Coffin figured that would keep him fed and dry and warm until spring came again. Then he could be on the move. To where he did not know. He would worry about that when the time arose.

He, like most of the other men in St. Louis—and everywhere else he supposed—spent much of his non-working time in saloons. They were warm and comfortable for the most part. Coffin found a few saloons that fellow workers frequented, and he usually went there. In such places, he was pretty much left alone.

Still, it seemed he craved excitement of a time, and so he would go to other saloons. Though he didn't exactly start fights at those times, he certainly prodded men enough that it became inevitable.

In the mornings after nights on which he did so, he would sit in his room quietly, full of pain, and wonder why in hell he would do such a damn-fool thing. It was insane, and Coffin began to think that perhaps he should find himself an asylum and move in.

When the hangover—and the pain of bumps, bruises and swollen knuckles—faded, he would be his old self again for a week or so, and then the drive for excitement would push him into foolishness again.

There were other excitements, too, though with working there was little time—or money—for indulging in gambling or in visiting some of the fallen angels, of whom the town had quite a selection.

Most nights Coffin just went to a saloon and sat by himself for a few hours, trying not to think of a life that seemed to be going nowhere.

Because some of his adventures could escalate quickly into a more serious fracas—and because quite a few of the other men went about armed—Coffin began carrying his pistols openly. He felt a little more secure that way, and no one looked askance at him.

Once Christmas was behind him, though, he began to look forward to spring with somewhat renewed spirits. He still had no idea of where he wanted to go or what he wanted to do, but he did feel a resurgence of a desire to be on the move.

With such thoughts in mind, he spent less time in saloons and in other low amusements. It wasn't born of any renewal of morality; just a desire to make sure he had enough cash to supply himself reasonably well when he bid farewell to the city.

Still, that did not keep him out of saloons and bordellos entirely. He had never thought of himself as a saint. With the promise of spring, even some of his gloominess lifted. He enjoyed life a little more, took more pleasure in such daily events as eating.

As winter's grip finally eased, Coffin began making his plans to leave. He quit at the meat market after drawing his pay on a Saturday evening. He spent the night getting drunk with some of his cronies. Sunday was spent mostly in recovering from the previous night's revelry.

He planned to leave on Monday, but late Sunday a storm blew in. A wicked wind swept over the city, and being this close to winter yet, it was a bitter wind. It brought with it thunderous, heavy rains, and even some sleet and snow. Temperatures plummeted.

Standing in his room at Smith's Boardinghouse, he looked out at the storm and wisely decided that he was not in all that much of a hurry to leave St. Louis. Instead, he braved the storm long enough to get to Farrel's Tavern.

"Goddamn," he muttered when he was back inside. He slapped the water off his hat and slicker. He clapped his hat back on and then hung his rain slicker on a peg along with the two dozen or so others. He greeted several of his former work mates as he clumped to the bar, where a shot of bourbon and a mug of beer awaited him.

Several hours later, he was back at the bar after having lost twelve dollars and seventy cents over poker. As everyone else did whenever the door opened, he looked to see the new arrivals.

Something was vaguely familiar about one or two of the men, but they were bundled up against the weather. Before the last one entered, Coffin turned away and was paying them no mind. He was just taking a sip of beer when someone clapped him on the back and started tugging him around.

Coffin let himself be pulled, but his hand dropped to one of the pistols in his belt. He stared up a little at a rugged, ruddy face. It was one of the five men who had just come into the saloon. "Somethin' I can do for you, pal?" Coffin asked as politely as he could manage.

"What's your name, boy?" the man countered, his voice grating.

"Abe Lincoln," Coffin said sarcastically. "Yours?"

"Tice Toomey, you fest'rin' little snake fart. Now what's your name, goddammit all?"

"You don't get your hand off me, boy," Coffin said flatly, "I'm . . ."

"Yeah?" Toomey asked cockily, "just what the hollow hell you gonna do to me?" He smirked.

Without Toomey knowing he had done so, Coffin had slid a pistol out. He thumbed back the hammer but said nothing. He just sneered at Toomey.

Toomey's eyes narrowed, and his bulbous Adam's apple bobbled some as he swallowed. He did not look afraid, just half-crazed. He released Coffin's shoulder and with exaggerated care, brushed off Coffin's shirt. "There now, ya see, bub, ain't no call fer nastiness and harsh words, now is there?"

Toomey took a step back, as if expecting Coffin to holster his pistol. When Coffin did not do so, disappointment flickered over Toomey's face for an all-too-brief moment before he could cover it up.

"You mind tellin' me just what in hell you're doin' comin' up and layin' hands on me like that?" Coffin finally asked.

"I was thinkin' you was somebody."

"I am. Now either tell me what the hell you want with me or get your ass out and leave me in peace."

Toomey looked like he was thinking it over. While he did, Coffin sized up Toomey and his four companions.

They were a mean, filthy-looking lot in whose eyes intelligence and goodwill did not reside. They seemed to be inbred, with that anfliction's moronic, slack-jawed face. All were tall and ungainly. Two wore remnants of Confederate uniforms, and Coffin was sure the two had not had those articles of clothing off since they donned them during the war.

"Your name wouldn't be Joe sumpin', would it, bub?" Toomey finally asked

"My name ain't no concern of yours."

"Now, dammit, you're bein' a mighty unreasonable feller. All I ast was your name Joe sumpin'. That's all."

"And I told you it was none of your goddamn business." He paused. "Now why don't you take them knobheaded peckerwoods back there and get the hell out of the saloon."

"Lord all-goddamn-mighty, but if you i'nt a ball-bustin' little son of a bitch," Toomey said with a low whistle and a shake of his head. "Goddamn if you ain't."

"What I am is one annoyed little son of a bitch, and I'm fast losin' my patience with you."

Toomey looked like he wanted to chew out chunks of the bar. " 'At ain't neighborly of you, bub."

"I got no desire nor willingness to be neighborly with the likes of you. I ain't even of a mind to talk to you. So, if you'd be so kind as to get the hell out of here, I can go back to my beer."

"Well 'at ain't gonna do. No sirree, no sir. It just plumb purely won't."

Coffin shrugged.

"You ever been in Cincinnat'?" Toomey asked, as if the question had just popped into his head.

Coffin shrugged again. Talking to this oaf had done no good so far, so he figured he wouldn't say anything else. Maybe that would force Toomey and his friends to leave him alone.

"Well, me'n my boys there is to think you was. Yep siree. Was 'long about the end of last summer. Come to think on it, you was holdin' a pistol in your hands then, too." He scratched at his furry chin, his eyes heavenward, as if he had just stumbled on the fountain of youth or something equally momentous.

Coffin shrugged again. He knew damn well who this man and his fellows were and why they were here. And he was not about to be civil toward them in the slightest.

"You was thuh pukin' little shit who kilt my brother Earl there in Cincinnat'. Shot 'im right inna back."

Coffin shrugged again. He was tired of the game. There would be gunplay here sure as anything, he knew, and he just wanted to get it over with now. "That's the chances you take when you hold up a bank, now ain't it?"

"Then it *was* you," Toomey said. He seemed surprised, as if he had never thought of such a thing before. That amazed Coffin.

"Yeah, it was me."

"Why'n hell'd you hafta get involved in 'at? Huh? Jesus, bub, that was a dumb thing to do."

"Not half as stupid as robbin' a bank in a big, busy place like Cincinnati." Coffin was vaguely aware that someone had opened the saloon door, took one step inside, saw the tableau and bolted back outside again.

"Well 'at's spilt milk under the bridge," Toomey mused.

Coffin shook his head in wonder. "It is that," he said evenly. "So what're you gonna do about it?"

"Well," Toomey said with a brilliant grin, "we come here to kill your ass dead."

"Then maybe you should be gettin' to the doin' instead of trying to kill me of boredom."

"You got us makin' a disadvantage here," Toomey protested mildly. "You got your gun out already and is ready fo' action."

"I found that's a good way to keep alive."

Toomey nodded in understanding. "That's a fac'. But 'at don't change the fac' you got an advantage on us."

"I'd say things're about even."

"How's 'at?"

"There's five of you idiots and only one of me."

Toomey nodded.

To Coffin, Toomey seemed to be actually trying to think, another source of amazement to Coffin, who seemed calm as he waited. He was, however, more than a little nervous. He knew he was good with a gun, but there were five of them, and he was nowhere near certain that he could get all five before one of them plugged him good. He also was not sure how the other saloon patrons would react either. Some were men he had worked with, but most he did not know, and it was possible that they could be kin of Toomey. Or they might be sympathizers of the South in the late unpleasantness, and so would join with any like-thinking person.

Coffin finally pushed the thoughts away. There was nothing he could do about any of that. What he needed most right now was to be alert, since he was absolutely certain that Toomey and his companions were going to try something. It was just a matter of when—and how.

The saloon was devoid of talking and most other noise. The thunder and pounding rain outside blocked out whatever other small sounds there might be.

"You mind was I to talk wit' my brothers and cousins back there a minute?" Toomey finally asked. With his limited intelligence, he was at a disadvantage in almost any situation. Having the comfort of his brothers' and cousins' advice was important.

"I would," Coffin said flatly.

Something in Coffin's eyes made Toomey realize that

Coffin was not lying. "But I can't make no . . ."

"Look, Toomey, you're an asshole. I know that, you know that, your brothers and cousins know that. Hell, everybody who's ever seen you knows that." He paused. "Since that's so well-known a fact, it's time for you to do somethin'. Either pull your piece and take your chances, or drag your sorry ass out of here, and take that rabble with you."

Coffin reached behind him, found his beer with his left hand, grabbed it and brought it around. He drank a little, eyes alertly watching Toomey over the rim of the mug.

As Coffin sipped, Toomey edged backward some. He had been only a few feet from Coffin and knew he would be blasted into oblivion at that range. With even a bit more distance between him and Coffin, Toomey thought he might have a small chance.

"Now!" Toomey suddenly shouted.

Chapter Four

Coffin flipped his beer mug toward Toomey, who jumped in surprise. It kept him from drawing his pistol for a few precious moments. Coffin figured he could use those few heartbeats to concentrate on the other four.

As Toomey shifted to the side out of the way of the beer mug, Coffin noticed that two of the other four men had drawn their pistols while Toomey had been blocking Coffin's vision. He went for them first, blasting each man twice. Then he dove to his right, and rolled, coming to a stop when he crashed into a table near the door.

Coffin noted that the two men he had fired on were down and apparently out of the fight permanently. But Toomey and both other men had unlimbered their pistols.

The saloon seemed empty except for the opponents. Coffin knew that was not true, but most of the saloon's patrons had fled earlier, racing out into the storm without coats or sometimes hats.

Shoving to his feet, Coffin snatched out his other pistol with his left hand. He fired four times, feeling the comfortable buck of the old Remington in his hand.

Toomey and one of the others went down, but Coffin was not sure how badly they were hit. He leveled the revolver in his right hand at the man still standing. Coffin was about to drop the hammer when his target suddenly started and then dropped his own pistol.

Coffin was confused by that, but he figured to fire anyway. There was no telling what the enemy might be up to, and Coffin was not sure that all the men he had hit were dead. Better to drop this one, he figured, than to risk being killed through some trickery.

The thoughts burst through his mind in less time than it took to blink, but the possibilities had been considered and the decision made. His finger started to tighten on the trigger.

Then something pounded him a good shot on the back of the head. As Coffin dropped, his finger jerked on the trigger. He heard the gun go off, but had no idea where the lead ball went.

He awoke with the storm still roaring around him. Once he got to his feet, he found that walking was not easy with the pounding of the rain on his thumping head. He realized that he was out back of Farrel's Tavern.

"Son of a bitch," Coffin snapped as he slipped in some mud and went down on a knee. He pushed to his feet again, shaking water off his hands. He finally made it to the wood walk in front of the saloon. He stopped in front of the saloon for a moment, trying to steady himself. As his hand reached for the doorknob, Coffin realized he did not have his pistols. He turned and splashed to the boardinghouse.

Glad that no one was in the sitting room, he checked the grandfather clock there. He had been out little more than half an hour. He hurried to his room, trying to ignore the throbbing ache at the back of his head.

Shivering a little from the cold, Coffin stripped down and dried himself off. He pulled on his only other shirt, long johns, socks and pants. Pulling out the two .36-caliber Colts he had taken from that Rebel so many years ago, he carefully loaded them and then shoved them into his belt. He slapped on his soaking hat and headed out. At the door he grabbed a slicker that someone had left there. It was way too big, but Coffin didn't care. All he wanted was to keep the powder in his pistols dry until he was inside Farrel's Tavern again.

Once more he stopped just outside and took a deep breath to settle himself. For the first time, the moisture-laden air smelled sweet and fresh, as if the pounding of the rain has washed away the city's foulness.

With his hand on the butt of a Colt still in his belt, he pushed inside. The place was nearly empty, and what little conversation there had been quickly was stifled. The bartender—known only as Stapely—smiled warily.

Coffin saw nothing amiss, really, and there was nowhere for an assailant to hide, so he figured he was safe. He pulled off the borrowed slicker and pulled on his own before marching to the bar. He passed several bloodspots.

Waiting for him at the bar—as if nothing had happened—were a shot and a beer, and his two Remingtons. He jolted down the whiskey and took a few sips of beer. Then he fixed an icy stare on the bartender and said, "What the hell happened?"

"It was the damnedest thing," Stapely said, shaking his head. "You was about ready to pop that last fella there, when these two guys come in. Bounty hunters they were. We found that out later. Anyways, the one bangs you on the back of the noggin, and a moment later, the other shot the last one down."

"Seems I recall that one feller looked funny right there at the end, as if he saw someone he knew all of a sudden."

Stapely nodded. "Yep, that was it. We found that out later, too." He refilled Coffin's shot glass and beer mug. "Them two—they said their names was Laidlaw; Dewey and Daryl—said they'd tracked the five of them here from somewhere back in Kentucky or Tennessee or somewhere."

Coffin could understand that. The Toomey clan most likely had as many enemies as friends and kinfolk.

"They was polite fellas, too," Stapely continued. "Once they'd conked you and made sure all those other boys really were dead—one of 'em wasn't, and they took care of that right quick—they picked up your guns and brought 'em over here." He paused. "Well, they stood there a minute lookin' at wanted posters. I told 'em you was a worker here, at the meat market," Stapely added, as if he were proud of the fact. "Apparently you wasn't among 'em, so they dragged you out back and dumped you there"

That made no sense to Coffin. "Why didn't they just leave me where I was?" he asked.

Stapely shrugged. "They seemed to think things'd be easier if you wasn't layin' around gettin' in the way."

Coffin figured that was reasonable. Bounty hunters like the Laidlaws probably worked efficiently and as safely as they could. If they had left Coffin where he was, they'd have to keep on stepping over him. Of course, they could've just moved him to the side, along the wall, but Coffin figured the men had to think of him as a danger. After all, he had just taken on five men and was standing untouched when the Laidlaws entered the saloon. Men like the Laidlaws would be wary with a man like Coffin around, thinking that if he awoke, he might get hold of a gun and open fire. The easiest thing for the Laidlaw brothers to do would have been to kill him, but Coffin figured they didn't do that since there were witnesses around, and they more than likely would not want to explain his shooting to lawmen. By dumping him outside, they had him out of the way, and there was a chance he might drown or something, in which case they would not really have much explaining to do.

"Why didn't you come bring me back?" Coffin asked. He reached up almost absent-mindedly and touched the still-swollen knot at the back of his head.

"I did," Stapely said. "Soon as those boys left, me and a couple others went out lookin' for you, but you wasn't there."

Coffin nodded. "Where'd them two get off to?" he asked casually. He had the thought that he might go after them for giving him the big knot on the back of his head, and for leaving him to die out in the storm.

Stapely shrugged. "All I know is that they took the five bodies—after they'd taken everything of value from them dumb bastards—and said they were gonna go get their bounties from the law. They didn't sound like they was plannin' to stay around."

"Why not?" Coffin asked, somewhat surprised. If he had just chased down five outlaws and gotten the bounty in the midst of a driving rainstorm, he would've been real fond of spending a few days in civilization.

"Said they was lookin' for another outlaw—a fella named Elwood Fox. You know him?"

Coffin shook his head. "Why the hell would I know him?" he asked sharply. He resented the assumption that because some outlaws had come gunning for him that he knew every outlaw.

"I don't know," Stapely said lamely.

"You know how much they got for that band of scum?" he asked idly. He had never seriously thought of bounty hunting, but it might be a possibility if there was any money in it.

"Hell yes," Stapely said with an impressed whistle. "Showed the posters around. Totin' it all up, them two fellas took in near three thousand dollars. Whoo, boy, that's a heap of money."

A burst of rage flooded through Coffin, so hot and so

big that it wiped the pounding ache of his head away for a moment. It wasn't bad enough that the two Laidlaws had smacked him on the back of the head, but they had made three thousand dollars for work he had done, even if he had done it with no knowledge of how much the Toomey clan was worth.

Coffin stood stock still, knuckles white where his hand gripped the beer mug. He was outraged at what the Laidlaws had done, and it took him some seconds to get a handle on the anger.

"Hey, Joe," Stapely said nervously. "Joe, you all right?"

Coffin got his rage under control somewhat. "I'm fine. Just fine," he mumbled. He finished off his beer and picked up the two big Remingtons. "Thanks for takin' care of these for me, Stapely," he said. "Be seein' you." He turned and headed outside.

The rain had lessened only minutely. It seemed to Coffin, though, that it somehow felt less powerful. Maybe there would be a break in the storm soon, he thought. The roaring sheets of rain did help to cool his temper some, and that allowed him to think more clearly. He had every intention of tracking the Laidlaws down. He had enough sense, though, to know that leaving now would be foolish, and perhaps suicidal.

Coffin wandered down to the local constable's office and popped in. "You have a couple fellers named Laidlaw come in here a little bit ago?" he asked the constable on duty.

The burly lawman nodded disinterestedly.

"You know where they went?" Once more Coffin had to battle his fury.

The lawman shrugged. "They picked up vouchers for some bounties, and asked if a man named Elwood Fox had been around."

"Has he?" Coffin asked in exasperation.

"Nah. I told them boys that he'd been seen out around St. Charles." He paused, then glared at Coffin, eyes squinted. "What's all your interest in this anyway?" he asked.

Coffin shrugged. "Got some personal business with them. I'd heard they come into town and tried to find 'em. Then some feller said he'd seen 'em down to Farrel's. I went there and the bartender told me the Laidlaws had killed a couple of wanted men and were comin' over here to get the bounty due 'em."

"I gave 'em the voucher to take to the goddamn bank, and they left." The lawman glared. "And that's all you're gonna get from me, goddammit."

"Where's St. Charles?"

"Northwest," the lawman growled, annoyed. "Eighteen, maybe twenty miles and across the Missouri."

"Thanks," Coffin said sarcastically. "You've been a big help."

"Don't get snotty with me, boy," the constable snapped. He started to push himself up out of the chair.

Coffin had taken just about as much as he could take. His hand went to one of the Colts in his belt. "I think you need to just keep where you are, Constable," he said tightly. He knew he was risking a lot. It would go hard on him if he stood here and shot down an upholder of the law, but he could take no more guff for this day.

The lawman eased himself back into the chair. He did not look happy.

"I got nothin' against you, Constable," Coffin said mildly. "And I sure as hell don't want to shoot you, but I've had me one piss-poor day."

The lawman glared at him for a few moments, and then grinned just a little. He nodded.

Coffin eased toward the door backward. He didn't figure the constable would try anything, but until he was sure he would use caution. Outside, he slipped around the side of the building and into an alley. He walked swiftly, through several bleak alleys and streets before he finally slowed. The lawman would have to be *loco* to come chasing him out in this weather. Coffin figured that while the constable might be ornery, he probably was not mad.

Coffin had a direction to head now, but he still figured it would be foolish to leave tonight. He decided to eat well and then have a good night's sleep. He could get an early start.

Chapter Five

The rain stopped sometime in the late afternoon or evening. Coffin was not sure which. He had eaten well and then gone straight to sleep. He awoke before dawn and headed for a restaurant that served workmen on their way to their jobs. It was a loud, rambunctious place, which Coffin could have done without, but he ate quickly and then headed back to his room.

His headache was gone, and the knot on the back of his head had shrunk somewhat. With the headache gone, a full belly and a long night's sleep, he was feeling better. Still, his renewed spirits did not in any way lessen his anger and his determination to get the men who had treated him so cavalierly. Each time he thought of it, his stomach would do a flop and the rage would rush through his veins.

Since he had planned on leaving today anyway, he had his supplies already. After breakfast, he went back to his room and packed. Done with that, he sat down to clean his pistols.

As he worked, he thought back on yesterday. He realized that he had two pistols and damn near used them all up in his gunfight with the Toomeys. It was an uncomfortable feeling. He recalled seeing a Confederate during the war who had taken two plain, simple holsters on thin belts and hung them around his neck from side to side, so that each pistol rode under an armpit, butt facing outward. Coffin thought that might be something to try.

Once he finished cleaning his pistols, he dug through his stuff and pulled out the two old holsters for the smaller Colts. He had only one belt, however, and that was holding up his pants. Thinking himself foolish for all this, he headed to a dry goods store, where he purchased two slim belts.

Back in his room, he hooked himself up and looked in the mirror. He still felt silly, but it gave him more firepower. He decided, though, that he would wear them once he got out of town, away from all the people who would, he was convinced, laugh themselves silly at him. With relief, he packed his newfangled contraption of a holster away.

He took a final look around his room. There was nothing he had forgotten, so he grabbed his saddlebags and the two burlap sacks of supplies and headed out.

The walk to the livery was a sloppy and ginger one. The mud in most of the streets seemed to be at least a foot thick. It clung to his boots, and tried to hold him down with each step. He made it with getting splashed by passing wagons and carriages only five times. It did wonders to improve his sour humor.

He took his time saddling and bridling his horse before he realized he was just stalling for time. He didn't know why, but he did know there was only so long it could take in getting ready. Finally he pulled himself onto his horse and rode out.

The day was still thick with moisture, and the clouds hung low and heavy over the swarming humanity. It kept the stench of the city down low, where it could most offend. It clung to his body, too, chilling him as the wind whished and whooshed in frigid fits and starts. Coffin felt miserable.

It was just about dark when Coffin pulled into St. Charles. The ride had seemed interminable, and the wait for a ferry across the Missouri River took an eternity. He found a hotel and then took his horse to a livery. Tired and cold, he found a restaurant and stopped in to eat a hasty meal. Afterward, he hit a saloon and spent an hour or so trying to wash away the surging anger inside.

Coffin felt different in the morning, and he was not quite sure why. But as he strapped on his newfangled shoulder holster get-up, he realized that he felt eager, calm and cool. It was like being back in the war, on the night before a battle. At those times, serenity came over him. It wasn't that he looked forward to battle, really; it was more like having an incredible amount of focus on the impending fight, as if his mind and body were preparing him for the horrors to come.

He headed for a restaurant. He ate, quite conscious of the surreptitious stares and comments directed his way. He bore it silently, trying to manage his embarrassment while eating.

Stepping outside afterward, he paused and then headed back to his room at the hotel nearby. It was still cool and humid, leaving a clammy chill in the air, so Coffin picked up his long slicker. That way, he figured, he was not only warm and dry, his rigged-up shoulder holsters were hidden from view, and thus from ridicule.

He asked a passer-by where he could find the town marshal's office. A deputy was the only one in the office. "Howdy, Deputy," Coffin said politely. "I was wonderin' if you could help me out?"

Deputy Jules Belmondo bore not only the name but the looks of his St. Charles French ancestors. He spoke with no French accent, though he did drawl a little. "What can I do for you, mister?" he asked.

"I was lookin' for a couple fellers. Dewey and Daryl Laidlaw."

"Couple of boys was in here yesterday. Didn't give their names." He glared balefully up at his visitor.

Coffin took the hint. He held out his hand. "Joe Coffin."

"Jules Belmondo," the deputy said, shaking Coffin's hand. "Have a seat if you're of a mind."

Coffin nodded and sat.

"Those two appeared to be bounty hunters, though they didn't say so. Just asked about a fella named Elwood Fox," Belmondo said.

Coffin nodded. "That'd be them."

"What's your business with them?" Belmondo asked.

Coffin thought the next few moments might be touchy. It was obvious that Belmondo had little liking for bounty hunters, but he wondered just how much of a story he should concoct for Belmondo. Then he decided that essentially the truth would be best. "They took some money I'd earned," Coffin said slowly. "A fair good amount." That was basically true. Coffin had earned the bounty money, even if he hadn't known it at the time.

"You a bounty man, too?" Belmondo asked bluntly.

"No, sir," Coffin said. That, too, was the truth. That he might become a bounty hunter after he found the Laidlaws did not count. "I'm just lookin' to square things."

Belmondo sat staring at Coffin for a few moments. Then he nodded slowly. A man had to square things if he was to be a man at all, Belmondo figured. "I don't know where they got off to, but we heard a couple days ago that Elwood Fox was spotted over in Crooked Creek."

"That a town?" Coffin asked.

"Yep. Over on the Gasconade. It runs into the Missouri a couple, three days ride from here. Crooked Creek's a couple miles south of the Missouri."

Coffin nodded. "There a ferry near there?"

"Half mile this way from the confluence."

Coffin stood. "I'm obliged, Deputy." They shook hands again and Coffin left. He took his time until he was outside, then speeded up. The Laidlaws still had about a full day's start on him. He hurried to the livery and had them saddle his horse while he went back to the hotel and packed his few belongings. By the time he had done that, a boy from the livery was outside with his horse. He gave the boy two bits, which sent the youth away happy.

Coffin rode slowly out of town, once again not wanting to give away his urgency in case anyone was watching. But once outside of the sprawling town, he put his spurs to the horse, keeping a good pace. He rode until after dark before pulling up in a stand of willows near the bank of the Missouri. By the time he unsaddled his horse and tended it, he was in no mood for making a fire. He would have appreciated hot coffee, but the effort was not worth it, he thought. He settled for a few pieces of jerky washed down with river water and a quick cigarette.

He got an early start after a breakfast of jerky and water. He pushed well into the night and had to roust the ferryman to take him across. The man growled and grumped, until Coffin handed him a double eagle. That changed his attitude in a hurry.

Coffin arrived in Crooked Creek near midnight. The only thing he saw open was the Twisted Water Saloon. It might not have been going full blast, but the small place was fairly crowded.

Coffin stopped at the bar and ordered a shot of bourbon and a glass of beer. When it was brought, he asked the bartender, who had introduced himself as Rudy Schmidt, "There any place to get a bite to eat this hour?"

"We can whip somethin' up for you if you ain't too

choosy."

"Beefsteak and taters'll do if you can manage that. Coffee, too."

"Won't take but a few moments." He started to turn away, but Coffin called him back.

"You seen two fellers named Laidlaw? They should've come through here yesterday, or maybe today."

"Not nobody that give his name that way," the bartender said with a shrug. "You know what they look like?"

Coffin dredged up the descriptions of the Laidlaws that Stapely had given him. "Brothers. Both're maybe six-foot, one seventy. Dark, unfriendly eyes, big noses. The older's got a touch of white in his hair and he's got a scar from a bullet in his left cheek."

The bartender nodded. "Yep. They were in here late this afternoon. They were lookin' for some fella named Elwood Fox They was bounty men. Showed around a paper on this Fox fella." The bartender wondered if he should be telling this short, hard-looking man anything, but then he decided that Coffin was a heap more friendly than those other two had been, so he didn't mind.

"Know what happened to 'em?"

Schmidt shrugged. "They had a couple of drinks, went and ate over at Landsberg's down the street there, and then rode on. Don't know where they were headin', but they left by the road south."

"That road follow the Gasconade?"

The bartender laughed. "Hell no. Any road followed the Gasconade, it'd take you a week to go a mile, twisty as that goddamn river is. But it goes in that general direction."

Coffin nodded. "Just one more thing—those boys do anything else while they were in town?"

The bartender shook his head. "Not that I know of.

Unless they had the blacksmith do somethin'. They left their horses there for the little while they was here."

Coffin nodded again. "Thanks."

"Sure. I'll have your supper out here in a jiffy. You gonna eat standin' up?"

"Not if I can find a table. You look pretty busy, though."

"We'll find you somethin' if there's no place open when your supper comes."

Coffin worked on his beer slowly, feeling the tiredness weighing heavily on him. His eyes were gritty and his body felt slack. Sooner than he expected, the bartender came out with a plate on which sat a sizzling beefsteak so big it hung off two sides of the plate and some steaming potatoes, as well as an iron knife and fork. In his other hand, the bartender held a plate with several biscuits and a bowl of butter.

"Come on, mister," Schmidt said with a jerk of the head. "We'll get you a place to eat your supper in peace."

Coffin nodded gratefully and followed the bartender, who shooed two men from a small table near the back of the saloon. Coffin sat, and Schmidt placed the plates in front of him. "I'll be back directly with your coffee. Anything else?"

"Another beer wouldn't hurt none."

"You got it."

Coffin dug into the food, finally realizing just how hungry he was. He didn't even slow when Schmidt returned with a mug of foamy beer in one hand and a pot of coffee and a cup in the other. Coffin nodded his thanks and kept on shoveling food in.

He was still doing so when one of the working girls sidled up and sat at the table. She was plain-looking despite the face paint, and was wearing some form of undergarment that Coffin knew was not designed for wearing as a sole article of clothing. It did, however, offer a quite considerable view of her perfumed flesh.

"You lonely, sweetheart?" she asked after a few moments to size him up. She decided she liked what she had seen so far. She wondered, though, why he had not taken off his long rain slicker.

"Not right at the moment," Coffin said, words garbled by the mouthful of steak and potatoes. He swallowed and then grinned. "But you give me a few minutes, and I might be."

"A girl can't just sit around on her ass waitin', ya know," she said with a smile to soften her words.

"Expect not. How's about I buy you a drink or two to tide you over?"

"That'd do, sweetheart." She turned and waved to Schmidt, who brought her a shot of whiskey. Looking at the glass, Coffin wondered how watered down it was.

Chapter Six

By the time Coffin had finished his meal, the scarlet woman—Blue Gladys—had polished off three shots of whiskey. Coffin leaned back and rolled and lit a cigarette. "Best slow down on that stuff, girl," he said, pointing to the empty whiskey glass. But he smiled as he spoke.

Blue Gladys looked around to make sure the bartender was not around. "I ain't supposed to say, but Rudy there and the other bartenders make sure we don't get too much."

Coffin grinned again. "I suspected. After all, it wouldn't do to have a bunch of drunk workin' girls, would it?"

Blue Gladys giggled.

Coffin wondered how she had gotten the nickname "Blue." She certainly didn't seem melancholy. Then he figured it didn't matter. He would be here just a few hours and then be on his way. Schmidt strolled up with another mug of beer for Coffin and another shot for Blue Gladys.

"Any way I can get my horse tended to, Rudy?" Coffin asked.

"The livery."

"It looked closed when I rode on by it before."

"Probably is, but for a five I can rouse one of the boys who works there."

"You trust 'em?" Coffin asked, looking up with eyebrows raised in question.

" 'Bout as much as I trust anyone else in Crooked Creek."

"And how much is that?"

Rudy laughed. "Most folks 'round here is respectable. 'Course, there's always a few bad eggs."

Coffin nodded. He dug in a pocket and pulled out a coin. He flipped it to Rudy, who deftly caught it and glanced at the gold eagle. "That enough?" Coffin asked. Funds were getting a little low already, but he wouldn't worry about that just yet.

Rudy nodded. "More than enough, but when you need things after hours, that's only right."

Coffin nodded. "Make sure he's grained good and curried, too. Tell the boy to take his care with the tendin', and with my belongin's, too. Have him bring my saddlebags to me here. Or you can, if you'd rather. I'll be by for the horse . . ." he glanced at Blue Gladys. ". . . in the morning."

Blue Gladys nodded. So did Schmidt. Then the bartender left. "It's gonna cost you some, sweetheart, for the night."

"Is everybody around here a thief?" he asked with a laugh.

Blue Gladys pinked up. "A girl's got to make a livin', ya know, Mr. . . . ?"

"Joe Coffin. And I understand. Just makin' a little joke." He dropped his cigarette butt into the mug of beer and stood. Schmidt was just approaching with his saddlebags. Coffin took them with a nod, then looked at Blue Gladys. "Ma'am," he said, holding out his left arm for her to take.

They headed up the stairway against the back wall of the saloon and into one of the rooms. Coffin dropped his saddlebags on a chair after Blue Gladys had lit a lantern, throwing a smelly yellowish light around the room. Then Coffin peeled off his slicker and self-consciously removed the shoulder rigs and dropped them on the chair, too.

Blue Gladys watched as Coffin removed the gunbelt with the two holstered Remingtons and the hard leather case with two extra loaded cylinders for the Remingtons and two for the Colts, as well as a couple handfuls of paper cartridges for the revolvers. Then he sat on the bed, shoulders slumping.

"You look tired," Blue Gladys said quietly.

Coffin nodded. "Been on the trail long hours the past couple of days," he said, rubbing his face.

"Well you just set there, sweetheart, old Blue Gladys'll take care of ya."

"Where in hell'd you get the name 'Blue' anyway?" he asked.

Blue Gladys had gotten off the bed and stood back toward him, bent over and grabbed his right boot. She looked back over her shoulder—a position Coffin found considerably enjoyable—to see if he was making fun of her. She decided he wasn't. With Coffin's left foot on her rump pushing, Blue Gladys tugged on his right boot. It popped off.

She straightened and looked back again. "My folks was well-off when I was a kid," she said quietly. She didn't seem to be downcast, just stating facts that she had gotten accustomed to over the years. She bent again and grabbed Coffin's other boot. A moment later, that one was off, too.

Blue Gladys turned and smiled. "In fact, they was better than well-off. Lots of old-time money from what I gather. Some of the girls I work with got wind of it one time and started calling me 'Blue'—short for 'Blue Blood.' "

Coffin was surprised. "How'd you ever come to be in

this business, then, if your folks was rich?" he asked, curious.

"They come on hard times when I was thirteen or fourteen. Pa killed himself soon after. Ma couldn't care very well for me, my brother and my sister. I found out soon after that men'd pay for what I wasn't supposed to be doin'. Ma looked the other way during such times, but I know it hurt her. Still, it kept a roof over our heads for a while."

Blue Gladys sighed. "By the time Ma up and married again, I was too far gone to the devil's ways as far as she figured. Everybody else, too, I guess. I joined up with a man headin' out this way. We got as far as here, and he was shot down one night for cheatin' at cards. But there's always a spot for someone like me in a busy town."

Blue Gladys had looked sad, but she brightened now that the tale was told. It used to make her sad to think of the way her life had been, but she wouldn't have it any other way now. She was pretty well treated by her customers, many of them regulars. The bartenders—who also acted as bouncers when the need arose—took good care of her and the other girls. Sure, she was snubbed by the respectable ladies of Crooked Creek, but not by the men. She had her own money to do with as she pleased, and she had come to enjoy some of her liaisons. Not all, by a long shot, but enough that she knew she would've been terribly disappointed at being married and so faithful to one man. Of course, now that she was getting a little older, she might have to set her sights on getting married. A girl couldn't last forever in such a profession. But there was time yet for that. Right now she wanted to explore the possibilities of this short, tough-looking young man.

Coffin looked at her and saw only a flicker of sadness. He grinned lopsidedly. Blue Gladys slid up to him and stood in front of him. Gently she placed her hands behind his head and pulled his face toward her until it stopped in the small valley between her breasts. She stroked his hair for a few moments.

She finally stepped back and shucked her shoes and her only garment. Then she helped Coffin get undressed. Naked, the two tumbled onto the bed, lips locked. Moments later the bed was creaking and squeaking under their excited thrashing.

Even Coffin's youthful strength and vigor could not keep him going after the second time. Cuddled in Blue Gladys's warm embrace, he fell asleep, feeling better than he had in a long time.

He awoke much later than he had wanted, and as he lay there looking at Blue Gladys's plain-pretty, soft face, he felt like he should be up and moving. The Laidlaws were getting farther away with each minute.

Then he pushed those thoughts aside as Blue Gladys awoke and pulled him to her one more time.

Half an hour later, Coffin was dressed—having done so under Blue Gladys's alert gray eyes. He wrapped the shoulder holsters in his slicker and stuffed the wad into one of his saddlebags. He still felt too self-conscious to wear the shoulder guns out in public much. He placed another double eagle on the small night stand, then winked at Blue Gladys. She blew him a kiss as he grabbed his saddlebags and headed out.

There was a different bartender on duty, so Coffin did not bother to stop. He just headed outside into the sunshine. It seemed that the storms had finally blown away and let some of spring's warmth poke through, and it felt good.

As he walked toward the livery, he came on a general merchandise store and swung in. He was low on some items and figured he might as well replenish here. He poked around the store as the clerk waited on a young woman. At one point, he got a good look at her, and he nearly stopped in his tracks.

She was, Coffin figured, sixteen or maybe seventeen. She had a small, heart-shaped face with a nose that was a tad too long and a chin a tad too pointed. They did not detract from her beauty; rather, he thought, they added to it. She had hair the color of spun gold, a high, smooth forehead, soft, golden eyebrows and a pouty lower lip. He could not see her eyes in the dimness of the store, but he wagered himself that they were soft, pale blue. Her figure under the plain wool dress was lithe and supple, and curvaceous enough for even the most exacting man.

For a few moments, Coffin stood there looking at the young woman's profile, stunned by her beauty and the desires she raised in him. Never had he been so struck by a woman.

The vision stayed with him a long time. It even took him some moments to push it out of his mind in order to get what supplies he needed. He stuffed the supplies into his saddlebags and moseyed over to the livery stable.

While a boy saddled and bridled his chestnut horse, Coffin talked with the stable's owner, asking about the Laidlaws.

"Yeah, I remember them boys," the livery man said. "They were in some hurry."

"They have any work done on their horses?" Coffin asked.

"I think so. Let me check." He turned and bellowed, "Johnny!"

A moment later, a short, burly man wearing a blacksmith's leather apron came out of the shop. He was sweating from the heat of the forge. In one hand he carried a blacksmith's small hammer. Coffin judged him to be in his late twenties or early thirties, but the man was going bald already. He had a cherubic face made red by the heat. And, despite his ready smile, Coffin figured the man would not be one anybody would want to tangle with.

"You remember them two fellas was in here yesterday? One had a sorrel mare, the other that ugly skewbald."

"Yeah," the blacksmith said. "Why?"

"Didn't you do some work for 'em?"

"Yeah. The skewbald had a bad shoe on the right foreleg. I put a new one on for him. Cleaned out the others, too, but didn't find no more problems except a couple loose nails I replaced."

"The other shoes worn some?" Coffin asked.

"Yep. Why?" The blacksmith impaled Coffin with a stony glare.

"Need to track 'em," Coffin responded flatly.

"Why?"

"That's none of your concern."

The blacksmith glared a moment, then grinned, face bright. He nodded. "Anything else you need to know?"

"Reckon not. Obliged."

The blacksmith turned and walked off.

Coffin paid the stable owner, mounted his horse and then rode out of town. Half a mile out, he stopped and got down. He had never been much of a tracker, had never needed to learn such a skill. So he wasn't sure what he was looking for. Finally he spotted what he thought was the print from a new shoe surrounded by old ones. He was far from certain that it was the horse he was looking for, but he had to assume it was. He pulled up into the saddle and rode off.

He rode at a good pace, not paying much attention to the ground. Around here, the road was fairly well marked, and got a lot of use. About the only thing he might be able to tell by going slowly was if the men he was chasing had gone off the road.

Coffin had closed some of the time gap that had separated him from the Laidlaws, but he seemed to not be able to pick up any more time. He began to think, as he made himself a small camp that night, that they had gone off some way that he had missed. That bothered him, and kept him from getting as restful a night's sleep as he had wanted.

In the morning, he was in poor humor, but he forced himself to do what needed to be done—cooking bacon and beans, drinking coffee, breaking camp. But before he rode off, he scouted the area in the sharp bend of the Gasconade, up and down as well as on both sides of the road. He was about ready to give up when he suddenly spotted a print that looked familiar.

On foot, he followed it a little bit, until he came to a campsite. He felt a rush of excitement as he hurried back to his own campsite and mounted up. He was sure he would find the Laidlaws by nightfall.

He didn't, though. Nor did he find them the next day or the next after that. He finally came to a town and asked around. No one had seen such men, nor heard anything about the Laidlaws' quarry—Elwood Fox.

Disgusted with himself, Coffin swung back on the trail, covering ground he had just come over. He forced himself to stop every ten or fifteen minutes and check the ground, looking desperately for the track of the new horseshoe.

Just as he was about to give up, he found it. The track led east, away from the creek.

Chapter Seven

Coffin was moving slowly, trying to sense what—or who—was out there. He didn't know what had tipped him off that there was something out there. He just knew it was time to take it easy. It had been like that in the war, too. He seemed to have a sense, something unconscious, that alerted him to unexpected danger before it happened—the first few scouts of the advancing Confederate Army; traps that had been set; ambushes lurking ahead. Because of that, Coffin suspected he was close to the Laidlaws.

Dark was approaching fast, and Coffin decided that it was time to call it quits for this day. He pulled into a patch of trees along Bourbeaus Creek, whose knotty, twisty length ran roughly parallel to the Gasconade a day's ride or so east. Coffin had followed the Laidlaws' track to the Bourbeaus, and then sort of followed it southward for almost two days.

As much as he wanted coffee and hot food, he knew he could not risk a fire, so he once more settled for hardtack, jerky and water. As darkness spread over his small, cold camp, Coffin walked to the water's edge and looked upstream and down. He saw nothing out of the ordinary. Then he moved through the trees to the path out beyond the stand of trees. In the quiet, soft night, he looked and listened.

A sudden sound off to his left made him freeze. Now that the trees blocked off the rushing sound of the swift-flowing creek, he could hear other things. Like voices. He was sure that was what he had heard. He waited, not moving. After an unknown time, he heard it again. It was laughter.

He knelt and pulled off his spurs and went back to drop them with his supplies. Back at the trail, he stopped and checked his pistols in the light of the half moon. Then he turned left and walked swiftly, surely, until he spotted the flicker of flames.

Coffin melted into the trees and edged close to the camp. It was tough going because of the dark. The half moon threw little light here under the canopy of the tall cottonwoods and thick willows. He moved inch by inch, testing each footstep so that he would not snap a twig or grunt out a curse brought by a turned ankle.

Finally stopping behind a good-sized cottonwood, he eased out a Remington and peered toward the fire, ready to plug the Laidlaws. But only one man sat at the fire. That stayed his hand. He waited, absolutely calm and still, until he could sort it out. He finally concluded that he was not all that sure it was one of the Laidlaws sitting at the fire. He couldn't see the man very clearly.

He headed back toward his own camp, keeping his pistol out until he was almost there. He moved silently, the small sounds that were impossible to stop masked by the creek's bubbling nearby. Coffin was alert; if that was one of the Laidlaw brothers back there, the other might be roaming around.

At his camp, Coffin sat on the ground, leaning his back against a fallen log. He puffed a cigarette, as he waited to hear if anyone was coming for him. He cupped the burning cigarette in his hands so the glowing tip would not be seen even from a few feet away. Finally he spread out his bedroll. With a Remington in hand, he dozed off.

He jerked awake just as dawn was edging into his camp in the trees. He lay frozen, trying to place the sound that had woken him. He couldn't so he pulled his head up a little and looked around. He smiled when he saw a deer drinking skittishly at the creek.

Still making no sudden moves, Coffin eased himself up. He went to make water, but walked around the area before he did. He had seen no one. He splashed water from the creek on his face and then patiently gnawed down a few strips of jerky and two pieces of hardtack. With a sigh, he pulled on his rigged-up shoulder holsters, just in case, he told himself.

Finally he saddled his horse, wondering just how he should approach that other camp. He was at a disadvantage since the Laidlaws had seen him back in St. Louis, though he was not sure what they looked like other than the descriptions Stapely had given him.

He decided that worrying about it would get him nowhere. He would just go along and see what happened. He rode toward the other camp, and then, just before getting there, pulled into the trees and dismounted. He went forward on foot, still without his spurs. He stopped behind the same tree he had used last night, and he looked into camp. Again there was only one man at the fire. He was not sure it was the same one as last night, but he was sure now it was one of the Laidlaws.

He swore silently, worried about Laidlaw's brother. He stayed there a while, until he picked out where the brother was, nodding to himself when he had the man placed. Pulling both Remingtons, he stepped into the little clearing.

Laidlaw—it was Dewey, Coffin figured—looked up, startled, but he covered it well. "I know you from somewhere, boy?" Laidlaw asked harshly.

"Where's your brother?" Coffin countered. He aimed the Remington in his right hand at Laidlaw.

"Around." He paused as he rose slowly, not wanting to spook the gunman.

Coffin cocked his pistol. "Where is he?" His tone was harder. He also caught snatches of sounds as Daryl Laidlaw circled around the camp to get behind him.

"Hey, you're that little feller gunned down them boys there in St. Louie, ain't you?" Laidlaw said, as if he was celebrating the fact. "Whoo-ee, boy, that was some shootin'." He grinned, as if greeting a long-lost friend.

"Yes, it was," Coffin said flatly. "And then you went and walloped me on the back of the head and threw me out into the storm. Even worse," Coffin spit, "was that you went and took all them bounties. Three thousand worth."

Laidlaw looked sharply at Coffin. "You followed us all this way and all this time just 'cause we made off with some cash you thought you was gonna get?" he asked. He was incredulous.

Coffin nodded. "I don't take kindly to peckerwoods like you pullin' such stunts."

Laidlaw shrugged. "We coulda just kilt you straight off, boy, and been done with it."

"That was your mistake, Laidlaw." He paused a heartbeat. "Now I ain't gonna ask you this but once more: Where's your asshole brother?"

Coffin heard the soft click of a pistol being cocked. He whirled half a turn and thrust out the Remington in his left hand. He fired once without seeing where Laidlaw was, just to protect himself. It took him less than a blink to see Daryl Laidlaw. He fired twice more, knowing instinctively that both lead balls had found a home.

Without waiting to see the effect of his shots, he cranked his head around. Dewey Laidlaw had dived to the side and rolled as he tried to yank out his pistol. He had just gotten his pistol in hand when two shots from the Remington in Coffin's right hand hit him in the head.

Coffin rose slowly, turning toward Daryl Laidlaw. Coffin knew Dewey was dead; he wasn't sure about Daryl, though. A few steps brought him to Daryl, and he knelt.

"Son of a bitch bastard," Daryl Laidlaw gasped, and then he died.

Coffin got his horse, brought it up and put it with the Laidlaws' animals. He pulled his tin cup from his supplies and poured himself some coffee. He sat and drank the thick liquid slowly, puffing a cigarette as he did.

When he was done with that, Coffin moved to Daryl's body and went through all his pockets. He pulled out a little over two hundred dollars plus some worthless personal items. He did the same with Dewey, and found just about the same. With a growing sense of annoyance and urgency, he went through all the Laidlaws' supplies. When he was done, he had the grand total of five hundred sixty-three dollars and eighty-two cents. It was more money than he had ever seen at one time, but it was a far cry from the three thousand dollars the Laidlaws had gotten in bounties for the Toomey gang.

He plopped himself down at the fire again and poured some more coffee—the last in the pot. He sipped it as he thought. He had been almost obsessed with finding, and killing, Dewey and Daryl Laidlaw. Part of that obsession was in the pot of gold he expected to get when the deed was done. But now there was almost nothing, he found.

He wondered what had happened to the rest of the money. The Laidlaws had not been in any one place long enough to have spent twenty-five hundred dollars, an amount that would be a fortune to any working man. The only thing he could think of that would account for it is that they had stopped somewhere, maybe even when they cashed in the voucher at the bank in St. Louis, and made arrangements to send the money home.

Coffin had not realized until now just how important that money was to him. He had braved a gunfight with five armed men, tracked and killed two experienced bounty hunters, and all for a paltry five hundred dollars.

Suddenly he laughed, something he hadn't done in a while. Here he was, a young man who had never had more than fifty dollars in his hand at one time grousing when he had "only" ten times that. It was ridiculous. Five hundred-plus dollars could take him a long way. Trouble with that, though, is he didn't know where to go. He was sure he would find a way to use the money.

With a sigh, he got up. He grabbed a shovel from the Laidlaws' supplies and found a spot that looked like it would not offer too hard a time digging. Three hours later, the Laidlaws were laid to rest. Coffin considered giving them a little service, but he did not think they deserved it.

Sweating from the work, he stripped down and jumped in the creek, enjoying the feel of the cool water flowing over him. Naked, he sat on the bank, letting the air dry him. Afterward, he dressed and then set about cleaning and reloading his Remingtons.

When he was done with that, he decided he no longer needed his shoulder holster rigs. Besides, he still felt foolish wearing the contraptions. So he wrapped them up in his slicker again and stuffed them into his saddlebags.

With a shrug, he cooked up some biscuits and beans and made another pot of coffee. He ate slowly. When he was done, he decided he was in no hurry to be anywhere, so he unsaddled his horse. He made himself comfortable. The two nearby graves did not bother him; not after the slaughter of men he had seen during the war.

He tried not to think of what to do now. There would

be no easy answers anyway, but he wanted at least a little time to just relax. Still, the thoughts of what the future held for him would not stay completely away.

He could, he knew now, turn into a bounty hunter himself. The risks were high, of course, but so were the rewards. That had been shown in St. Louis.

He had no delusions about himself. He had no training in anything but surviving and killing. With his innate sense of justice and right, bounty hunting would be an ideal profession for him. Especially when one considered that he had no grand plan for life. It removed the necessity of roots and family.

In the morning, he took his time about breakfast and in striking camp. There was no hurry, but there was no reason to linger here either. He finally mounted his chestnut and gathered up the Laidlaws' two horses. Then he sat, wondering just where he could go.

It did not come as a flash, but as a gradual awareness. He held a vision of a young woman with honey-gold hair and a perfect heart-shaped face. With a smile, he said softly, "Crooked Creek's as good a place as any."

He might not be able to court that pretty young woman he had seen in the general store. If not, well, Crooked Creek had seemed a nice enough town. Besides, there was always Blue Gladys to turn to for occasional comfort. He rode off with a lighter heart.

Chapter Eight

Coffin stopped at Harry Carstairs's livery stable in Crooked Creek four days later. He had taken time on the ride back, having no cause to hurry. With the Laidlaws' supplies he had more than enough food, coffee and cigarette fixings. He even had some whiskey. About all he didn't have was a woman.

He dismounted at the livery in mid-afternoon and acknowledged Carstairs's greeting. The livery man and his twelve-year-old son, Randy, walked up. Carstairs pointed to the two extra horses. "You found them fellers?" he asked.

Coffin nodded. "You interested in buyin' 'em?"

Carstairs looked the two horses over closely, checking them swiftly but thoroughly. He patted the sorrel one on the neck when he had finished and nodded. "Don't see why not," he said. Then he fixed Coffin with a stare. "Unless I'm gonna get stuck with two angry bastards come lookin' for their horses." His eyes turned the statement into a question.

"You don't have to worry about that," Coffin said flatly.

Carstairs stared at him a few moments more, then nodded. "I'll give you thirty each."

"Seventy-five."

Carstairs shook his head. "Forty."

"Fifty and I'll throw in the tack."

"Done," Carstairs said with a firm nod. They shook hands on the deal. Then Carstairs took the reins to his two new horses and handed them to his son. The boy began leading the horses into the stable. "I ain't got that kind of cash on me . . ." Carstairs said. He stopped. "You know, I never did get your name, mister."

"Joe. Joe Coffin. I take it you're the Harry Carstairs whose name is on the building?"

"That's me. As I was sayin', Mr. Coffin, I ain't got that much cash on me. You want to come back a little later today, or in the mornin', I can have it for you then. Or I could give you a bank draft, if you'd rather."

"Will the bank cash it if I bring it in? I'm a stranger in these parts."

"Tell you what, I'll send Randy over to the bank with you. That way if Warren Yarnell—he owns the bank—gives you a hard time, Randy can vouch for you."

"Sounds fine. I'll just leave my gear here and pick it up later."

Carstairs nodded and called his son. He explained to Randy, and then the boy and Coffin left.

As the two walked, Randy, who was only a few inches shorter than Coffin, asked shyly, "You use them guns of yours much, Mr. Coffin?"

Coffin looked at the boy in surprise. "When needed," he finally said. "Why?"

"Well, you're a pretty short feller for a full-growed man, and I figure I ain't gonna get much bigger'n you, though I still got a little ways to go yet. I was just wonderin' . . . well . . ."

"Go on and say it, boy," Coffin said more heatedly than he had meant to. He was annoyed at Randy's impertinence, but he figured he should give the youngster the courtesy of saying whatever it was he wanted to say.

"Well," Randy said slowly, "I'd . . . Well, dang it all, since I'm not gonna be much bigger'n you, I figure, I want to know if them guns . . . if they . . . if you need 'em to stop from bein' . . . bein' . . ."

"Bullied?" Coffin finished for the boy.

"Yeah, that's what," Randy said firmly. "Well, do ya?"

"I use 'em when I need to." He paused, mulling the question some more. "I expect just wearin' 'em helps some to keep folks from botherin' you, especially if they can see that you'll use 'em."

"Then I'm gonna tell Pa to get me a gun," Randy said firmly.

"I wouldn't do that was I you, Randy." When he saw the confusion on the boy's face, he added, "At your age, that'll bring a hell of a lot more trouble than it'd avoid." He paused. "You been bothered by a bully?"

Randy nodded and looked glum.

Coffin stopped and looked at his young companion. "Your Pa might be awful angry at me for this, but I'll tell you a few things. For one thing, you can't show fear. Don't mean you can't *feel* scared, you just can't show it. Another thing you got to do is not to let anybody make fun of you 'cause you ain't tall. Not serious makin' fun of you. It's all right if it's somebody you know, and he's only joshin' you. But somebody makes light of your size, you got to do somethin' about it."

"You get in a fight every time somebody makes fun of you 'cause you're short?" Randy asked, surprised but interested.

"I try to give 'em a chance to back off. Trouble is, most bullies, who're generally real chickenshits to begin with, take that as a sign that you ain't much of a man. That happens, you best be ready to go after 'em full and hard. Don't matter too much if you get the tar whaled out of you. Most folks'll respect that."

"So what should I do?" a perplexed Randy asked.

"Give yourself some time. Along the way, though, work hard. Hard as you can. That'll build up your strength and stamina." He paused, thinking. "There ain't anything anyone can teach about fightin', except to say that you do anything you can. Kick, bite, scratch, poke 'em in the eye. Do whatever you need to do."

They began walking slowly again. "You get a little older's time enough to learn how to use a gun. But whether a gunfight or a brawl, you got to know when to fight and when to swallow whatever insults're heaped on you. For that, you need to use your judgment, and that's somethin' else you can work on. Not the judgment exactly, but stayin' calm enough to make a sensible judgment."

"Seems like a lot to learn—and to know," Randy said thoughtfully.

"It is."

They walked a few moments in silence, then Coffin asked, "Why didn't you ask Johnny, the blacksmith, this? He ain't no bigger'n I am."

"I did, sorta." Randy grinned a little. "He didn't take me serious. Besides, nobody ever picks on him. Not with all those muscles."

"That's what I told you," Coffin said with a chuckle. "I figure he also keeps his nose out of situations that might lead to trouble." He grimaced. "Some of us ain't that smart."

More silence. Then, "Did you fight in the war?"

"Yes," Coffin said quietly.

"What side was you on?"

"Doesn't much matter now, does it?" Coffin countered.

Randy thought about that for a moment. "I guess not. But I figure it'd be better to be on the winnin' side."

"There is somethin' to be said about that."

"That where you learned to shoot?"

"Yes."

"You ever get shot?"

Coffin nodded. "A couple times." He sighed. "Last one was the worst. It happened just a couple weeks before peace was called."

"You kill many men?"

"You ask a heap of goddamn questions, son," Coffin said. He was more annoyed than angry, but he did not want to think about those times, either the ones during the war, or the ones after.

They entered the bank, and Coffin had to wait a few minutes for one of the two tellers. Then he stepped up and handed the thin, pale young man the draft. The teller looked at it carefully.

"It's okay, Mr. Carter," Randy said. "My dad give it to him."

"I'm sure you're right, Randy," Carter said officiously. "But I'll still have to clear it with Mr. Yarnell." He looked at Coffin. "I'll only be a moment, Mr. Coffin."

Coffin nodded. He rolled a smoke while he waited. Then Carter returned with a distinguished-looking man, who said, "You're Mr. Coffin?"

Coffin nodded. "And you're Mr. Yarnell, I suppose?"

"Yes. Yes, I am." Yarnell was medium height and slim except for a small paunch. His clothes were well-cut and expensive. Despite the lateness of the working day, Yarnell's red-cheeked face looked fresh. "Why do you have Mr. Carstairs's draft?" His voice was ever so polite.

"Sold him a couple horses," Coffin said flatly.

"That right, son?" Yarnell asked, looking at Randy.

"Yessir," the boy answered respectfully. "Pa says I was to come here with Mr. Coffin to vouch for him that the draft was all right."

"Thank you, son." Yarnell looked at Carter. "Pay the

man, Mr. Carter." Looking back to Coffin, he asked, "Anything else, sir?"

"I'm figurin' to stay around Crooked Creek a spell, so I thought I might open an account here with you."

"By all means." He still held the draft, and he waved it a little. "Are you planning to use this to open your account?"

"That and some other cash I have."

Yarnell nodded, as if giving benediction. "Come, then. I'll help you. Mr. Carter, you have customers waiting."

"I'll wait outside for ya, Mr. Coffin," Randy said.

Coffin nodded. Once Yarnell was behind his desk, and Coffin sitting in front, Yarnell asked, "How much will you be depositing?"

"Six hundred dollars," Coffin said flatly.

Yarnell whistled softly. "A goodly sum of money, Mr. Coffin." Yarnell very much wanted to know where Coffin had gotten it, but he knew he could not ask. "You've been traveling far with this much cash on you?"

Coffin shrugged. He dropped his cigarette butt on the floor and squashed it out. "Far enough."

"You were not afraid you'd be robbed?" Yarnell probed.

"Ain't nobody knows I had that much on me. Besides," he added boastingly, "someone tried to rob me, he might just get a bit more than he bargained for."

Yarnell nodded again, thinking. He tapped a pen on the top of the desk. "Do you have a job here, Mr. Coffin?" he finally asked.

"Nope. I expect I'll find something soon enough. I have the money to wait a spell."

"Indeed you do. Have you any trade?"

Coffin flinched inwardly at the question. "Not much I'm afraid. Or at least not much that doesn't include blood." He gazed evenly at Yarnell. He thought he saw the banker's thin mustache wriggle in something that might've been a small attempt at a smile.

Yarnell finished the paperwork, took Coffin's money and gave him a receipt. As the two men stood and shook hands, Yarnell said, "It's a pleasure doing business with you, Mr. Coffin. I hope we can do more."

"We'll see," Coffin said noncommittally. He headed out.

True to his word, Randy was sitting on a bench just outside the bank. He hopped up, and the two fell into step together. At the livery, Coffin grabbed his saddlebags and his two bags of supplies. "I can help you with those, Mr. Coffin," Randy said eagerly.

Coffin looked at Carstairs. "That okay with you, Mr. Carstairs?"

The livery man nodded. "Unless you think he'll bother you."

"Nope. Come on, Randy." Coffin handed the boy one of the two canvas bags of supplies. Just outside, Coffin asked, "You know of a decent place for a man to stay? One that's quiet, maybe has meals?"

"Hotel or boardinghouse?"

"Either. A hotel'll be more expensive but most likely more comfortable and secure."

"Well, there Eagan's and Sutter's. They're both hotels. Mr. Eagan's place ain't near as fancy as Sutter's, but Mr. and Mrs. Eagan've always been nice to me."

"That your recommendation then, boy?" Coffin asked with a small smile.

"Yessir," Randy said firmly.

"Then lead on, my young friend."

Eagan's Hotel was off the main street by a block. It was a two story clapboard place with a sitting porch out front. A restaurant, also named Eagan's, was attached. The street was lined with trees, mostly cottonwoods, and seemed quiet and peaceful.

Grady Eagan greeted him warmly, once Randy had announced to Eagan that he was bringing a customer and introduced the men to each other.

"You givin' this boy a tip every time he drags in some poor, unsuspectin' soul?" Coffin asked with a laugh.

Eagan grinned a little. "He's a good kid, as far as kids go. Now, Mr. Coffin, what can I do for you?"

"A room. Second floor, if possible."

"We got one. How long?"

"Ain't sure. What're you askin' for a night?"

"Fifty cents. Three dollars a week."

"How about a month?"

Eagan's eyebrows raised. "Don't know as if I ever had anyone stayin'—or payin'—for a month." He scratched on a small pad with a pencil. "Twelve dollars. What the hell, make it eleven, if you pay me up front."

"Meals included?"

"That's extra. Let's see here." He did some more figuring "Again, if you pay me up front, I can give you room and two meals a day for twenty dollars."

"Sounds fair enough to me," Coffin said agreeably. "Where do I sign?"

He scribbled his name in the ledger book and took a key from Eagan.

"That's the room in the southwest corner upstairs. You got a good view of the river on one side, and a good view of the street from another."

Coffin nodded. "Any rules or anything I should know?"

Eagan shook his head. "Just keep it peaceable. We don't mind you having whiskey up there, long's you don't get drunk and rowdy. Go on outside, Randy," he suddenly ordered.

Randy made a face but did as he was told. Once the boy

was gone, Eagan said, "You can have women up there, if you're of a mind, but don't advertise it and keep the noise under control. Mrs. Eagan's willin' to look the other way, but she—and I—can only be taken so far."

Coffin nodded. "Hey, Randy," he shouted. "Come give me a hand with these here bags."

Chapter Nine

The first thing Coffin did—after unpacking his few personal items and cleaning himself up some—was to pay a visit to the Twisted Water Saloon.

Rudy Schmidt was tending bar again, and he grinned as Coffin stopped at the bar. "Couldn't stay away?" he asked.

"Hell no," Coffin said with a small laugh. "You got the best rotgut and the best grub I've had in a dog's age."

"No other reason?" Schmidt asked.

"Well, there is one other reason."

Schmidt laughed again. "She's upstairs right now, but I expect she'll not be busy too much longer. How's about a beer . . . and a snort of bourbon while you wait?"

"Sounds good to me." Coffin pulled his hat off and dropped it on the bar. A moment later Schmidt slapped two glasses down in front of Coffin. "You plannin' to linger a while this time?"

Coffin nodded. "Might even make my home here, things work out."

"Then this one's on me," Schmidt said. "And help yourself to the vittles down there at the end of the bar."

"Thanks, Rudy." Coffin strolled to the end of the bar and looked over the selection of food. He picked up a tin plate and piled on some smoked beef, catfish, two kinds of cheese and a boiled egg. Juggling the plate and utensils, he went back to where his drinks and hat were. A tall, beefy man dressed in a neat suit was standing there, back to Coffin.

"Excuse me," Coffin said. He got no response. "Excuse me," he said again, more loudly this time. Still no response. Coffin calmly set his plate on the bar, and then gave the beefy man a hard punch to the kidney.

The man gasped and sank, but caught himself with his right arm on the bar and managed to push himself back up.

"Now," Coffin said evenly, "get your fat ass out of the way."

The man turned, his face red. "You goddamn little shit, I'm gonna mash you."

"I don't think so," Coffin said calmly.

The big man looked down, and saw the muzzle of a cocked Remington brushing the vest across his sizable middle.

"Back off, Mike," a voice said.

The big man shuffled backward two steps. Then another man materialized. He was tall, thin, strong looking and had a mean cast to his handsome, unmarred face. He held out his hand. "Name's Rupert Lyons," he said.

Coffin glanced from Lyons to Big Mike, as he thought of the other man. Then he eased the hammer of the Remington down and slid the pistol away. He shook Lyons's hand.

"Mike here gets a little feisty of a time," Lyons said easily. "But he don't usually mean no harm. Still," Lyons added, musing, "Finnegan don't take kindly to folks pullin' guns on him."

"Then he should keep his fat ass away from other folks' things," Coffin said flatly. He waved a hand toward his hat and two drinks.

"Well, I can see how that'd go against a man's grain. Don't you, Mike?"

The big man nodded, but Coffin could see and even feel the insincerity.

"What's your name there, fella?" Lyons asked politely.

"Joe Coffin."

"You in town to stay? Or you just passin' through?"

Coffin shrugged. "Ain't decided yet. Not that it's any of your affair."

"I got a little piece of advice for you," Lyons said with exaggerated politeness. "You plan on stickin' around here, I'd be a good man to be friends with. And a man not to get on the bad side of."

"That right?" Coffin said, with only a little sarcasm.

"Yes indeed."

"Fine," Coffin said with a nod. "Now, if you're through tryin' to impress me, my beer's goin' flat and I'm hungry."

Lyons glared at him but then nodded. "We can chat another time, then," he said. Turning, he added, "Come on, Mike." The two walked off, but not before Finnegan shot a withering glance at Coffin, who grinned insolently back at him.

Coffin turned back to his food. A few minutes later, Schmidt wandered back toward him, stopped and refilled the two glasses.

"Who—or what—was that?" Coffin asked, cheek bulging with food.

"Rupe?" Schmidt said with a laugh. "He owns about half the town. Or so people say."

"Includin' this place?" Coffin asked, curious.

"Well, like with everything else he supposedly owns, not 'officially,' you might say. Word is that he owns a major chunk of the Twisted Water, but silently. Just like other places. No one knows for sure. As far as the 'real' owner, the one who plays the role, anyway, is Rex Sutter."

"Owner of the hotel?"

Schmidt nodded. "I'll be back in a minute." He walked off to take care of some thirsty customers. "Anyway, Rupe carries quite a bit of weight around Crooked Creek," Schmidt said when he returned.

"And I suppose that ox that was with him helps enforce whatever Lyons is up to?"

"Ain't many men around here gonna stand up to Big Mike Finnegan."

Coffin shrugged. "The bigger they are, the farther they got to fall. And they'll fall. It might take some time and a bit of equalizin', but they'll fall."

Schmidt grinned. "Feisty little bastard, ain't you?"

Coffin returned the grin.

Schmidt went off again, and when he returned, he was serious. "Another word of advice, Joe," Schmidt said quietly. "Watch your step around Lyons."

"He don't scare me."

"He should." Schmidt held up his hand to forestall more protest. "I ain't sayin' you should back down from him or kiss his ass or anything like that. Just be wary of him. He has a lot of friends around town. Worse, he's got a lot of people who owe him and are scared shitless of him."

Coffin nodded. He was cocky and tough. But he was not crazy. A man with a lot of scared folks at his beck and call could cause a lot of trouble for someone. Especially if that someone was in a town where he knew no one and had no friends.

Schmidt went back to his work, and Coffin went back to his eating. When he had finished, and still not seen Blue Gladys, Coffin strolled off to one of the two faro tables and watched a while. He even managed to lose a few dollars after a while. But it quickly paled on him.

Coffin was thinking of dropping out of the faro game

when Blue Gladys walked up behind him and gently placed her hands on his shoulders. He looked up and grinned, then reached up and patted her one hand.

"So, you just couldn't stay away, could you, sweetheart?" she asked in that slightly mocking tone that was normal for her.

"Nope. Had me a great urge to come on back here and do a little pokin' dance."

"Well, let's get to . . . unless you'd rather set here and play some more faro?"

"Well, I reckon I could break off my playin' if you're gonna stand there naggin' me. Lordy," he added as he stood and swept his money up, "I should've got married if I was gonna have to listen to this."

Blue Gladys laughed. It was a surprisingly strong sound from such a thin woman. They headed up the stairs together.

"What're you doin' back here, sweetheart?" Blue Gladys said when they were done and lying relaxed.

"Come to see you." Coffin smiled.

"Ah, bullshit," Blue Gladys said. "You ain't gonna go ten feet to find some pitiful fallen angel," she said bitterly. "Now, why'd you really come back?"

Coffin flipped the covers off him and swung around so he was sitting on the edge of the bed, feet on the floor. He reached for the cigarette fixings in the pocket of his shirt lying on the table. He rolled a smoke quietly, and then lit it. Once it was going, he spoke, more like he was talking to himself than talking to Blue Gladys.

"I got no place else to go, really. I got no kin except some folks back in Pennsylvania I don't really know and who don't want nothin' to do with me. I've got no wife, no sweetheart, no roots and, I sometimes think, no future."

He paused, taking a couple of deep drags on the cigarette and then blowing the smoke out with a long, drawn-out sigh. "When I come through here the other day, I wasn't here long, but I felt more comfortable in Crooked Creek than I've ever felt anywhere else that I can remember. Hell, I know that don't mean nothin', and that I just got me a dose of the melancholy, but, since I didn't have no place else to go, this seemed as good a place as any."

Coffin grabbed the bottle of whiskey on the table and slugged back a good mouthful. He finished the cigarette and stubbed it out on the table and lay back again. Then he grinned. "Besides," he said impishly, "there was this nice-lookin' and mighty willin' woman just a-sittin' here in old Crooked Creek waitin' for me." He laughed a little.

"That she was . . . I mean is . . . Well, that is, if *you're* willin' again."

"Hell, a man don't get an invite like that too often," he said with a laugh, reaching out for her.

It was near noon the next day before Coffin left Blue Gladys. He was tired but happy and hummed a tune as he strolled out into the balmy sunshine. For the first time he could really believe that spring was here. He strolled toward his hotel, taking in the sights around the town. He had never really looked at the place before.

The main street was wide and seemed well-kept. Large cottonwoods rose up in the middle of the street in two places, and someone had taken the time to ring them with small wooden fences. Stores lined the street, many with wood sidewalks out front and a few with porticos.

Coffin turned west on River Street toward his hotel. Suddenly Randy Carstairs trotted up beside him.

"Hi, Mr. Coffin," the boy said exuberantly.

"Hi, Randy. How're you doin'?"

"Just fine. Where you been?"

"You're awfully nosy," Coffin said with a laugh.

"Well, I come lookin' for ya before, and you wasn't in your room. Mr. Eagan said he didn't see you at all today."

"I had some business down in town early," Coffin said quietly, but firmly.

"I looked all over town for ya, too."

Coffin stopped and looked at Randy. "You ought to know, Randy," he said sternly, "that there's many folk who don't take to bein' asked questions. Not everything a man does is of concern to others."

"I'm sorry, Mr. Coffin." He looked crestfallen.

"It's all right, Randy. I'm just lettin' you know that I don't like too many questions, and also to save you some grief in later times." He started walking again, with Randy alongside. "Why ain't you helpin' your pa?"

Randy shrugged. "It's a lot of work."

"It'd help you build your muscles up. Help toughen you, too."

"Yeah, I know," the boy complained.

They arrived at Eagan's. "I got more things to do, Randy," Coffin said politely but firmly. Actually, all he really wanted to do was get some sleep, something he had had precious little of the night before. But he didn't want to tell that to his young friend.

"You sure?"

"Yeah, I'm sure. Tell you what, though. You go on back and help your pa today. Then you come by tomorrow about noon. Me'n you'll go do somethin'."

"Like what?"

"I don't know," Coffin said with a shrug. "We'll think of somethin'."

"All right." Randy ran off, whooping and hollering. Coffin watched him for a minute, wondering what he had gotten himself into. He wasn't sure he wanted a friend that age. Nor did he want to be a substitute for Randy's father. He also did not think it was good for the boy to go hanging around with him all that much.

He sighed. He growled at himself for worrying too much about things that would work themselves out somehow anyway. He turned and headed inside.

Chapter Ten

Coffin was walking down Cottonwood Street—the main street of Crooked Creek—enjoying the late autumn crispness. He had been in Crooked Creek six months or so and had found it a good place to be, all in all. He had not met the young woman he had seen that one time, and for a while he had wondered if seeing her perhaps was a dream. He had finally concluded, though, that she had been passing through Crooked Creek. Maybe on her way west; maybe on her way back east, her family beaten by the hardships; maybe a girl from one of the nearby farms, come into town for supplies of a time.

He did not give up his hope of seeing her again, though. Not this soon. In a way, it was almost good that he had not seen her since it was almost like a dream, one he could conjure up anytime he wanted. He was half doing so now, strolling down the street.

He stopped suddenly, intently watching a wagon down at the far end of town. Something seemed wrong. It took a few moments to realize that the freight wagon was out of control, racing hellbent up the street.

Coffin started walking again, more quickly. The wagon continued its headlong rush, though it was still two hundred yards or so away. Coffin stepped up his pace a little more.

People were beginning to stop and point at the wagon. Coffin quickened his steps still more. Then he spotted a plump woman stepping out into the street. She was bundled up against the cold and appeared to be oblivious of the charging wagon.

Coffin began to run, dodging gawkers rooted to the cold ground, watching in fascination as the woman blithely walked to an almost certain death.

He jumped off the boardwalk, slipping on the thin rime of ice on the ground. He rcgained his balance and charged on, breath puffing out in frosty little clouds. He glanced up and saw that the wagon was less than fifty yards off.

The woman had finally become aware that something was wrong. She stopped, looking at the gawkers on the sides of the street. Many were beckoning urgently to her. She slowly turned, as the sound of the thundering wagon washed over her. Then she screamed as she found herself frozen in fear.

Coffin slid, trying to stop. Still skidding, he slammed the side of his shoulder into the woman. He did not bother to see if she fell or not; it was sufficient that she was out of the way, at least a little.

The wagon was only twenty yards away, and Coffin saw that the driver was frantically trying to stop the four racing mules, but he only had one line in hand.

Coffin tore open his waist-length blanket coat and jerked out a Remington. He cocked it and fired all five rounds in the chamber. The front two mules were down, either dead or dying. It did not matter. The two rear mules immediately trampled on the front two, though they tried not to. Then all four were jumbled in a squirming, squealing knot of mule-flesh, chains, wood and leather.

The wagon's front wheels hit that roiling mess and flipped the wagon up and over. The driver jumped, landing hard on the cold ground and rolling. Crates, boxes and bales flew in all directions.

Coffin had seen his shots take effect, and in the few heart-stopping seconds that all hell broke loose, Coffin spun to his right and dove, landing mostly atop the woman. Then something landed hard on his back. He grunted, the sound muffled by the woman's heavy cloak.

Suddenly the world seemed almost serene. The only real sound in the hushed aftermath of the action were mules braying wildly. Coffin pushed himself up, quietly groaning with pain as whatever had hit him fell off. He helped the woman up, though it hurt his back considerably.

"My apologies, ma'am," he said. "I didn't mean to be so rough."

"Think no . . ."

A scream of "Mother!" stopped the woman. She and Coffin turned. Coffin managed to keep from gasping as he saw the young woman he had come to Crooked Creek to find rushing toward the woman.

"Mother, are you all right?" the girl asked, breathless from the cold and her mad dash.

"Yes, yes, dear. Yes. I'm fine. Haven't hurt anything but my dignity." She brushed herself off. "If it wasn't for this young man here, I'd have been squashed flat as a flapjack." She looked at Coffin. "And what is your name, sir?"

"Joe Coffin, ma'am," Coffin said quietly, as if afraid to talk.

"Well, Mr. Coffin," the woman said, "I am most grateful for your saving intervention."

"It was nothing, ma'am. Though I apologize again for bein' so god awful rough on you."

"Pshaw. I'd rather you did that than allowing the alternative," she said with a small laugh. She paused, then said, "Dear me, I've forgotten my manners. I'm Edith

Yarnell. And this is my daughter Edna"

"Pleased to meet you, ma'am. You, too, miss. You'd be related to Mr. Yarnell, the banker, then?"

"My husband," Edith said. "You know him?"

"I met him a couple times when I've had business in the bank." He realized he was standing there still holding his pistol. He stuck it in his holster and pulled his coat closed. "Well, ma'am, miss, I should be pushin' on. And I expect you'd like to compose yourselves after all this."

Edith smiled a little. "I must admit, it did get my old heart ticking faster."

Coffin was surprised at the woman's earthiness. She was not as old as he had originally thought, but she was middle-aged, and seemed not to mind being middle-aged.

Edith looked at Coffin's face. "You think I'm not proper enough?" she said with a laugh.

"No," Coffin said hastily. "No, not at all."

"Pshaw, Mr. Coffin." She smiled. "I didn't get to be my age without taking some of life's misfortunes. I wasn't born in any fancy circumstances. I've come far, Mr. Coffin, and I think I've managed to do so without being too awful snooty about it."

"Mother!" Edna said in a little shock.

"Hush, daughter. You're not all that snooty either."

Edna blushed, and Coffin thought she looked wonderful.

Sudden gunshots made them all jump. Coffin whirled, hand reaching for his other pistol. He stopped and turned back to face the two women once he saw that it was just someone who had shot two of the mules that had still been alive and suffering.

"Well, Mr. Coffin, what can I do to repay you?" Edith asked.

Let me marry your daughter, he thought. But he said, "Payment's not necessary, ma'am."

"Pshaw again. Certainly there must be somethin' I can do."

"Have him over to supper, Mama," Edna suddenly said.

Coffin glanced at her out of the corner of his eye. He could not believe it, but she seemed to be interested in him. He fought back the hope, though, not wanting to be crushed when he learned she was just being polite to the man who had saved her mother.

"An excellent idea, Edna," Edith said. "Yes. Come to supper, Mr. Coffin. Will tonight be all right?"

"Yes," Coffin stammered. "Yes, sure."

"Our house is over on Winding Road. You know where that is?" When Coffin nodded, Edith added, "It's the two-story brick house. Five o'clock."

"I'll be there." Coffin walked away befuddled by his sudden fortune. The jumbled profusion of the horses and wagon brought him back to reality.

The wagon driver was leaning against a hitching rail, holding a rag to a cut on his head. He pushed off the rail and limped toward Coffin, his hand out. "Goddamn if I ain't glad you come along there a few minutes ago, mister. Hell yes I am."

Coffin nodded and shook hands with him. "I don't imagine the man you work for's going to be quite so grateful."

The man laughed. "I figure he'll be a lot happier this happened than if we'd run down Warren Yarnell's wife. There'd be hell to pay over that, I can guarantee."

Coffin nodded.

"I'd be obliged if you was to let me buy you a drink or two. Or more. Kind of say thanks."

Coffin nodded again. "Next time you see me. I usually go to the Twisted Water."

"Vern Moore."

"Joe Coffin." He walked off, back still hurting, but not

as bad as before. He wasn't sure if he was getting over it or if the cold was just numbing him some. He was grateful, though, that he had been wearing the heavy blanket coat when that bale of cotton goods had landed on him.

He stopped at one of the mercantile stores and bought himself a new outfit. It was time for it anyway, but his impending supper at the Yarnell house made it almost imperative. He walked slowly back to Eagan's with his packages, and asked Eagan if he could get a tub and some hot water up in his room.

"We ain't set up for that, Mr. Coffin," Eagan said apologetically. "About the only place I know of you can get a bath—and a shave, if you're of a mind to—is Hennessey's down on Cottonwood Street. A couple doors down from the Catfish Saloon."

Coffin nodded. "I've seen it." He walked up to his room and set his things down. Moving slowly, he cleaned the Remington he had used and reloaded it. Then he napped for two hours.

He felt a little better when he awoke. He headed out with his packages again. He stopped at Hennessey's and had a haircut, a shave and a hot bath. Afterward, he dressed in the new store-bought suit and derby. The outfit—especially the hat—made him feel ridiculous, but he vowed to suffer through it, if only for this one night. He felt sillier when he buckled on his gunbelt.

Annoyed at being so concerned about his looks, he checked his pocket watch. He still had plenty of time before he had to be at the Yarnells' house. Gathering up his old clothes, which he did not think were ready for the dust bin yet, he headed out. He dropped his old clothes at Ling's Laundry and then headed back to the hotel. There he peeled off his gunbelt. With a sense of foolishness, he grabbed his saddlebags and pulled out the shoulder rig he had made up. He checked the two Colts to make sure they were loaded. He pulled the contraption on and then put his suit coat on over it. He looked into the small mirror on the bureau and nodded. It wasn't perfect, but it would do, he figured.

Finally it was time to leave. As he walked along the chill streets of Crooked Creek, he realized he was more worried about this supper than he had ever been about anything. Then he was at the house and knocking on the door. He shifted from foot to foot, feeling the cold air filter in through his coat.

The door opened and a tall, regal-looking black man stood there. "You're Mr. Coffin?" he asked.

Coffin nodded.

"Come with me, sir."

Coffin followed him down the hallway and into a sitting room. Warren Yarnell stood from his heavy chair and came to greet Coffin, hand outstretched.

"Welcome, Mr. Coffin," Yarnell said jovially. "I hear I have a lot to thank you for."

"No, sir."

"You're much too modest. You saved my wife from a horrible death, and you say it's nothing?"

"Well, maybe I did save her, but I wound up dumping her on the ground in the doin'."

Yarnell laughed, and Coffin's opinion of him rose quite a bit.

"Yes, Edith did mention that," Yarnell said. "And, while many respectable folks might have been horrified by that, I, like my wife, am grateful you did so. I'd rather have her here and unhurt, if a little mussed, rather than having to bury her in any condition." He smiled. "Now, sit, sit. Would you like a drink?"

"If you don't mind," Coffin said from the big upholstered chair Yarnell had indicated.

"Cigar?"

"How long before supper?"

"Not long. Hungry?"

"Well, yes, but mainly I'd hate to waste a good cigar if supper is due soon."

"A wise thought." Yarnell handed Coffin a glass of bourbon. He held up his own glass. "My heartfelt thanks, Mr. Coffin," Yarnell said in salute. They both drank.

"Have you found a job, Mr. Coffin?" Yarnell asked after he had sat again.

"Not really. I've been helping Harry Carstairs over at the livery, but that's just something to pass the time. I'm afraid now, though, that I'll have to pass even on that."

"Oh?"

"He took quite a blow from something that flew out of that wagon today, Warren," Edith said.

"Oh?" Yarnell was surprised.

"I'm not sure what it was, but it hit him—and would've landed on me if he hadn't flung himself on top of me at the last moment."

"Well," Yarnell said with a hearty laugh and a note of gratitude in his voice, "your heroics grow, Mr. Coffin."

"Anyone would've done the same," Coffin said modestly.

"Then how come none did?" Yarnell countered. "From what I was led to believe, dozens of people were standing around just watching. You were the only one who acted."

Coffin nodded and took a sip of bourbon.

"Edith said you would take nothing for your heroics today. Is that right?"

Coffin nodded.

"I—we all—would feel slighted if you did not let me do something for you in payment. Come now, there must be something we can do for you."

Coffin polished off the small glass of bourbon. He had an icy stillness in his stomach, as he often had had when preparing for battle. It was an interesting feeling, and he rather enjoyed it. "I'd be obliged if I'd be allowed to court your daughter, sir." He paused a moment as a shocked stillness spread around the room. "But only if she's willin'," he added. "I wouldn't want to put her or you folks out any. I'd understand if she was to say no, since I know I don't have the best prospects in the world, but I think I'd . . ."

"Hush, Mr. Coffin," Edna said boldly. "You make too light of yourself. I'd be happy to have you come a-courting—if Father doesn't mind."

"I have no objections," Yarnell said. "Edith?"

"Your visits will be welcome, Mr. Coffin."

"Then it's set," Yarnell said.

Coffin wasn't sure, but Yarnell seemed to actually cotton to the idea. Coffin felt a lot better about things.

Chapter Eleven

Coffin felt like a king when he squired Miss Edna Yarnell around Crooked Creek. The only trouble was, winter was on them, and it made their walks first uncomfortable and then almost impossible. So Coffin had to settle for spending time in the Yarnells' sitting room, more often than not under the watchful, though somewhat tolerant, eyes of Edith Yarnell.

Still, it irked Coffin a little. He was not used to being under such constraints any longer. He thought all that had ended when he left the army. Then again, he had never had such a reason to be tied down. He tried not to let it bother him much, and he was usually successful, mainly because he was able to spend quite a bit of time with her. It helped that Warren Yarnell offered Coffin a job two weeks after Coffin had begun courting Edna.

"Doin' what?" Coffin had asked, surprised.

"Guard."

"What kind of guard?" Coffin was intrigued.

"The bank. We haven't had much trouble there, but you never know. Occasionally, we might have you ride along with a shipment over to the Missouri."

"Shipment?"

Yarnell shrugged. "We have no real gold here or other precious metals, but we do have to ship money on occasion. Townsfolk also sometimes need to ship things of value."

"Why me?" Coffin asked. He was skeptical.

"Anybody who can use those pistols like you did when you saved Edith is a benefit to me." He smiled. "Besides, I need to know that a prospective possible son-in-law has a job."

Coffin laughed. "Might be a job of mighty short time once I'm shootin' it out with all them bank robbers and such."

"I'll give you sixty dollars a month—to start." He paused. "You know, Joe, I wouldn't mind being your father-in-law one of these days. Now, I'm not forcing the issue. I know how much you care for Edna. And I know she cares very much for you. If it should come to pass that you two do tie the knot, I'd probably like to bring you into the business one day. Starting out as a guard at the bank will give you the opportunity to see how things work."

"I ain't so sure about that part, Mr. Yarnell, but I'll give it a try, if you want."

"I do." Yarnell laughed. "Sort of a fateful phrase, isn't it?"

It took a few weeks, but sometime around Christmas, Coffin began to think that there was more to Warren Yarnell than just a prosperous banker. He began to notice short, almost furtive, meetings between Yarnell and hard-looking men. He noticed a few small confrontations between Yarnell and Rupert Lyons. It all puzzled Coffin, but he kept quiet about it, at least until he could learn more.

Yarnell had told Coffin that if he wanted to frequent a saloon, he should use the Eagle, rather than the Twisted Water. Coffin nodded and visited the Eagle. It was on par with the Twisted Water. It might've been a little newer, and the bar and back bar a little finer. The whiskey was no more—or less—watered, and the women working there were no more or less desirable than those at the Twisted Water.

It did not take long for Coffin to figure out that Yarnell owned the Eagle. Coffin wasn't sure if Yarnell was the sole owner or part of an ownership group, but it didn't matter. For all intents and purposes, the Eagle belonged to Warren Yarnell.

Coffin did go into the Twisted Water of a time. He enjoyed jabbering with Schmidt. But more, Coffin wanted—or maybe needed—to see Blue Gladys every now and then. Edna was, of course, a good girl, and could not be expected to do such things. Not until she was married anyway. Besides, with Edith always hovering nearby, there would be no opportunity even if Edna had been willing. So, periodically, Coffin would visit Blue Gladys, sometimes for just a short while, sometimes for the night. He did not think he was doing anything wrong. He even figured that Edna would be glad for it, since his time with Blue Gladys would keep Coffin from pestering Edna too much.

Between his time with Blue Gladys, his infrequent chats with Schmidt and from listening to others in both the Twisted Water and the Eagle, Coffin began putting pieces of the puzzle together. He finally realized there were two leaders in the town—Warren Yarnell and Rupert Lyons. Each had money, each was tough and unyielding, each had a few gunmen at his disposal, and each hated the other.

Coffin didn't know quite how to feel when he realized that he had become one of Yarnell's gun hands. In one way, it annoyed the hell out of him. He supposed that was because he had been reeled in like a fish. He would not have been angry if Yarnell had simply come up to him and told it to him straight. On the other hand, it kept him close to Edna, and, since Yarnell treated him very well, he knew he was in Yarnell's inner circle, or would be soon.

Once he knew all this, he could pretty well relax in the Eagle Saloon. In the Twisted Water, however, he was always on the alert. Lyons and his henchman, Mike Finnegan, had confronted Coffin inside the Twisted Water, but it never got too troublesome. Coffin finally figured that Lyons had suspected that Coffin knew far more about Yarnell's dealings than he did. Once Lyons realized that, he backed off some, while still keeping an eye on Coffin, particularly while Coffin was in the Twisted Water.

Yarnell didn't take kindly to Coffin's visit to the rival saloon either, and told him so one night after they had eaten. Yarnell handed Coffin a glass of whiskey and a cigar. When Coffin's and his own cigars were going, Yarnell said, "I hear you've been spending time at the Twisted Water."

"Occasional."

"I'd rather you didn't."

"Why?"

"Because I'm asking you not to."

Coffin's eyelids narrowed. He held the cigar up, as if studying it, then said quietly, "Just because you pay me a salary, doesn't mean you own all my time."

Yarnell considered that for a moment. "You're right on that." He paused. "But on the other hand, I've taken you into my family, or at least I am thinking of doing so."

Coffin shrugged.

"What's the appeal of the Twisted Water anyway?"

Coffin shrugged and smiled. "It ain't the Twisted Water itself. It's what's in it."

Yarnell looked baffled.

"I enjoy chewing the fat with one of the bartenders."

"That all?" Yarnell asked skeptically.

"Well, if you really got to know, there's Blue Gladys."

"She one of the fallen angels over there?" Yarnell did not sound shocked or bothered.

Coffin nodded and took a sip.

"There's plenty of such women at the Eagle."

"I know. I just like Blue Gladys is all," Coffin said without apology.

"You like her?" Yarnell asked, voicing some alarm.

"Yep," Coffin said with a chuckle. "It ain't like I'm gonna marry her or . . ."

"I should say not," Yarnell huffed.

". . . it's just that she's fun to be with."

"I'd still rather you kept away from the Twisted Water."

"I ain't over there much. Just once in a while. I figured you'd rather have me go visit Blue Gladys than . . ."

"That goes without saying. Look," Yarnell added in some exasperation, "I don't give a damn how many whores you bed, Joe. But I don't like my money going to . . ." He suddenly clamped his mouth shut, inwardly cursing himself.

Coffin smiled in his head. It was the closest Yarnell had ever come to admitting his feud with Lyons. "I wouldn't want someone spending my money in a rival's place neither," he said flatly.

"You know?" Yarnell was surprised.

Coffin nodded. "Some. I expect there's a hell of a lot I don't know. And that gets my hackles up more than a little." He allowed just a bit of his temper to show.

"What the hell are you angry about?" Yarnell said.

"I don't mind bein' one of your hired guns, Mr. Yarnell. I don't even mind bein' told what saloons I can—and can't—use. But what really ruffles my feathers, dammit, is the fact that you didn't see fit to play straight with me"

"But . . ."

"Don't give me no 'but' bullshit, Warren. I'm young, but

I'm not a goddamn fool. Like I said, I don't know much of what's going on exactly, but I'm bright enough to figure out that you're more than what you seem to be, and that you and Rupert Lyons're at loggerheads. I have no idea why."

Yarnell nodded. "You're right, of course. Rupert and I don't go back far, but we've never been peaceable toward each other. He likes to think he runs the town, and to a certain extent he's right. On the other hand, I have my influence, too. I can hire as many guns as he can, match him in anything. So it's a Mexican standoff of a sort. We keep circling each other like a couple dogs meeting for the first time. We keep snarling and yapping at each other and not accomplishing a whole hell of a lot."

Coffin nodded. "There somethin' you want me to do about it?" he asked. "Somethin' you've been warmin' me up for?"

"No," Yarnell said with a shake of the head. "No, I just want you on my side if something happens."

"Are you expectin' somethin' to happen?"

"Yes. But I have no idea what or when."

Coffin nodded. He stood, setting down the empty glass. "I don't mind bein' around in case somethin' happens, Warren. I'd be mighty damn put out if you didn't count me in, considerin' my feelin's for Edna. But I'd be obliged," he added pointedly, "if you wouldn't give me no more bullshit. You got somethin' you want me to do—or not do—tell it to me straight. If I ain't willin', I'll tell you straight, and we can jaw it out like two reasonable men.

Yarnell also stood. He nodded firmly. "I will do that, Mr. Coffin. Now, come, the ladies are waiting."

Christmas came and went. Going with it was a truce that had existed as part of the Noel season. But not long after the new year began, the old enmity returned. To an outsider, nothing really seemed to be amiss. If it was noted at all, it was just put down to two hardheaded businessmen having their differences.

Coffin could feel more tension, though, in the Yarnell household, in the Eagle Saloon, and in the Twisted Water. It was a strange kind of thing, nothing that one could get a grasp on, just a sensation as if everyone was waiting with baited breath for something to happen. Only nothing did.

In mid-January, Coffin went with a wagonload of freight and cash, heading for the Missouri River. He made another trip in mid-February and a third a few days into March. He hated the trips, but did not feel right in refusing them. He missed Edna on the journeys, and he was bored—and frozen—stiff.

There was no excitement on the treks. The journeys were just slow, jolting rides with him sitting on a hard piece of wood and cradling a cold scattergun in his arms. At the end of the outward trip, he could expect several hours of backbreaking work unloading the wagon, a foul, rancid meal and then a few hours sleep in a log and sod house with no windows.

He was always glad to get back. Edna always was waiting for him at the edge of town, standing in front of Gelman's Book and Stationery Store. She would be bundled up against the cold, and her pert face was flushed from it. He thought her a lovely sight, even though her lips were a little chapped, both from the cold and from her nervous chewing on them.

She was not there when he returned from the March trip, though. As the wagon got farther down Cottonwood Street, an icy fear began to build in his stomach. Then he spotted her. She was backed against the wall of Oversham's Millinery Shop by Rupert Lyons and

Big Mike Finnegan.

Coffin hopped off the slowly moving wagon and hit his stride. In moments, he was on the boardwalk right behind the two men. "Afternoon, boys," he said evenly. "Nice of you to keep a watch on my fiancée durin' my absence."

The two men turned, ready to pound on Coffin—until they saw the shotgun Coffin held. It wasn't exactly pointed at them, but it was close enough to give them a considerable dose of concern.

"The least we can do for a friend, Joe," Lyons said tightly. He was aware that a little crowd had gathered. He was embarrassed, and that gave rise to his temperature.

Edna had taken the chance to slide out from behind Lyons and Finnegan and move to just behind Coffin. "Well, I'm obliged, Rupe. You and Mike get down to the Eagle one day, and I'll stand you a couple of drinks." He tried to keep from smirking, but it was difficult. "Good day, boys."

Coffin watched as Lyons and Finnegan walked away. When he figured they had gone far enough, he turned, offered his arm to Edna, and they strolled off.

Chapter Twelve

Coffin's hand headed toward one of his pistols as he heard the door latch rattle a little. His hand had barely touched the butt of his revolver, hanging over the bed post, when he heard Rupert Lyons say, "Don't do it, sonny boy."

Coffin froze, empty hand outstretched, still half kneeling, half lying between Blue Gladys's legs. He and Blue Gladys were as naked as jaybirds.

"Get up there, sonny boy," Lyons said in a voice that quivered with excitement.

Coffin did so gingerly. He was certain Lyons would shoot him at his first false move. Then he was standing next to the bed, trying to keep the embarrassment off his face. He stood with his hands at his side, feeling his manliness shrinking rapidly.

"He don't look near so big now, does he, Rupe?" Big Mike Finnegan said with a chuckle as he pointed to Coffin's groin.

"Damn small if was you to ask me, which you just did," Lyons offered with a raspy, delighted laugh. "Stay right where you are, bitch," Lyons suddenly snapped, looking toward Blue Gladys.

An ashen-faced Blue Gladys stopped trying to rise and instead lay back, afraid, her legs spread and bent at the knee.

"Now," Lyons said, his humor returned, "Mike, you and

Albert there keeps your guns on Mr. Shrinkin' Man here while I tend to some business." He dropped his own pistol into his holster, peeled off his gunbelt and dropped it around the post at the foot of the bed. Then he climbed onto the bed, between Blue Gladys's legs. He skinned down his pants. Lyons grabbed one of Blue Gladys's hands and placed it on his manhood. "Now be nice," he said in a choked voice.

"What the hell do you think you're doin'?" Blue Gladys asked, even as she handled him. "I get paid for such favors."

Lyons laughed loud and hoarsely. "You been paid, bitch. Mr. Little Dick there paid you. He never got to finish, so I'm gonna finish for him." He turned hard, nasty eyes on Blue Gladys. "That's enough now, bitch," he said gruffly, "except for helpin' me in."

Coffin kept his face as flat as he could, trying not to betray any of the rage that seethed inside him. As surreptitiously as he could, he kept an eye on Finnegan and Albert Reece, another of Lyons's men. Reece was an odious little man, looking like nothing more than bones and clothes, except for the thin, long peaked nose, which constantly ran. He watched, hoping that both of the men would get distracted by Lyons's bouncing and grunting. It would take Coffin no more than a few moments to grab a Remington and blast Finnegan and his moronic little partner. Then he could take his time finishing off Lyons.

Reece's attention wavered from watching Coffin to watching his boss with wheezing pleasure. Finnegan's eyes never wavered from Coffin.

Within minutes Lyons was sounding like a dying hog, and moments later he was done. He lay atop Blue Gladys until he caught his breath. Then he rolled back and pulled up his pants as he got off the bed. With his pants buttoned, he buckled his gunbelt back on.

Grinning like an ape, Lyons drew his pistol again and

pointed it at Coffin. "I'll watch the little bastard for a spell, Mike, if you want to have a go at her."

"Don't mind if I do."

Blue Gladys once again endured the disgusting though enthusiastic rumblings of what passed for lovemaking for Mike Finnegan. Then he, too, was done, and it was Albert Reece's turn. He was a little quieter, and he squeaked rather than grunted. He also lasted no more than a few seconds.

"You owe me for two more, Rupe, you cheap son of a bitch," Blue Gladys said flatly.

"Another time, bitch. Now, if you know what's good for you, you'll stay here for a while."

"What're you gonna do with him?" she asked, eyes wide with fright. She pointed at Coffin.

"Hell, I ain't gonna hurt him none, if that's what you're worried about," Lyons said soothingly.

Blue Gladys didn't believe him any more than Coffin did, but neither said anything.

Lyons looked back at Coffin. "You know, Mr. Coffin, that you hurt my feelin's the other day when you threatened me with that scattergun. Took me down a peg or two with the good folks of Crooked Creek."

Coffin shrugged. "I didn't know you had any feelin's to be hurt," he said flatly.

"Well I do, Mr. Coffin," Lyons said reasonably. "Yes, I do." He paused and stroked his neck a few moments with his left hand. "Now, had you *really* humiliated me, I would've killed you straight as soon as I could. But you didn't, and I expect you really didn't know any better. Because of that—and because I'm just a friendly sort of fella—I ain't gonna kill ya. Nope." He shook his head, looking like every man's best friend doing a painful but necessary task.

"Nice of ya," Coffin said sarcastically.

Lyons nodded, as if he agreed with Coffin. "Besides, you

was kind enough to pay Miss Gladys here for my sportin'. I expect you'll be happy to pay for Mike's and Albert's turns, too." He sighed. "But that can wait."

"You mind tellin' me what you got planned for me?" Coffin asked nonchalantly.

"Naw, don't mind a-tall." He paused, smiling as he thought of what he had planned. "I'm aimin' to humiliate you some, like you done to me. Now, march. Outside and downstairs."

Coffin stalled a second, expecting Lyons to tell him to hurry up and get his pants on. Then he realized that Lyons was going to humiliate him by making him walk around the saloon in his birthday suit. He could accept that without too much discomfort, he figured. He shrugged and moved toward the door.

They made a strange little procession: Joe Coffin, naked as the day he was born, followed by three grinning men holding pistols on him, and then Blue Gladys who had jumped out of bed pulling the sheet with her. As the parade came down the stairs, she hastily wrapped the sheet around her.

"Take a turn around the place there, Shorty," Lyons said. He followed Coffin fairly closely, wanting to make sure Coffin didn't grab someone's pistol or something. Finnegan and Reece were right behind him.

Coffin could feel his ears burning, and he hoped the rest of him was not as red as he felt with the embarrassment. Still, it wasn't all that bad. Of course it didn't help him any with the hoots, catcalls, whoops and other assorted noises emitted by the saloon's patrons.

Coffin finished his circuit of the saloon and stopped at the foot of the stairs. Blue Gladys was standing there, sheet still wrapped loosely around her. She grinned at Coffin, who returned the smile. He placed a hand on the banister and put a foot on the first step.

"Not so fast there, Sonny Boy," Lyons said.

Coffin turned his head to look at Lyons. There was a light in Lyons's eyes that Coffin did not like at all.

Lyons waved his pistol. "Outside," he ordered, his voice turning suddenly harsh.

Coffin turned and glared at him, trying almost desperately to bottle up the sudden flash of rage.

Lyons grinned maliciously. He lowered the pistol some. "Or I could shoot 'em off here and now," he said, sounding as if he were really enjoying himself.

Coffin hesitated, wondering if he should take the risk. After all, there was no reason to think that Lyons would not do what he had just said after parading Coffin around for his perverted humor some more. Then Coffin sighed mentally. It would be a certain thing now if he gave Lyons any trouble. And if that happened, he would probably not live long enough to kill Lyons. As long as he was still alive and whole, there was always a chance to do something about his situation.

The thoughts lasted no more than the blink of an eye. Still managing to keep his temper in check, Coffin moved his foot off the step.

Lyons grinned vacuously again and wagged the pistol barrel. Coffin sucked in a deep breath and then eased it out. Then he marched off. The parade was a little longer, and a little more strange than it had been. The naked Coffin was followed by three gunmen, one prostitute wrapped in a cheap bed sheet, several of her fellow painted women and a half-dozen men with various drinks in hand.

"Where to?" Coffin asked tightly just outside the doors.

"A parade up and down Cottonwood Street would be about right, don't you think?"

Coffin shrugged and stepped off the boardwalk into the cold street. It was close to spring, but winter was making a last gasp effort before being shoved aside. A weak afternoon sun provided mild heat. The temperature was just at the freezing point. A light, sifting snow was falling, and the ground was still frozen. The wind and snow chilled him quickly, and then the cold seeped up from the hard ground into his feet. Coffin fought as hard to keep from shivering as he did to keep his fury in check.

Time lost meaning for Coffin. He just marched along, occasionally prodded by Lyons or Finnegan. He was aware, but only in a vague sense, that quite a few people had stopped to watch and point, many of them laughing. Women gasped and whispered, pointing in shocked amusement.

At the intersection of Cottonwood Street and River Street, Lyons and the steadily growing parade of onlookers turned Coffin back the other way. Somewhere after having passed the Twisted Water again, Lyons finally told Coffin to stop.

Coffin did so, and turned to look at Lyons. Nothing could be seen in his face, but Lyons was a bit uneasy at the hard sheen over Coffin's eyes. Then he shook off the gloom. He had had himself a hell of a time here, and provided the citizens of Crooked Creek with an entertainment that did not come along every day. Besides, he always felt better when he was able to shame or abuse someone this way.

"Well, sonny boy," Lyons said magnanimously, "I hope you've learned somethin' today. It doesn't pay to publicly humiliate me." He grinned, enjoying the limelight. "Now, why don't you go on back to your room over there at Eagan's before your pecker freezes off. You can come get your things tomorrow. Oh, and Blue Gladys will be takin' the money due her from your pockets. Just so you know and so you don't go accusin' folks of stealin' from you."

Lyons whooped once, loudly and fired his pistol in the air. "Drinks're on me, folks!" he bellowed. He turned and led a cheering crowd away, leaving Coffin virtually by himself.

One who remained was Edna Yarnell. She stood a hundred yards away, on the other side of the street, looking toward Coffin. Then she, too, turned and walked away, into Markham's Dry Goods Store.

Coffin stood for another minute, while the wind whispered gently around him, brushing him with soft, freezing snowflakes. Then Coffin began striding up the street, refusing to give in to the chills that racked him. People began trickling out of the Twisted Water. Coffin figured that Lyons had only bought one round. A few of the people saw him and laughed. Most who spotted him, though, walked away with heads down, as if embarrassed themselves.

Almost directly across the street from the Twisted Water was Mueller's General Store. Coffin pushed inside, clamping his jaw tight to keep his teeth from chattering. Two old women turned at the sound of the door and then turned away immediately when they saw him. They muttered to each other while shading their eyes.

Coffin ignored them as he headed for a table on which pants were piled. He generally had trouble getting trousers to fit, at least as far as length went. He found one pair that fit his waist right. They were long, but he didn't care right now. Nearby were socks, and he pulled a pair of those on and then some boots, tucking the too-long legs of his pants into the boots. He did not worry about a shirt.

Coffin clomped up to the glass-fronted counter to his left of the cash register. Otto Mueller stood with arms crossed across his chest, glaring at Coffin. Mueller was a tall, distinguished-looking man with a mane of white hair and matching mustache. He had piercing blue eyes and a permanent hard cast to his face.

Coffin gave him an equally hard stare, then lifted a fist and punched it through the glass counter. Mueller jumped as if struck. He moved to grab Coffin.

"You keep the hell away from me, Otto," Coffin growled. "Don't even think of layin' a finger on me."

"But my counter," Mueller protested.

"I'll make it good. Everything else, too. Now stay away from me, dammit."

Mueller did not like it, but he had never had trouble with Coffin before. He wanted to see what Coffin would do.

Coffin was no longer paying attention to Mueller. He reached into the glass case and picked up a .44-caliber Remington. He brushed shards of glass off a package of paper cartridges and opened the box. Methodically, he tore open the paper, poured the powder into the cylinder, and then rammed the lead ball home. He filled all six cylinders this time. There was no need for safety right now. He pulled out the small tin of percussion caps and set one on each nipple of the pistols. He grabbed another Remington and loaded that, too. He was about ready to leave, when he shrugged and grabbed a .44-caliber Colt and loaded it. Once more he dipped into the box of paper cartridges and pulled out a handful.

He was about to shove them into a pants pocket when Mueller said, "Here, you can use this." The storekeeper held out a small buckskin pouch.

Coffin nodded and took it. He dropped the cartridges into the pouch and then dumped the tin of caps in the little sack. He tied it to a belt loop on the pants. Coffin shoved the Colt into the waistband of his trousers at the small of his back. With the two Remingtons in hand, he nodded again at Mueller, and then headed for the door.

Chapter Thirteen

Randy Carstairs could not understand how a man like Joe Coffin, a friend the likes of which he had never had, and probably would never have again, could allow himself to be so mistreated and humiliated.

Randy hadn't spent nearly as much time with Coffin in the past couple of months as he had earlier. Randy didn't fully understand it, but he had some inkling of courting and such. He hadn't been too upset at Coffin's many absences. After all, a man had to work.

He did, though, miss spending time with Coffin. The short, powerful man had taught him much in the way of handling himself and dealing with bullies. Indeed, Randy had even managed to fight his nemesis—Howie Magee—to a draw one day when Magee had been taunting him unmercifully. Randy had started to get angry, ready to just leap on Magee. But slowly Coffin's words had asserted themselves in his mind. He shut down his anger as best he could, and appeared to be calm and unconcerned. Magee increased the volume and enmity of his epithets. Then, when Magee was highly frustrated because Randy seemed nonplused by all the taunts, Randy jumped on him. Surprised, Magee had quickly managed to gain an almost upper hand. Together the two had decided to call it a draw. Howie Magee had not bothered Randy much after that.

So Randy stood on a box in the small space between Medved's Hardware and the Twisted Water wondering how Joe Coffin could allow himself to be so humiliated. He stood there watching, until almost everyone was gone into the saloon. Still, he stayed there and watched as Coffin walked slowly up the street. When he saw Coffin turn into Mueller's, Randy was ready to leave. It was cold, and he was totally dispirited by what had happened to Coffin. But something kept him in place. He watched and waited and hoped something would happen.

Then Coffin had come out of Mueller's, a big pistol in each hand, and Randy felt a ripple of excitement.

With a Remington in each hand, Coffin left Mueller's and stalked across the cold, almost barren street. He stopped only a moment outside the door of the Twisted Water. He took a deep breath and then slammed the door open, with a kick hard enough to knock the bottom hinge off.

There were not that many patrons in the saloon, and those took one look at the hard set of Coffin's face and began scrambling to get back against the side walls. That way they would be out of the line of fire, or more hopefully, be able to get out once Coffin moved away from the entrance.

That left Lyons, Finnegan, Reece and a man known only as Rickets, another of Lyons's hired hands, standing near the bar. They were all looking toward the door.

"Well, well, well, look at this, boys," Lyons said with a laugh, "if it ain't Nature Boy himself come back for another round."

"A little overdressed, ain't you?" Finnegan said with a satisfied laugh.

Coffin moved a dozen steps inside the saloon and a few

yards to his left to get away from the door a little. He did not notice that Randy Carstairs had slipped inside and crouched against the wall next to the door.

Coffin lifted a Remington and shot Rickets twice. The scabrous reprobate of uncertain lineage looked at Coffin with wide, blank eyes. Then his bowed legs lost their strength, and he crumpled as he wheezed his last breath on the sawdust-covered floor.

"Jesus, Mary and Joseph," Finnegan breathed in awe. He, Lyons and Reece stood, stunned, drinks held in hand in midair.

"Hey," Lyons finally said, trying to recover some semblance of equilibrium, "why the hell'd you do that?" He was incredulous.

Coffin stared unblinkingly at the three men.

"Jesus, Sonny . . . I mean, Christ we were just havin' some fun is all." Real fear began to creep up Lyons's spine. He was beginning to think that he had made a major miscalculation. He had seen Coffin as just a small, unimportant smart-mouth; a cocky young man who thought he was better than he was. Now he was not so sure. No, not sure at all.

"A man don't mind bein' taken down a peg or two of a time," Coffin said coldly. "But what you did was more than just parade me around for the enjoyment of others. You stripped me of my pride, and that's often all a man like me has got—pride."

"Hell, Mr. Coffin—Joe—we didn't know you'd take this all so poorly," Lyons said unctuously. "I mean, we figured to march you around the saloon here and kind of get back at you for having embarrassed me that time when . . ."

"That time you accosted my fiancée, you stupid bastard," Coffin snarled.

"Well, I expect we were wrong there. Yes indeed," Lyons said more firmly, "we were wrong that time. And we were wrong today. Yes, sure we were." He laughed uneasily. "Things just kinda got out of hand, ya know. I mean, we . . . I didn't mean to let things get that far, but, ya know, with everybody havin' a high old time and all . . . well, it just kind of kept on goin'."

"You're a lyin' sack of shit, Lyons."

"Hey, that ain't fair, now."

"I ain't fair." Coffin knew that Lyons was trying to draw his attention to the conversation so that he, Finnegan and Reece could have a chance at getting their guns out and blast him. So he was not taken in by it, but he decided that he didn't need to let Lyons and his two cronies know that he knew.

"Come on, Coffin," Lyons said, a plaintive note edging into his voice, "we were just havin' a good time. Can't you take a . . ."

Reece, the most nervous of the three, made his move. His shaking hand had never been far from his pistol that was lying on the bar. He grabbed it and started to turn. "Now, Rupe!" he screeched. "Now!"

But the only other one to move was Coffin, who raised the Remington in his left hand, and fired twice. Reece screamed as one ball hit him in the thigh, breaking the bone. He fell sideways, and Coffin's second shot missed him, going over his head to thud into the bar.

As Reece struggled to cock his pistol, Coffin shot him in the face.

Lyons's eyes were as wide as saucers. Neither he nor Finnegan had moved. Finnegan's face was blank, but Coffin was sure he could see fear—or maybe it was craziness—in the big Irishman's eyes.

"You still havin' fun, Rupe?" Coffin asked. There was not a hint of warmth in his voice.

"I . . ." Lyons squawked. He found that his voice would not work right.

"How about you, Finnegan? You want to laugh at me some more? Make a few more jokes about my manhood? As I seem to recall from when you was pokin' Gladys up there that you didn't have much to boast about that way."

"You smart-ass son of a bitch," Finnegan hissed. "I ought to . . ."

"Don't tell me what you ought to do chickenshit. Just do it," Coffin challenged coldly.

Finnegan stood there for a moment looking at Coffin. Then a slow smile began creeping across his face. He had been leaning an elbow on the bar, but now he pushed off it. "Seems like you got yourself a little advantage there, boy," he said, waving a hand at Coffin's two pistols.

Coffin shrugged. "You got to take your chances," he said flatly.

Finnegan nodded. If he were in Coffin's shoes, he wouldn't give someone like him a chance either. "Mind?" he asked, pointing to his glass. When Coffin shook his head, Finnegan drained the whiskey and set the glass down. Suddenly he whirled, crouching as his hand darted for his pistol.

Coffin fired the last shot in the Remington in his left hand, and missed. Finnegan had moved far faster than Coffin had expected. He swung the other revolver up, though and fired twice. Again he missed once, but the second bullet hit Finnegan in the throat.

Finnegan's eyes widened, and he jerked from the ball's impact. He tried to say something, but all that came out was a strangled, bloodchoked gargle.

Coffin watched Finnegan for a moment, to make sure Finnegan would not be able to do anything. Then he turned his hate-filled gaze on Lyons. "Looks like you're all alone now, Sonny Boy," he said sarcastically.

Lyons could not remember having ever been this scared before. He hoped he didn't show it. "So where does that leave us?" he asked. Even he could tell that his voice was quavering.

Coffin shot Lyons in the right leg, just below the knee.

Lyons sucked in a breath at the sharp pain as his tibia broke. He managed to catch himself on the bar, though.

Finnegan was moaning and moving a little. He seemed to be trying to get his pistol in hand. Coffin was distracted by it, and did not like it, so he shot Finnegan again before turning his attention back to Lyons.

"You wait till the goddamn marshal hears about this," Lyons spit. "You'll goddamn hang."

Coffin shrugged. "When's the last time that useless old fart ever stuck his nose into anything?" Coffin asked rhetorically. In the eleven months Coffin had been in Crooked Creek, he had only seen the lawman a few times. He didn't even know his name. If any laws needed to be enforced in Crooked Creek, either Lyons and his cronies took care of it, or Warren Yarnell did.

Lyons shook his head. "You've done more than enough damage here, Coffin. Why don't you just go on about your business, and we'll forget all about this. What do you say, huh?"

Coffin laughed hollowly. "Right. And in a couple of months or so, you'll be mended and hire a new crew of guns to come kill me."

"I wouldn't do that. I swear."

Coffin caught sight of someone behind an overturned table edging a pistol out in his direction. He whirled and fired once. The ball tore a chunk of table out. The man's head jerked backward. "Toss out the piece, or the next one goes through your head."

A revolver suddenly flew over the rim of the table and landed with a clatter on the floor. Coffin was relieved it did not go off. "Now stand up and let me see you're unheeled."

An elderly man stood up, hands half raised.

"Hold your coat open." The man did. "Hold the back of your coat up and turn." When the man had completed that, Coffin asked, "There any others behind there?"

The man nodded timidly.

"You others come on out and do the same."

Two other aging men stood and went through the routine. Coffin nodded, satisfied, and turned back to face Lyons.

Lyons had gotten a pistol out, but he was having trouble cocking it while trying to keep himself upright with one arm on the bar. He was muttering curses.

Coffin was mentally debating whether to just finish Lyons off right away or make him suffer a little longer, when he heard a frightened, shouted, "Watch it, Joe!"

Coffin did not worry about who had said it or why. He just knelt where he was and then swung toward the door. He spotted Randy Carstairs next to the door, and Freddie Moore, a low-level gunman in Lyons' employ, standing in the doorway, a pistol out. He fired three times.

So fast had it all happened, that Moore was shooting at where Coffin had been, not where he was. Coffin popped off the last two shots in the Remington. Moore staggered back outside and fell off the boardwalk.

Coffin looked at Randy and nodded solemnly. "Thanks, boy," he said as he rose. "You keep watchin' out."

Wide-eyed, Randy could only nod.

Standing again, Coffin looked at Lyons, who was grinning. He had managed to get himself balanced on his one good leg and had the broken leg resting lightly on the brass rail near the bottom of the bar. He was still struggling to cock his pistol, but almost had it done.

"Somethin' funny?" Coffin asked.

"Yes," Lyons said, laughing almost hysterically. "Yes,

you dumb bastard, yes." The pistol was cocked now, and Lyons was shakily bringing it to bear. "Your pistols are empty, you sorry bastard." He was gloating, and enjoying it immensely.

"I expect you're right," Coffin said evenly. He tossed the pistols down.

"I'm gonna shoot your nuts off first, you son of a bitch, and then I'm . . . I'm gonna shoot you, you little bastard. Several times and let you die slow, while I watch."

"There's one small problem with that," Coffin said icily.

"Oh? What's that?" He was as sarcastic as Coffin had been earlier.

"This." Coffin reached back and pulled out the Colt that had been stuck in the waistband of his pants. He fired, breaking Lyons's other leg. Lyons dropped his revolver as he fell to the floor, groaning.

Coffin walked up and stood over Lyons. "Damn fools like you never stop amazing me. You think that because I'm smaller than you are, that it somehow makes you better. And as if that wasn't bad enough, you have to humiliate people." He shook his head. "It's a little late now, but you should've shot me either upstairs when you started this, or else down at the end of the street there when you left. Stupid, stupid bastard."

Coffin shot Lyons through the right eye.

Chapter Fourteen

Coffin stood for a few moments, looking around the saloon. No one made a move against him, though one man raced to the door and then out, tripping over Moore's body. Coffin slowly rose and walked toward the three bodies. He stopped at Reece's and went through his pockets. He pulled out eighteen dollars and change, a pocket knife and some cigarette fixings. He dropped them and the knife on Reece's chest.

Methodically, Coffin went through Finnegan's pockets and then Lyons'. Altogether, he had one hundred fifteen dollars and some change. He placed the fifteen dollars and change on the bar, picked up Reece's knife, opened it and jammed it through the dollar bills and into the bar, holding the money down. He shoved the rest of the money in a pants pocket. He looked at Rudy, who was behind the bar, and who had not moved during the whole altercation. Coffin nodded at the bartender. "That's for Blackburn to bury this scum," he said, pointing to the money on the bar.

Rudy nodded. "I'll have someone fetch him directly."

Coffin looked straight at him. "Thanks," he said quietly but firmly. It would have been easy and probably more beneficial for Coffin if the bartender had hauled out one of the several loaded scatterguns stashed behind the bar for when trouble erupted, which in a place like the Twisted Water was fairly commonplace.

"It's nothin'," Rudy said.

"Bullshit." He grinned tightly at the bartender, who returned it. Coffin turned and headed toward the door. As he did, he stuffed the Colt into the waistband of his pants again like before. He paused long enough to grab the two Remingtons from the floor before he stopped in front of Randy.

"You were a big help, boy," he said gruffly.

"It wasn't so much," Randy said, though inside he was so full of pride that he felt like he was going to explode with it.

"Hell, it wasn't for you, boy, I'd be layin' dead over there with the rest of those bastards." He paused, staring at Randy. He could see how proud the boy was, and in a way it made him feel bad. A man should never feel good about killing, he believed, though one should not hesitate to kill an enemy if need be, and do so with swift certainty. Still, Coffin did not like killing as did many men, including Lyons and Finnegan.

What bothered Coffin so much now was that he had presented a very poor image to Randy, who well might think killing four men was an acceptable way to avenge some humiliation. In the cool calm of hindsight, Coffin knew he had overreacted today. On the other hand, he knew with absolute certainty that it would have come down to this sooner or later. He and Lyons were bound to go at each other.

He felt he had to try to explain that to Randy, but he wasn't sure this was the time for it. He held out the two Remingtons, and noted that Randy's eyes looked like they would pop out. "Take them over to Mueller," he said.

Randy looked crushed.

Coffin pulled the money out of his pocket and peeled

off forty-five dollars in paper money. He held it out to Randy, who had a little trouble juggling the two big guns while trying to take the money. He finally managed, though.

"The money's for Mueller, too," Coffin said. "Tell him I'm obliged for the loan of the guns. The money's for the display case, the pants and boots." He paused. "And some to pay for the guns," he added.

"You want me to bring these guns over to you at Eagan's?" Randy asked. He was still crestfallen. He had thought that Coffin was going to give him the guns for his very own.

"Nope. Leave 'em with Otto." He paused. "Then have him pick out a couple smaller ones for you in their place. A couple Colt .36s might be good. Or even some .32s, if he's got any. Your hands . . ." He stopped, his words overwhelmed by Randy's whoop of joy.

Coffin let the boy's shouts of joy run on for just a bit, then barked at Randy to stop his foolishness. Randy stopped and looked at Coffin with large, suddenly frightened eyes.

"Listen to me, boy, and listen good," Coffin said harshly, wanting to make sure he cut through Randy's excitement so that he would be able to digest the words. "You're to use them guns only if it's life and death. You don't go shootin' anyone—don't even go shootin' *at* someone—unless you're in danger of dyin' right there. Or if your pa or some other kin or friends'll die if you don't act. You got that?"

"But you . . ." He cradled the guns against his chest with one hand and arm and pointed with the other hand, in which he still had the money Coffin had given him, toward the bodies.

"I'm a goddamn fool for that," Coffin said roughly. "A goddamn fool. Don't heed what I've done here today, boy.

Heed what I told you. Don't shoot at no one unless there's danger of some innocent dyin'. This here isn't the way to handle affronts to your dignity."

"How do I know when . . ."

"I don't know, boy, I really don't," Coffin said wearily. "But you ought to learn more self-control than I have." He sighed. "I think a lot of it's due to the war, boy," he said, almost speaking to himself. "Most times there it was kill somebody or take a bullet yourself. It just got to a point where all there was in the world was shooting and blood, and gunsmoke and pain. And death. There was always death. It seemed like there was never a day without dyin'."

He shook away the harsh, blood-soaked memories. "Anyway, boy, just heed what I said. I don't want you turnin' into somebody like Lyons or Finnegan, men who like killin'. I don't want you turnin' into a man like me neither. I ain't . . ."

"Don't say that, Mr. Coffin," Randy said as harshly as he could manage. "You ain't like them others. You ain't!" he insisted.

"Listen to the boy, Joe," Schmidt said, walking up. "You hadn't of killed them boys today, you would've had to do it another time."

Coffin looked at the bartender and nodded. "I know that," he said sadly. "I didn't want Randy to know that, though."

Schmidt shrugged. "Those bastards hurt a lot of folks over the years, Joe. Today they only got what was coming to them for a long time." He looked at Randy and smiled. "But it'd be a good thing was you to heed Joe's words. He's been through it."

"So've you," Coffin said.

Schmidt nodded a little.

Randy looked from one man to the other and then nodded solemnly. He felt like he had been given a weighty responsibility. "I'll try'n do good, Mr. Coffin," he said in a hushed voice.

Coffin nodded. "One other thing—your pa don't want you to have them guns, you come give 'em to me or give 'em to your pa for keepin'. Don't you argue with him on this or go sneakin' about behind his back."

"I will." Randy could not believe his good fortune.

"Oh, while you're at Otto's, tell him I'll be in later or tomorrow to settle up over the Colt."

Randy nodded.

"All right, boy, go on about your business," Coffin said. When Randy had run off, tightly clutching the guns and money, Coffin turned and looked back across the bar.

Blue Gladys had watched the gunfight and its aftermath from halfway up the stairs. She realized how lucky she had been. Only moments before Coffin had entered the saloon she had been with Lyons and his men, arguing with them over what they had done to Coffin. They had laughed, as they had all along, and ignored her. Finally tired of being snubbed, she had turned and started up the stairs. The sudden, gasping silence had stopped her halfway up, and she had turned to see Coffin.

She smiled tentatively at Coffin now. "I got business to tend to, Rudy," Coffin said quietly.

The bartender turned and spotted Blue Gladys. "Reckon you do, boy," he said with a small laugh. "So do I, but not nearly as pleasant as yours," he added.

Coffin headed to the stairs and up, stopping on the step just below Blue Gladys's. "You still of a mind to finish what we started before?" he asked quietly.

Blue Gladys nodded without hesitation.

Coffin silently escorted Blue Gladys up the stairs and then into her room.

"I never touched nothing of yours in here," Blue Gladys

said as they entered the room. "I haven't even been up here since we . . . I was down there arguin' with that son of a bitch."

Coffin nodded.

Blue Gladys was still wearing nothing but the bed sheet. She dropped it and sat on the edge of the bed. She twisted, bringing her legs up, and then was lying down, legs spread and knees bent. "This about where we left off, sweetheart?" she asked with a smile.

"No, not quite," Coffin said, grinning. He skinned off his boots, socks and pants and climbed into the bed, positioning himself between her thighs. "I believe this is where we was interrupted."

It was dark when Coffin finally left Blue Gladys two hours later. He had pulled out the cash taken from Lyons and his men and held out a twenty-dollar gold piece and a ten-dollar bill. "That ought to about cover it," he said quietly.

"You don't owe me any money, Joe," Blue Gladys said, eyes downcast. She looked up at him. "You won't have to pay for it no more. You come around for me another time."

He grinned. "Well, that's mighty nice of you. But this ain't payin' for me. I paid you for that last night. This is to pay for Lyons and his cronies."

Blue Gladys looked hesitant, and Coffin grinned again. "Hell, girl, this ain't my cash. I took it from those bastards down there."

Blue Gladys smiled and reached for the cash. "Thanks, Joe," she said happily. A little more somberly she said, "I can sure use it."

"I expect you can." He set his hat on. "I'll be seein' you around." He left, wearing his old pants and shirt, though he kept the new boots and threw the old ones out. His familiar gunbelt was around his waist.

Coffin had spent more time with Blue Gladys than he had planned but a little less than he had wanted. He was glad that it was dark outside. He would admit only to himself that he did not want to face the people of Crooked Creek, at least for a while, and so he was pleased that the darkness would hide his movements at least to some extent.

Eagan was at the desk when Coffin got to the hotel, but to Coffin's relief, he said nothing about the afternoon's incident. Coffin tossed his extra clothes and the Colt revolver on the bed and then washed up in the basin. He felt tired and drained and just wanted to sleep for a week. But he felt he had to go to Edna's and talk to her. He had missed dinner at the Yarnells' house, the first time he had done that for a reason other than being out of town on business.

Still, he hesitated. It was bad enough that he was embarrassed when walking down the street at night after what had happened. It was going to be very difficult—and discomfiting—to face Edna and her parents.

He shook off the gloom a little and headed out the door. The walk to the Yarnells' house seemed to take less than half a minute, where normally it took five or ten minutes, depending on how quickly he felt like walking.

Then he was standing on the Yarnells' spacious front porch and rapping on the door. He waited for Mordecai Jefferson—the Yarnells' black servant—to answer the door. It seemed to take a long time, and Coffin knocked again.

Finally Jefferson opened the door a little and stood in the space. Coffin started to step inside, but Jefferson did not move.

"May I help you, sir?" Jefferson asked in his wonderful

baritone voice.

"What in hell's gone wrong with you, Mordecai?" Coffin asked, torn between anger and bewilderment.

"Mr. Yarnell says he don't want to see you. Miss Edna says the same."

"Why?" Coffin asked, more baffled than ever.

Jefferson shrugged. "You have to ask them about that," he said calmly.

"And how the hell am I supposed to ask them anything if you don't let me in the house?"

"I don't know, sir." Jefferson's face was blank.

Coffin almost shook with the intensity of rage that swept over him. His right hand came up and began tracing slow little circles on his stomach. It was a habit he had picked up, but when or from where, he never knew. It seemed like he always had done it in times of stress or danger. It seemed to calm him. It also kept his hand fairly close to both Remingtons. He felt like just up and shooting Jefferson, but he knew that would do no good.

"They say I could talk to them another time?" Coffin asked, mouth tight.

"Tomorrow. You come after supper, when it's dark. Mr. Yarnell says you come to the back door."

Once more fury ripped through Coffin like a buzz saw. He managed to get it in control. He had nothing else to say, and apparently neither did Jefferson. Coffin nodded and turned away. He knew now, though, that today's episode with Lyons and the others was on the Yarnells' minds. He didn't know what they thought of him now, but he knew it wasn't good. He was tempted to not bother going back the next night. Not if it meant going to the back door like some poor servant.

Then he sighed, the breath coming out in a frosty white cloud in front of him. He had to go back at least one more time. He just had to confront them about it.

Chapter Fifteen

Coffin stayed holed up in his room at Eagan's for the night, and throughout the daylight hours the next day. He did not want to meet anyone just yet. He knew that as angry and humiliated as he still was, that as soon as someone—and there would be someone for certain—poked fun at him for yesterday's doings, that he would kill that person. Coffin could get away with killing Lyons and his pals, since it was basically self-defense, but killing one of Crooked Creek's respectable citizens was another story.

So he stayed in his room and had Eagan or his wife bring him food from the restaurant. He did have two visitors. Randy Carstairs stopped by early, face bright with excitement.

"I got me two new guns," the boy said excitedly.

"Well, where are they?" Coffin asked.

"Right in here," Randy said, holding up a burlap sack.

"So show me," Coffin said with mock exasperation. "I can't see 'em inside the sack."

Randy grinned even more, though Coffin would have sworn that was impossible. The boy put the bag on the bed and opened it. He reached in and pulled out a cloth and lay that on the bed. He pulled out another cloth and set that down too. Then he almost reverently began unfolding the cloths until the two pistols were revealed.

Coffin picked one up and turned the cylinder slowly, making sure it was not loaded. Then he hefted it. "A .31-caliber Colt pocket model," he said, nodding. "Good little pistol."

"It ain't too light?" Randy asked seriously.

"Too light for what?" Coffin asked, glaring at his young friend.

Randy shrugged, embarrassed. He had thought Coffin would understand such things, and would not talk to him in that tone of voice that made fun of him.

"Let me tell you somethin', boy," Coffin said more harshly than he had wanted. "A .31 can kill somebody just as dead as a .44. All a .44 really does is give you a bit more range. It does give a little punch up close, which can help you. But this here gun'll do the job just about as good. With your small hands and your skinny arms, this .31's ideal. It'll be easier for you to learn how to shoot with it. You get a little older, a little bigger, maybe strengthen up your arms, you can look for a bigger, heavier pistol."

"Will you show me; teach me, I mean?"

"If I'm around," Coffin said flatly.

"What's that mean?" Randy asked, bewildered.

"After what happened yesterday, there might be more than a few folks'd think Crooked Creek'd be better off without the likes of me. I ain't sayin' that'll happen, but it might."

Coffin put the one pistol down and picked up the other and checked it over. "Both of 'em are in good shape," he said. "They're fairly old, and used, but they've been well cared for. You know how to keep 'em in good shape?"

Randy nodded.

"Good. How much did Otto charge you for 'em?"

"Three dollars each, plus two more dollars for a flask of powder, a pouch of lead balls, a tin of caps, cleanin' stuff and a bullet mold. You think I paid too much?"

Coffin shook his head. "What about the rest of the money I give you?"

"Oh, yeah, I almost forgot." He pulled some dollar bills and then some change from a pants pocket. He held it out. "Six dollars and fifty cents left."

"That don't sound like nearly enough."

"Darn," Randy said. "I'm just pure foolish today. Can't remember nothin'. Mr. Mueller said for you to keep the Colt you borrowed yesterday. He charged fifteen dollars for the gun and fifty cents for him havin' to clean the Remingtons. He said the glass in the case'd cost you ten dollars. He took five dollars for the boots, a dollar for the pants, and he threw in the socks for nothin'."

Coffin nodded. "Sounds right. Keep it." He grinned at the wonderment on the boy's face.

Randy stammered thanks and carefully put the money back in his pocket.

"Your pa know you got them pistols, boy?" Coffin asked.

"Yessir."

"You ain't lyin' to me now, are you?"

"No, sir," Randy said with a firm shake of the head.

"I'm gonna ask him, you know."

"You can do that. He'll tell ya." His face sagged. "He says I can't load 'em or carry 'em unless I'm with you or him."

"Don't be so glum, boy," Coffin said a little sourly. "You wear them pistols, and you'll most likely breed more trouble than you'd stop. And I can say that for certain."

"I know," Randy groused. Then he grinned a little. "That don't mean I have to like it none."

Coffin laughed. "That's a fact, boy. Sure is." He looked at his pocket watch. "It's just about time for noonin'. You want a bite of food with me?"

"Yessir!"

"We're gonna eat it up here, since I ain't in no mood for settin' in a restaurant with a bunch of other folks."

"That's all right by me."

"Good. You go on down and tell Mr. Eagan that you'll be eatin' here with me. Tell him I'll have some of that roasted chicken his wife makes up so good. Taters and biscuits, too. And tell him what you want."

"Yessir!" Randy said smartly. He hurried out the door.

Lunch was a quiet, though not a very solemn, event. Randy pestered Coffin for stories, and Coffin told him one or two, then told him to get to eating. Coffin enjoyed eating and did not like to be disturbed any more than necessary.

Soon after eating, Coffin said, "You best get on back to your pa now, boy. He'll be needin' help."

Randy was reluctant, but he knew that if he didn't get back soon, he'd be in real trouble. He packed his guns carefully in the cloth and put them in the bag. Then he was off.

Coffin's only other visitor was Blue Gladys. She showed up about mid-afternoon. She smiled shyly when Coffin opened the door and stood there surprised. "I can leave if you want, Joe," Blue Gladys said quietly.

"Why would I want you to do that?" he asked.

"I don't know," Blue Gladys said with an accompanying shrug.

"Come on in," he said, stepping back and opening the door all the way. He uncocked the Remington he had in his hand. After Blue Gladys was in the room, Coffin returned the pistol to its holster.

"You sure you don't mind me comin' here, Joe?"

"Hell no."

"I saw your friend, that kid . . . ?"

Coffin nodded. "Randy Carstairs."

"Yeah, that's him. I asked him about you, and he said he'd been here, but you weren't aimin' to leave your room."

"That's true," Coffin admitted. "I don't want to face most folks right now. A couple days or so and most of 'em'll forget what happened yesterday."

"You mind me stayin' a while?"

"Nope. I'd be obliged to have your company. All night, if you're of a mind."

"I am," Blue Gladys said with a saucy smile.

The smile faded when Coffin said, "I do have to go out for a bit tonight. Just after dark."

"What for?" Blue Gladys asked nervously.

"Need to meet some folks."

"Who . . ." Blue Gladys nodded unhappily. "Oh, yeah, Miss Hoity Toity."

Coffin considered getting angry, but decided he had no call for such. "Yep," he said. "But I'm figurin' she won't want a hell of a lot to do with me after yesterday."

"How can you say that? If she loves you, she'll be there for you."

"That's what I thought. But I went over there last night, and their servant wouldn't even let me in the house. Said to come back tonight."

"What're you gonna do if she does cast you off?"

Coffin shook his head. "Don't know." He looked closely at Blue Gladys. She seemed a little worried.

She was. Blue Gladys liked Joe Coffin very much. But it was not love. She didn't want him to think that if he lost Edna, then he could turn to her instead. "I ain't in the market for marriage, Joe," she warned softly.

"I don't know as if I can say the same," Coffin said with a boyish, lopsided grin. "Depends on what Edna says. She turns me down, I won't be in the market for a wife."

Blue Gladys nodded, relieved. "I didn't want you to think that . . ."

"You're a fine woman, Blue Gladys," he said honestly. "But I don't think we'd make a good mix for the long run."

"Me either." Then Blue Gladys grinned impishly. "On the other hand, there's a lot can be said for the short run." She stood and began pulling off her dress.

Coffin's anger was renewed as he rapped on the back door of the Yarnell home. Moments later Jefferson opened the door. "Follow me," he said officiously.

Jefferson stopped outside the sitting room and "offered" Coffin inside with a regal wave of the hand. Coffin glared at the servant a moment before entering the room. He pulled off his hat as he did so.

"Sit," Yarnell said, pointing to a chair. There was no warmth in his voice.

Coffin remained standing. "Where's Edna?" he asked harshly.

"She has told me that she no longer wishes to see you under any circumstances," Yarnell said coldly.

"I want to hear it from her," Coffin responded just as icily.

"What you want is of no consequence to me, Coffin," Yarnell said, trying to inject a note of threat into his words.

"You either get her in here to tell me herself, or I'll go get her."

"You'd be stopped. Permanently."

"By who? Jefferson back there? Or that big, ugly ape you got in that other foyer over there?" Coffin said sarcastically. "Jefferson ain't gonna shoot me in the back, and I'll plug lard ass there before he gets a shot off. And I ain't adverse to sending you to the boneyard either."

Yarnell sputtered and fumed for a few moments, then sat angrily behind his desk "Mordecai, bring Miss Edna in here. And be quick about it."

Coffin strolled to the sideboard near the other foyer door. He poured some bourbon into a glass and gulped it down. He refilled the glass and set it down as he picked out and lit a cigar. He turned to face the room, leaning back against the sideboard. With the door on his right, whoever was in that foyer could not get a shot at him without coming into the room. Coffin swept the room with his eyes, making sure there were no immediate dangers.

A moment later, Edna entered the room, and Coffin's heart beat faster. She sat demurely in a chair, facing him. She left her hands in her lap, and her eyes were downcast.

"Your pa says you don't want to see me no more. That might be true, but I ain't gonna believe it till I hear it from your lips."

"I don't want to see you anymore," she said, not lifting up her head.

"This something your pa put you up to?" Coffin asked harshly. "If it is, we can fix that fast enough."

There was an uncomfortable silence of several moments' duration. Then Edna looked up at him. Her face was red, and she looked like she had been crying. "I loved you, Joe," she said. "I really did. But after . . . after . . . yesterday . . . I just can't . . . I don't know." She dabbed away a few new tears. "I was humiliated by what happened yesterday."

"*You* were humiliated?" Coffin asked incredulously.

"More than you were."

"Lordy, Edna, I can't believe that."

"Nevertheless, it's true," she said adamantly. "After what you done yesterday—or what was done to you, it don't matter which—I can't hold my head up in town any more." She stopped to nibble her lower lip a while. It looked to Coffin to be half chewed through. "It was bad enough that you let Lyons parade you around stark naked in front of the whole town, but then you went and brutally killed four men. I can't live with the shame of your debasement, and I can't live with a man who's so ruthless . . . so bloodthirsty. God, Joe," she wailed, "you killed four of them. Four."

"I suppose you would've felt better had I slunk out of town? Would that've been better?"

"No," Edna said reasonably. "No, that wouldn't have been better. Nothing would, I guess."

"We can leave here, you know," Coffin said, making one more effort. "I got a little money saved. We could go someplace where nobody'd know us. I could start up a business."

"No, Joe, it just won't work." Edna stood. "Good-bye, Joe," she said as if she were in deep pain. She walked out of the room, her tears flowing freely once more.

Chapter Sixteen

Coffin looked over at Yarnell, who wasn't quite gloating but was close to it. "Well, you've heard it from her lips," Yarnell said sarcastically. "Now you can leave. And, if I might offer some advice, I'd leave Crooked Creek, if I were you."

"Why?" Coffin asked, surprised. "I think Edna's crazy for feelin' this way, and it's likely she'll get over it sooner or later." He swallowed the whiskey in his glass and puffed his cigar a moment. "What I can't understand is why you want me out of town. Hell, I just got rid of your main enemy in Crooked Creek. Now the way's clear for you to take over the whole goddamn town."

"That's true, Joe," Yarnell said, seemingly at least a little apologetic. "And I do appreciate it, believe me. It solves a lot of problems for me, but it also creates something of a dilemma for me."

"How's that?"

"I can't be connected with you now. If I keep you on as an employee, everybody'll think I ordered you to kill Lyons and his men."

"But with you controlling Crooked Creek now, what difference will that make?"

"Somebody's sure to tell the county sheriff. Maybe even the governor. Then I'd have a lot more trouble than I'd be comfortable dealing with." He sighed.

"Bullshit," Coffin said flatly.

Yarnell's eyebrows raised. "Is it?" he asked. "Lyons still has friends here—and in other places. They'll be sure to spread the word about this. If I send you packing—or better yet, if you 'decide' on your own to leave Crooked Creek, the county or state officials would be much more easily convinced that while you had been an employee of mine, I had nothing to do with your killing Lyons and his men. In proof, I can say I sent you packing. Or that you were so remorseful that you hit the trail on your own account. Then those nosy, busybody officials'd most likely leave me be. I can lay quiet a bit, just keeping tabs on the rest of Lyons's men here. A couple months from now . . ." Yarnell clenched a fist, as if crushing a small, unimportant enemy.

"All this goes against the grain, Warren," Coffin said quietly.

"I suppose it does," Yarnell agreed with a nod. "Tell you what, I'll make it worthwhile for you."

"How?"

"I'll give you a few hundred dollars. Say, five hundred. But you'd have to leave Crooked Creek and not come back."

"Sounds like you're buyin' me off," Coffin said, not sure he liked the idea.

Yarnell shrugged. "It is, I suppose, if one wanted to look at it that way. You could look at it as a bonus. Something a little extra for some 'special services' you provided."

"I still ain't sure, Warren. It smacks too much of runnin' away. I ain't ever done that before, and I ain't inclined to start now."

"How'd you get that five hundred you deposited in my bank that day you rode into Crooked Creek?"

Coffin shrugged. "None of your business."

"Come, come, Joe, we are men of the world. From what I understand, you had come into town once before and were asking questions about two men. A couple weeks later you come ridin' back into town with five hundred dollars in your pockets. And nobody's heard of those two since." He drummed his fingers on the desk, waiting for a response from Coffin.

None came, so Yarnell continued, "I figure you either killed them two boys and took their money. Or you killed them and collected a bounty on them."

"It's still none of your business how I got that money."

"Hell," Yarnell laughed a little, "it doesn't matter to me how you got it. But if you are—or were—a bounty man, then the offer I just made to you could be taken as a bounty on Lyons's head. So what do you say, Joe?" Yarnell looked mighty earnest.

Coffin thought about it for a few moments. He had gotten the money as a bounty more or less. There was no reason to not take the money from Yarnell. Still, he wasn't sure. "Tell me, Warren," Coffin suddenly said, "was Edna's rejection of me her idea? Or yours?"

"I could say it was my idea and let you hate me instead of her, but that would be a lie. And I don't like to lie. I do it as little as possible."

Like now, Coffin thought. "And you had no hand in it?"

"No, sir," Yarnell said earnestly. "She came to me just after it happened and told me she couldn't be courted by you any more. Just couldn't. And she asked me if I'd tell you, since she felt mighty bad about having to do it."

"What're Mrs. Yarnell's thoughts on all this?"

"She concurs, of course. Anything she can do to stand by her daughter she will do."

"You know," Coffin said as he stood there studying his cigar, "it's a good thing you don't lie too often, Warren, 'cause you do it so dang poorly."

Yarnell looked as if he had been slapped, and his eyes narrowed in anger. "You watch your mouth around me, boy," he growled. "I don't cotton to being called a liar."

"Then don't lie," Coffin said levelly. "I'm absolutely certain that you put Edna up to this. Probably ordered her not to see me any more. I figure you probably browbeat your wife into accepting it, too." His hard glare shut off the protest Yarnell was set to launch. "Just let me finish."

Yarnell nodded, though he looked nervous.

"All that doesn't matter much now. If I was to defy you and come courtin' Edna again, there'd be trouble with you. And then I'd have to kill you," he said simply. "Once I'd done that, Edna'd not want me anymore anyway." He could see a faint trace of a gloat beginning on Yarnell's face.

"But don't go gettin' too smug about all this, Yarnell," Coffin said roughly. "I hear that you're spreadin' the word that you run me out of town, and I'll be back to pay you a visit. You won't survive that visit. I guarantee you that."

Yarnell looked like he had swallowed hot coals.

"Now, I'll be by your bank first thing tomorrow. You're gonna give me a thousand dollars, in addition to what I already have in my account there. Anybody asks why, you tell 'em there was a reward on Lyons. Anybody asks why I've left, you can tell 'em anything you want as long as it's not that I run out—or was run out."

Coffin could see the scheming going on in Yarnell's eyes. "And, remember, old man, that I got friends here. You badmouth me, and I'll hear about it, don't you think not."

Yarnell seethed. It enraged him to see that Coffin was reading his thoughts.

"Oh, and one more thing—don't send nobody after me. I'll kill 'em and drop 'em on your doorstep." He paused. "Tell lard ass to come on out, hands empty."

"How'd you know he was there?"

"The fat pig breathes like a steamer ship."

Yarnell nodded. It was something else he would have to remember. "Ike," he called. "Ike, come on out of there. No guns."

A moment later, the door just to Coffin's right opened, and a big-bellied, slovenly hulk of a man stepped out, hands hooked into the holster belt that spanned his vast girth.

"Turn toward the window and ease your pistols out, one at a time."

Ike Kohlhaus looked big and dumb, but he was not the latter. He had no book learning, but he had been living by his wits for a good many years now. He had heard—first-hand—how Coffin had taken down Rupert Lyons, Big Mike Finnegan, and two others. And did it on his own. Kohlhaus appreciated such daring and flair. He knew that if he tried something now that Coffin would blast him into eternity without a second thought. So he did as he was told. He pulled one pistol out, bent awkwardly and set it on the floor. He did the same with the other.

"Kick 'em back here," Coffin ordered.

When Kohlhaus did so, Coffin knelt and picked them up. He dropped one of them on the sideboard. The other he flipped in the air and caught it by the barrel. He stepped up right behind Kohlhaus. "No hard feelin's, pard," he said quietly.

Kohlhaus nodded, and Coffin clubbed him hard on the back of the head. Kohlhaus grunted, swayed and then toppled. Coffin pulled the percussion caps off of Kohlhaus's pistol and dropped it on the sideboard. Then he did the same with Kohlhaus's other revolver.

"Tomorrow. First thing," Coffin said, impaling Yarnell with a hard glare. Then he left the room. He turned right in the hallway, heading toward the front door.

"Mr. Yarnell'd prefer you to use the back again," Jefferson said.

"And what do you prefer, Mr. Jefferson?"

Jefferson grinned. "I prefer to stay out of trouble when I can."

"An admirable pursuit."

Jefferson nodded. "However, I don't expect Mr. Yarnell'd make too much of a fuss about it."

Coffin stared calmly at Jefferson. "You figurin' to come

after me?" he asked quietly.

Jefferson looked around, making sure none of the Yarnells were around. "No, sir. Mr. Yarnell sends me out after you, I'm gonna visit some folks for a period of time and then come back here and tell Mr. Yarnell I couldn't find you."

"Obliged, Mr. Jefferson."

Jefferson nodded, and escorted Coffin to the front door.

Coffin walked slowly back to his hotel. His emotions were roiling in his head, and he wanted to try to sort them out. He had never cared for a woman the way he had about Edna Yarnell. At the same time, though, he was relieved in a way that he was no longer courting her. He didn't know why that was. He did care deeply for her, but courting, and a possible marriage to her would present no end of troubles. He also still felt as if he were running away, too, despite doing it on his terms. On the other hand, there was nothing he could really do about Yarnell spreading tales about him once he had left Crooked Creek. He would never learn about it.

Just before he got back to the hotel, he turned the other way and just walked some more, letting the still-cold air wash over him. It seemed to help after a little while. He still had not really resolved anything, but he figured that now at least he might be able to live with his troubles. It would take a long time for him to forget Edna, and Crooked Creek. Until he could forget, he would live as best he could.

At last he turned toward the hotel once again. Blue Gladys was waiting for him, which he appreciated. As much as he might want to be alone, he knew that would be bad for him. Blue Gladys was wise enough to not press him too hard for anything right now.

A rapping at the door woke Coffin. He noted the light coming from the window, and he figured it was an hour or so past dawn. He got up and pulled on his pants. There was another timid knock on the door. Coffin grabbed one of his pistols, thumbed back the hammer and eased up to the door. Standing a little bit to the side, he yanked the door open.

Randy Carstairs stood there grinning. "Mornin', Joe," he said happily.

Coffin smiled a little. "What the hell're you doin' here so early, Randy?"

"Come to get you for breakfast."

"Well, come on in for a minute while we get dressed."

"We?"

Coffin laughed. "Yes, we."

Randy entered the room and stopped, mouth gaping when he saw Blue Gladys. "Mornin', Randy," she said with a big smile. She was sitting up, and her covers had fallen down around her waist.

Randy was speechless. He had never seen anything like this.

"How'd you like to become a man today?" she asked with another bright smile.

Randy gulped. He might have been trying to say something, but no words came out.

"I think he's a mite young just yet," Coffin said with a short laugh.

"Judgin' by the state of his pants right now, I'd say you was a mite wrong," Blue Gladys giggled. She stepped out of the bed and gave Randy an eyeful. She laughed again. "He's gonna burst, Joe," she said.

Coffin nodded, distracted a little.

"Why don't you go wait outside a minute, Joe," Blue Gladys said quietly.

He glanced at her, a brief flash of anger arising. Then he looked at Randy, who at the moment was most aptly named. Randy had turned thirteen just after Christmas, and so was the same age Coffin had been the first time he'd had a woman. He smiled and nodded. "Enjoy yourself, boy," he said. And then he went outside, where he rolled and lit a cigarette. By the time he was done with it, Blue Gladys and Randy came out. Blue Gladys was happy; Randy, beaming.

"Well, boy, how's it feel to be a man?" Coffin asked.

Randy was still speechless, but if smiles told the tale, he felt on top of the world.

The three headed downstairs and to the restaurant next door. When they were done, and Coffin sitting back with a last cup of coffee and a cigarette, Blue Gladys asked, "What're you gonna do today?" He had not said a word to her about his plans last night.

"I've got to go to the bank. After that, I ain't sure."

Blue Gladys looked sharply at him, and Coffin made a barely perceptible nod in Randy's direction. Blue Gladys nodded. They would discuss it later—if Coffin wanted. He certainly owed her nothing.

Chapter Seventeen

The three stopped just outside the restaurant to let their eyes adjust to the sunlight. After the hard freeze of the past few days, today was warm and pleasant, with a light wind. No clouds marred the deep, rich blue of the sky.

"We might as well walk together part of the way," Coffin said. He turned left and took a step. A moment later, his hat went flying off and the restaurant window behind him shattered. "Get down!" he roared, as he ripped out a Remington and crouched, as he tried to spot the source of the attack.

Just as he picked out Ike Kohlhaus, Coffin heard Randy screech and then fall. "Shit," Coffin breathed. He cracked off one shot immediately, not caring if he hit Kohlhaus. He just wanted to put the fat man on the defensive. Coffin risked a quick look behind him. Blue Gladys was crouched over a sprawled Randy Carstairs, who seemed mighty still, and there was blood soaking into the wood beneath the boy.

"You dumb, fat son of a bitch!" Coffin bellowed. He pushed up and let fly the last four rounds in the Remington. Each ball hit Kohlhaus in the chest, shoving him back a half step each, until he hit the hitching post, and he hung over it, back arched.

Coffin shoved the Remington away and grabbed the other. He took a quick look around, but no one else seemed to be of a mind to try shooting at him. He ran across the street, as Kohlhaus fell into a fat puddle on the ground. Coffin knelt next to him and grabbed the man's shirt. Kohlhaus was still alive, but fading fast. Coffin slapped his face twice, trying to keep him conscious for a few more moments. "Did Yarnell send you, you fat bag of shit? Or was this your own goddamn stupid idea?"

"Mine," Kohlhaus gasped. "Wanted to get you back."

"For what? Conkin' you on the head last night?"

"Yeah. I also thought Yarnell'd think better of me."

"Damn stupid reasons for dyin', boy."

"Little late for worryin' 'bout now, ain't it?"

"It is. Makin' it all the worse, though, is you killed a boy, you big, fat stupid son of a bitch."

A few tears leaked out of Kohlhaus's eyes, which were deeply imbedded in his obese face.

Coffin was amazed to see it. He shook his head at the complexities of men. The tears stopped when Kohlhaus stopped breathing a moment later. Coffin rose and looked around. To his surprise—and great relief—he saw Blue Gladys and Randy standing. He walked swiftly across the street.

"You all right, boy?" he asked anxiously when he got there.

Randy nodded. His face was pale, and he seemed to be in shock. "It hurts," he whispered, as if afraid that using his regular voice would make his arm fall off.

"I told you it did," Coffin agreed, grinning. Part of the reason was relief. The other part was for Randy. If the boy could see Coffin laughing and joking, Randy might feel a little better. Maybe not less pain, but he would have the idea in his head that he would be all right.

Coffin tore open Randy's shirt and looked at the boy's shoulder. "Hell, boy, it's hardly more than a scratch," Coffin pronounced.

"It is?" Randy said. "Even thought it hurts so much?"

"Well, it's more than a scratch, but I reckon you'll be all

right. You go with Blue Gladys. She'll bring you to Doc Hanratty."

"What're you gonna be doin'?" Randy asked, still in a faint voice.

"I got business. I'll stop by when I'm done to see how you're doin'."

"But . . ."

"Don't you argue, boy," Blue Gladys said sternly. "Now, come on." She took Randy's hand and tugged him off.

Coffin turned and walked back across the street. A crowd had gathered around Kohlhaus's body. "A couple of you boys come give me a hand here," he ordered.

"Doin' what?" someone asked.

"Helpin' me sling skinny here over his mule so I can get rid of him."

Two men came forward grudgingly and helped. Soon enough, Kohlhaus's corpse was hanging belly down over his big gray mule. "Thanks," Coffin said. He was sure some of the men wanted to make fun of him, but after he had killed four men at the Twisted Water and now Ike Kohlhaus, they most likely were afraid to say anything. That, too, was a relief. He still didn't feel great about walking the streets of Crooked Creek in broad daylight, but he was a little more certain now that people would leave him alone.

Towing the mule carrying Kohlhaus's fat corpse, Coffin headed down River Street. People gathered along the street as they had only two days before. Now, though, the people were quiet, watching the procession in silence.

Coffin walked straight into the bank, with the mule behind him. The two tellers and six customers stood with gaping mouths, as Coffin headed for Yarnell's office. Then he—and the mule—entered the office.

"What the hell . . . ?" Yarnell exploded, jumping up. "Dammit, Coffin . . ."

"Shut up and sit down," Coffin snapped. When Yarnell did, looking mystified, Coffin said, "Where's my money?"

"I'll . . . I'll get it for you. Right now." He rose again.

"Have someone do it."

Yarnell nodded and called for Clark, one of the tellers.

While Coffin and Yarnell waited, Coffin said, "There's only one thing keepin' you alive now, Yarnell. Old Kohlhaus here was some sad when he found out that he'd shot a boy while he was gunnin' for me."

"That Carstairs kid?"

Coffin nodded. "If he hadn't shown any remorse, I would've come here and blown a big hole in you."

In less than five minutes, Coffin had closed out his account and had a pocketful of money.

"I can't say it's been a pleasure dealin' with you, Yarnell," Coffin said. He turned, pulled a pistol and calmly shot Kohlhaus's mule in the head. The animal fell, jerking and shuddering. Coffin slid the revolver away and headed toward the door. Once there, he looked back and said, "Oh, by the way, Yarnell, don't send anyone after me. I'd not look favorably on such a thing."

Outside the bank, Coffin headed for Doc Hanratty's. He found Randy and Blue Gladys still there. The boy was looking a little better, though he was still mighty peaked. "How're you doin' now, boy?" Coffin asked.

"I'm all right. It's still painin' me a lot, but the doctor give me something to help keep that in line."

"That true, Doc?" Coffin asked.

"It is," Hanratty said.

"Good. Can I take him home now?"

"Sure."

"Come on, Randy."

As they walked toward the livery, Coffin said, "I've got to be pushin' on, Randy."

"What?"

"I'm leaving Crooked Creek."

"Why?"

"A bunch of reasons, none of 'em anything you or I could

do much about."

"But I thought we was friends."

"We are. But friends have to part, too. I've got business to tend to in other places."

"You'll write to me?" Randy asked. He seemed subdued, and Coffin did not know whether it was because he was leaving or from the reaction to being shot.

"Occasionally." Coffin delivered the boy to his father at the livery. Harry Carstairs was not happy about his son being shot, but he accepted it, especially after Coffin told Carstairs that he was leaving as soon as he could pack his few things.

"You want your horse saddled?" Carstairs asked after he had sent his son heading toward home.

"Yep. I'll be back soon."

Forty-three minutes later, Coffin was riding his chestnut out of Crooked Creek, heading north toward the Missouri River. From there he turned west. He had no idea of where he was going, but going generally west was a logical choice for him. He realized the next day that it seemed he was being pulled west, and he felt a strange longing for the mountains.

That felt odd to him for a few days, but he finally puzzled it out. He had been born and raised in the Sierra Nevada. For fourteen years the Sierra Nevada had been his home. He felt now that it—or even the Rocky Mountains—would do. As long as there were towering peaks, and trees, game animals and rushing, tumbling, frigid mountain streams.

Once he had figured that out, he set his sights somewhat southwest. There he could find Independence and St. Joe—and the wagon trains of settlers heading for Oregon and California. If they were still running them. They had before, and Coffin figured they still were.

With at least a partial destiny in mind, he moved with a little more determination and speed. He was stopped one day by a hellacious late spring storm, but he had managed to wait it out in a barn on some farm. Two weeks after having left Crooked Creek, he hit St. Joseph, Missouri.

The first thing he did was find a hotel that had an open room, which was surprising considering how many people were in the city waiting to head west.

Then he hit several saloons, trying to see if he could hook on with one of the wagon trains heading west. In the fourth saloon he tried, a man told him that he had heard that Roy Denham, who had been elected a captain of a large wagon train, might be hiring.

It took a little while to track down Denham, but he finally found him in a saloon. Coffin bought a bottle of whiskey and got a glass. He went to Denham's table, pulled up a chair and sat across the table from the emigrants' captain. He poured himself a drink and did the same for Denham. "I hear you're hirin'," Coffin said.

"Might be. What do you propose to do?" Denham asked. He was a man of medium height with a big chest and stomach. A thick mustache covered both his lips, and Coffin thought Denham looked like a flapping caterpillar when he spoke.

"Whatever needs doin', long as it don't take no special skills other than handlin' a gun."

"You a good shot with a long gun?"

"I'm better with a pistol, but I can hold my own against most others with a long gun."

"You know how to butcher?"

"Worked in meat houses for a spell."

"Though we got a big train, we can't pay much." He was not embarrassed to say so.

"I got enough for my needs."

"Good," Denham said. "We've got a bunch of other hunters. That bother you?"

"I work best alone, but I can work with others. Long as they don't pester me too much."

"You fight in the late war?" Denham asked.

"Yes," Coffin said tightly. "What's that got to do with anything?"

Denham ignored the question. "You're mighty young for having fought," he said.

"I was fourteen when I joined a volunteer company."

"What rank did you attain?"

"Corporal."

"Then you've led men before?"

"Yessir. It's not a job I enjoy much, but I can do it if the need arises."

"You're hired, Mr. Coffin. We leave a week from tomorrow. Meet us in the big meadow on the north edge of town."

Coffin nodded and left. He went back to his hotel room and paid for a week's lodging. Then he went out on a drinking binge that lasted five days. It helped him forget much of what happened in Crooked Creek, but only because he was either drunk or severely hung over. As soon as he sobered up again, the hurtful emotions brought on by his stay in Crooked Creek flooded back over him, seemingly with even more pain.

It took two full days for him to clean the poisons out of his system after the binge, and as he rode out toward the jumping off place, he felt better physically. He was not sure he could say the same about mentally, though.

Coffin counted thirty-two wagons, plus a dozen or so men traveling on their own. Two of those were guides for the wagon train; and five more, including Coffin, were hunters.

Coffin stopped by to tell Denham that he was in camp and ready to leave the next day. Denham, busy with many duties and distractions, simply nodded and turned to shout more orders at someone. Coffin smiled a little, glad he had not been so blessed as to be in charge of this chaos.

Chapter Eighteen

The trip was about what Coffin expected—slow, tedious, and as uneventful as one could expect with such an undertaking. They saw Indians a few times, but the warriors seemed to know that attacking a wagon train of this size was foolish if not suicidal.

The Indians did catch four men and kill them. They were killed in two separate instances when two men went out to hunt and then butcher the meat. The four men had been shot repeatedly with arrows, scalped and mutilated. Each time, the wagon train stopped long enough to dig graves and say a few prayers over the dead.

It seemed that the men of the wagon train dug a lot of graves. Sickness and accidents were rampant in any wagon train of emigrants, and this one was no exception.

Coffin managed to stay mostly aloof from all that. He simply went about his job of hunting, riding out with a boy he had met. Thirteen-year-old Rolf Schottenheimer reminded Coffin a lot of Randy Carstairs. Both were about Coffin's height and filled with a boy's sense of wonder and eagerness. Coffin had been unable to find one of the men to help him with the butchering—it seemed very few of the men wanted anything to do with him. Coffin had helped Schottenheimer's father, Wilhelm, the first day out fix a small problem with the Schottenheimers' wagon. Schottenheimer invited Coffin to eat at his fire that night, and Coffin had agreed.

From that time, Coffin ate with the Schottenheimers. Then, when he mentioned to Wilhelm that he could not find someone to help him with the butchering, Schottenheimer had offered the use of his son Rolf.

"He know how to butcher?" Coffin asked.

"Yah. I am a butcher by trade," the father said in his thick German accent. "And so I show the boy how."

Coffin nodded.

He and Rolf found the first hunter and helper who had been killed by Indians three weeks out from St. Joseph. Coffin and Rolf had three of their four pack mules loaded with antelope meat. They used the fourth to cart the two bodies back to the wagon train.

"Didn't you go after 'em?" Denham asked.

"After who?" Coffin countered.

"The Indians, dammit."

"It ain't my job to go chasin' Indians. Besides, I don't know anything about them. Certainly not enough to track 'em down."

The men were not happy with Coffin after that, at least until the second hunter and helper were found by other hunters. Denham asked the same of them and received basically the same response. This time, though, it was accepted as making sense, and they backed off their criticism of Coffin.

Not that Coffin cared all that much what the others thought anyway. Still, it would make the journey a little easier if the travelers were not at each others' throats. There were enough problems without that.

Death was an almost everyday occurrence. People died in wagon accidents; from disease, especially cholera; accidental shootings; snakebite, drinking poisoned water, even heat stroke. Some just plain gave up on life and faded away.

Coffin was not fond of funerals and buryings at the best

of times. Seeing them with his own group, as well as the fresh graves dug by other wagon trains, was more than he could take. He had seen more than his share of graves during the war. He didn't need to see them now. The worst ones, though, were the ones for the children. The Schottenheimers lost a girl, 18-month-old Marta. When her grave was dug, Coffin saddled his horse and rode out with three pack animals in tow. He went alone, not wanting the company of even an exuberant young man like Rolf Schottenheimer.

It took a few days for Coffin to get over that one, but he did. It had, for a time, kept his mind off Edna Yarnell. Not much else did, though he realized a little while out that with each passing mile he could look back on his time in Crooked Creek somewhat objectively. The pain also lessened a little with each passing day.

Not all the days were filled with sorrow and death. Denham got dances up every once in a while, to let the tired people kick up their heels with some fun. There were Sunday services led by Parson Elijah Morrow, a feast now and then when the hunters had been especially lucky.

In general, though, the trek was hard physically and mentally. Coffin had it better than most, since he was not chained to one of the wagons. He often wondered how people like Wilhelm Schottenheimer and his family could bear the drudgery of each day. The tasks were endless. During the day they walked, mile after mile. Schottenheimer cracked the whip over the mules pulling the wagon that would be his family's whole world for five months or so. Everyone else walked, too, except the very young ones and the very old ones. Occasionally one of the travelers would hop on the lazy board on the side of the wagon for a short ride.

By the time they hit the Sweetwater River, Coffin was sick of it all. He was not really one of the travelers, and did not have the same destiny, hopes or dreams. He was tired of the endless miles of nothingness that lay before them still. He was tired of crossing rivers with shifting, quicksand bottoms, of ducking Indian war or hunting parties. He was tired of the constant bickering and jockeying for position or prestige, such as it was out here, especially since that meant a chance to move out five minutes before the next wagon, and stop that night five minutes earlier. No matter where one rode in the long wagon train one had to eat dust.

Coffin was also sick of the heat and the disease, the bad water and the monotony, the heavy rains and lightning-sparked prairie fires, the death and despair.

He sat at the Schottenheimers' fire one night and tried to analyze his situation. He had no yen to stick with the wagons all the way to California, and Schottenheimer's family was planning to go to Oregon, where Coffin had no desire to go. When he had first started his journey, he had done so urged on by some primitive yearning to go "home"—as in the mountains where he had spent his childhood. He was no longer concrete about that, though he still felt an uneasiness that was strange to him.

It finally came to him that he simply wanted to be in the mountains. It didn't have to be the Sierra Nevada of his childhood. Just tall, majestic mountains, with bubbly, running creeks, brash, powerful rivers—and gold. The last surprised him. He had never been bitten by the gold bug. But for some odd reason panning for gold in some lonesome mountain canyon held some appeal at the moment. He supposed that was more the idea of being isolated from people rather than some heretofore secret desire for gold that had prompted the thoughts. He did not want anyone counting on him, not for a while anyway. There had been far too much of that for his taste lately.

The next night, as he was puffing an after-dinner cigarette and sipping at some coffee, he mentioned it to Schottenheimer.

"But where will you go?" Schottenheimer asked, surprised. He was a family man, had been for a number of years. He could not understand that a man would want to move about unfettered, roaming wherever the wind pushed him.

Coffin shrugged. "Ain't sure. I hear there's plenty of gold up north of here. Montana Territory. Idaho Territory, too."

"You have the gold fever?"

Coffin shook his head, unsure. "I don't think so. But where there's gold, there's . . . I don't know. Not so much that there's people. Minin' camps just seem to have somethin' goin' all the time."

"Ach," Schottenheimer said with a knowing nod. "Beer and whiskey, cards and fancy women, gambling and gunfire."

"It's got all that for sure, Wilhelm," Coffin said with a small laugh.

"How will you get to this place, Joe? Answer for me this."

"I don't know," Coffin said honestly.

"It is not safe riding out here by one's self," Schottenheimer said firmly.

"That's a problem," Coffin admitted. He grinned a little. "I'm gettin' itchy feet, Wilhelm," he said. "But there are some drawbacks to adventurin' on my own." He paused. "Reckon I'll have to think on it a spell."

Coffin began paying more attention to the people with the wagon train, and within a few days had heard some grumblings from other young men. Finally one night he gathered them all around and told them of Idaho Territory and Montana Territory.

"What's that got to do with all of us?" one named Billy Poindexter asked.

"I hear you been spoutin' off about wantin' to leave this wagon train and go adventurin'."

"Yeah, so?"

"I'm of a mind to head north."

"What's that got to do with us?" Frank Bishop asked.

"Why don't we go up the trail together?" Coffin said.

"What in hell for?" Poindexter snapped. He was a dim-witted young man, not given overly much to actually thinking.

"Well," Coffin said, trying to keep his temper in check, "it ain't safe for any of us to go off on our own. But with the six, seven of us here, we should be safe enough from Indians and such."

"Where're you plannin' to go?" Bishop asked. He seemed interested.

"Ain't sure. Soon's we get to some of the minin' areas, I'll figure out what I'm gonna do. You boys'll be on your own there. I ain't proposin' we form some minin' company or anything. All I'm sayin' is we ride together for safety till we get someplace that's got folks. Then we all go our own ways."

"I'm in," Bishop said. "I've had too damn much of these goddamn crawlin' along wagons and squallin' babies and burials. It's time I was on my own hook."

"Any of you others?"

Six hands went up.

"When do we leave?" Poindexter asked.

Coffin shrugged. "Tomorrow? Or maybe you boys'd rather have a day to get your folks used to your plans?"

"Day after sounds good enough to me," Bishop said. The others agreed.

The eight young men rode slowly out of camp just after dawn. Each had his riding horse and a mule for what small supplies he had gotten from family or friends. This was no communal enterprise, so each man had to provide his own meat, coffee, guns, blankets, shot, powder and other food and personal supplies. Not that they were averse to sharing when one of them brought down an elk or a buffalo. It was just made clear to all that they were on their own unless they faced an attack. In preparation for that possibility, the men had elected Coffin as their "war captain," who would give the orders. The others had promised to obey him in such a case.

He had to assume that "office" three times. Two of those times ended up with no trouble. Once the Indians did not see them as they hid in thick brush along some creek; another time, the eight nervous white men had a small parley with six equally anxious Shoshones. Fighting was averted with the exchange of some small gifts.

The third time, though, the eight men hunkered down behind brush and fallen logs as they battled twenty angry-looking Crows. When the gunsmoke had finally cleared, Delbert Hardesty was killed, and Bishop and Coffin were wounded, neither badly. They had killed two Indians.

Poindexter spoke kind words over Hardesty's grave, and then the unfortunate young man was covered over with dirt, and his companions rode off, a little more quiet and subdued than they had been the day before. Still, with the resilience of youth, by the next day they were their normal old selves again. Hardesty's death would sit with them for a while, but they had to go on living.

They had ridden northwest since leaving the wagons, moving along the bottom of the Wind River Range. They soon began heading into mountains, ones still thick with snow on their caps above the timberline. They were hushed and awed as they moved through a land of bubbling mud and sulfurous emanations, and they were relieved when they got out of that piece of hell on earth.

In midafternoon one day three weeks after they had left the wagons, Coffin pulled to a stop, looking at a poor excuse for a sign. "Reckon this's where I turn off, boys."

"Where're you headin'?" Bishop asked.

Coffin pointed to the sign. "Virginia City."

"Why?"

Coffin shrugged. "Just seems right is all. Any of you other boys aim to come along?"

They all shook their heads. "We'll mosey on up aways, I

expect," Bishop said. "Good luck to ya, Joe." He pulled on his reins and moved off.

Coffin watched for a few moments. They had not been all that bad a bunch of men, and Coffin was a little sorry to see them go. He turned west, and by nightfall he was in Virginia City.

The city was total bedlam from all he could see. He could not believe it. It was as if somebody had taken all the worst from St. Louis, Cincinnati and Crooked Creek and rendered it down and stuck it here. He was awe-struck by the wildness of the place.

Coffin managed to find somebody willing to rent him a storeroom to pass as a bedroom. He put his horse up in the livery, ate and then headed to a saloon.

By morning he had decided Virginia City was not for him. He had nothing against some excitement, but total chaos seemed pastoral when compared with Virginia City.

After only a moment's hesitation, he continued west. Several hours later, he found himself in Madison. The town looked rambunctious enough for him, but it also had a more permanent look to it, as if people had come here to stay and grow. Women – wives and daughters rather than just fallen angels – walked the streets, and there were some stone and brick buildings. He nodded. He might not want to live the rest of his life here, but it would be a good enough place for the time being.

Chapter Nineteen

After some experimentation for several days, Coffin decided to do most of his drinking in the Pittsburgh Saloon. It was a large, rollicking place, with plenty of faro tables, roulette wheels, hurdy-gurdy girls, two bars, a piano, small stage and a plethora of fallen angels who plied their trade in the second floor rooms. For Coffin it was a comfortable place.

Like any other saloon in any mining town, even one that had been civilized to a small extent, the Pittsburgh had its brawls, gunfights and other trouble. Coffin generally managed to stay out of such melees, but he could not ignore everyone who got drunk and bothered him.

Like the fool who turned around and bumped into Coffin, and wound up spilling half his glass of beer all over Coffin. That was bad enough, but then the man snapped, "Goddamn, boy, why'n't you grow up some so's a body could see ya." It was not a question.

"Why don't you watch where you put your big feet, you dumb bastard!" Coffin snapped, also not making it a question.

"I'll tell you where I'll put my big feet, you shrunken little peckerwood," the man drawled. He was maybe six-foot-four and seemed all legs and arms. His eyes—what Coffin could see of them—were bloodshot. "I'll ram one of 'em right up your skinny little ass, boy."

"You'd have to take 'em out of your mouth first," Coffin said evenly.

"Goddamn, why is it that the smaller the man, the more petty he is?" the man mused aloud.

"Well, why is it that the bigger a man is, the dumber he is?" Coffin countered. "You so far up there you ain't got enough air? That it?"

The man laughed some, a deep, bearish sound. "Hell, boy, you got a lot of gumption for a little squirt. Now what say you buy me a beer, and we can go our own ways?"

"Why don't you just shit in your hat and pull it down over your ears. I hear tell you look good in brown."

Silence grew among the small circle of men standing there, though the rest of the saloon was still going full blast. Then the man's face mottled up in anger. "You smart-ass little bastard," he snapped.

"Pick on someone more your size, Harlan," a nearby bartender said.

"Go to hell, bub," Harlan Gilmore snapped. "A man goes through life tryin' to avoid trouble, goes out of his way to not pick on some half-pint little bastard, and all he gets is abuse."

"Christ, you are a windbag, which is hard to believe—considering you're so full of shit I didn't think there was room for so much wind."

Several men snickered. Gilmore snarled, then said in clipped tones, "You just bought yourself a peck of trouble, boy."

"Have at it," Coffin said quietly. He almost jumped when he suddenly heard a loud clanging nearby. He turned his head, muttering, "What the hell . . . ?"

One of the bartenders was banging on an iron bell with a hammer. Gradually the sounds of the saloon dwindled, until it seemed as if the only sound there was in the saloon was that infernal bell. Coffin became aware of people gathering around, having left their games of chance or whatever else they were doing. It was strange, but Coffin accepted it. The men would've gathered for the fight sooner or later anyway. The ringing of the bell and the gathering of the crowd just sort of made it all "official" somehow.

Gilmore slugged Coffin on the side of the head, and Coffin's right arm hit hard into the bar. Before Coffin could recover, Gilmore pounded him twice more, both punches catching Coffin on the jaw, rattling his head. But as Gilmore reared back to pelt him again, Coffin jerked himself forward, head lowered.

Gilmore's punch sailed over Coffin's head, just about the same time Coffin's head slammed into Gilmore's breastbone. Gilmore grunted more in surprise than in any pain.

It gave Coffin a moment's respite, though, and he took advantage of it by snapping three quick jabs to Gilmore's midsection. That opened up a little more room for him, and Coffin shoved Gilmore away. Then Coffin stood for a moment catching his breath.

Gilmore figured Coffin was about ready to quit, seeing as how the short man was just standing there looking winded. Confidently, Gilmore moved up a step and sent a bony fist at Coffin's head.

Coffin blocked the blow with his left forearm and then slammed three hard little punches to Gilmore's abdomen, knocking the taller man's wind out.

Gilmore staggered back a little, wheezing, and trying to breathe.

"What's the matter with you, big man?" Coffin said sarcastically. "Ain't so tough now, are you?"

Gilmore still couldn't breathe with any comfort or regularity, but the look on his face might have melted a lesser man than Joe Coffin. And he shook his head angrily.

"I couldn't hear you," Coffin said with a smirk. He balled up a fist and moved up, ready to put the finishing touches on Harlan Gilmore. Then someone landed high on his back.

The new assailant began flailing away at Coffin with one fist. His other arm went around Coffin's throat.

"You son of a bitch," Coffin muttered. He charged straight backward, smashing the new assailant's back against the bar. The man groaned and lost his grip around Coffin's throat.

Coffin surged away from the other man and charged at Gilmore, legs slipping some on the sawdust-covered floor. Gilmore tried to punch Coffin but had little strength back yet, and it was but a feeble blow. Then Coffin crunched into Gilmore, and both went down.

"Try and have someone help you, you goddamn son of a bitch," Coffin muttered. "Goddammit all to hell and gone." All the while, he was pounding on Gilmore's head and face.

Once more someone landed on Coffin's back. He rolled off, but as Coffin pushed himself up, someone else plowed into him. He went down, with the unseen attacker's grasp solid around him.

Coffin found himself with his face mashed against the floor. The sawdust was fouled by mud and dust, spilled beer and whiskey, and tobacco spittings. Coffin was not happy with being ground into the fetid muck. He managed to get his hands under him. With them and his legs, he shoved up until he was on hands and knees. He was barely aware of someone hitting him. Right now, all he wanted to do was get the one tenacious assailant off his back. He would worry about the others, however many of them there were, later.

With a roar, he pushed up some more. He could feel the man on his back start listing to one side. Coffin hoped he had a little room to get some leverage, and he jerked his left elbow back. It hit the man in the ribs, but there was no power to the blow. The man merely grunted.

The two strained and struggled, until Gilmore, who had gotten his wind back, came up and pelted Coffin a good shot to the solar plexus. Coffin had tightened his stomach muscles in anticipation, and so the punch wasn't too bad to handle. But it hurt nonetheless.

As Gilmore prepared to pound Coffin again, Coffin bent backward as much as he could while still being held, and then snapped himself forward, bending at the waist. The man holding him lost his grip somewhat and half tumbled off Coffin's left side—and right into the path of Gilmore's punch.

The man cursed and released Coffin as he stumbled. Gilmore's midsection was wide open to Coffin, who wasted not a moment in slamming two powerful punches into Gilmore's stomach again. Gilmore doubled up, wheezing once more.

Coffin swung around and another man charged into him. Both fell, Coffin hitting his elbow on the hard floor. Before Coffin could do anything more, one more man jumped on him, and then a third. Two half lay across him, while the third hastily stood, looming over the wildly struggling Coffin. He raised his foot, ready to stomp Coffin's stomach—or lower.

A shotgun roared. The man teetering on one foot fell sideways. The two men holding Coffin started at the noise, giving Coffin a little leeway. He jerked his right hand free and slammed a punch to one man's jaw. The other one tried to keep his grip on Coffin, but it was a tenuous hold. Coffin pounded him, too, and suddenly was free.

As Coffin began sitting up, Gilmore kicked him in the back of the head. It wasn't a hard blow, and it annoyed Coffin more than hurt him. He jumped up and spun. "Bastard," he snapped, just before smashing Gilmore's nose flat.

Coffin was ready to wallop Gilmore again when someone rammed into his back again. As he went down, he thought, *I've had about enough of this.*

The shotgun roared again as Coffin began pushing himself up once more. Just as he got up, two men came hard at him. Coffin ducked and grabbed the man nearest him, one arm over the man's shoulder, the other between his legs.

Coffin shoved upright, bringing the man up with him, and then he dashed the man to the floor.

Coffin whirled to face the second man, but a burly, middle-aged man had just thumped the butt of his scattergun against the man's neck. The burly man looked at Coffin, and his eyes grew wide. "Well sweet jumpin' Jesus. Joe Coffin."

Coffin stopped and stared, blinking rapidly to make this vision go away. Trouble was, it didn't. "Major?" Coffin said in surprise and wonder. "Major Pembroke."

"Marshal Pembroke now, boy," Pembroke said with a small laugh. He looked around at the mild amount of carnage. "Jesus, you still can't stay out of trouble, can you, Joe?"

Coffin shrugged. "Hell, Maj . . . Marshal, somebody asks me to dance, I just can't turn 'em down."

Pembroke laughed. "You always was a feisty cuss." He glared at Gilmore. "Damn, Harlan, you gotten so old and stove-up that it takes four of you galoots to whip up on one little man?"

Gilmore growled in annoyance.

"Don't you take that goddamn tone with me, you presumptuous snot," Pembroke said evenly. He neither looked nor sounded agitated, but there was a warning in his soft, fluid tones nonetheless.

Gilmore glared but said nothing.

"What caused all this ruckus?" Pembroke asked.

Coffin shrugged. "Ask that damn fool," he said, chucking a thumb over his shoulder at Gilmore.

"Harlan?" Pembroke turned his hard, blue eyes on Gilmore.

Gilmore shrugged. "He was gettin' on my nerves is all," he said lamely.

"Oh?"

"Well, he kind of bumped into me and . . ."

"Jesus, Harlan, you can't even lie good." He sighed.

"Take yourself—and those three pissant cronies of yours—over to the jail. If the marshal ain't there, stash your pieces in the desk and lock yourselves in."

"Ah, come on, Enoch," Gilmore pleaded. "Ain't nobody really got hurt or nothin'."

"Joe?" Pembroke asked after a few moments' thought. "What do you think about it?"

Coffin rubbed his jaw. It hurt more than a little. So did his back and several other body parts. "Well, I ain't a vindictive sort of man, Enoch, as you well know. But I don't take kindly to havin' four men set against me for no goddamn good reason at all. Still . . ." he paused, thinking. "Well, hell, Enoch, I don't know," he finally continued. "I could use some guidance here. I'm new in these parts."

"Well, let's see," Pembroke said expansively, "Harlan there is a royal pain in the ass. Causes more goddamn trouble than any three or four men, except for his dimwitted cronies there."

"Maybe I just ought to shoot 'em all. That'd solve things, I expect," Coffin said.

"Probably cause more trouble than it'd solve," Pembroke offered. "But it does sound enticin'." He sighed, as if he carried a heavy burden. "I'll tell you what, Harlan. You and your boys there buy me and Joe here a bottle and then keep yourselves away from us, and I'll not lock you all up. How's that?"

"Sounds good to me," Gilmore said firmly. "What about you boys?" he added, looking from one of his friends to the other. All three nodded eagerly. "You got yourself a deal, Marshal." He strode the few feet to the bar, slapped some coins down and grabbed the bottle that materialized where the coins had just been. He turned and held the bottle out. "It's the good stuff, too, Marshal, as you can see. Not that cheap shit Foster usually tries to foist off on everyone."

Pembroke took the bottle. "Now get your ass out of here and take that scum with you."

Gilmore looked angry, but he said nothing. Then he and his three friends headed toward the door.

"What say we find us a table, Joe, and talk of old times? And, what the hell, maybe some new times, too?"

Coffin nodded. He picked up his hat from the floor and slapped it on.

Chapter Twenty

"So," Pembroke asked as he poured whiskey into two glasses, "what brings you to Madison, Joe?"

Coffin shrugged. "Just kind of rolled in here." He poured tobacco into a wheatstraw paper and then licked the edge. He scraped a match across the rough wood of the table and then lit his cigarette. Once it was going, he explained quickly and with no frills how he had landed in Madison, Montana Territory.

While Coffin talked, Pembroke reloaded the muzzle loading shotgun.

"How about you, Major . . . Marshal . . . that's gonna take some gettin' used to, I think." He grinned. "Anyway, how'd you wind up in a place like this?"

"Wasn't much reason to stay back East. Jobs was scarce, and then Netty died."

"No," Coffin breathed.

Pembroke nodded. "The cholera took her, God rest her soul." He paused a moment, then said, "Anyway, that left me no reason a-tall to stay back there. Then I guess I got bit by the gold bug some. Don't know why exactly, but since I didn't have no strings on me . . ."

"Seems you're doin' all right," Coffin said, pointing to the star on Pembroke's chest.

"Hell, I sometimes think I'm the biggest damn fool in

Madison for wearin' it."

"What the hell're you doin' breakin' up bar fights if you're a deputy U.S. marshal?"

"You remember my brother Beryl, don't you?"

"Sure."

"He's town marshal here. We help each other out when we can. He's probably off in some other damn saloon stoppin' another damn fracas."

"Keeps you busy, I take it," Coffin said, making a question out of the statement.

"Hell, busy ain't the word for it." Pembroke took off his hat and tossed it down on the table. Without the hat's shade on Pembroke's face, Coffin could see the tiredness in Pembroke's eyes. "Christ, Joe, we can't keep up with it. Madison's a heap more civilized than Virginia City and some of the other places around here, but it's got more than enough rough edges. It's a big town and still growin'. We've got all kinds here from good, hardworkin' storekeepers to hell-raisin' miners."

"Sounds typical of such an area."

Pembroke looked sharply at Coffin, then he nodded. "I'd forgotten you were raised in places like this. It must seem like home to you."

"A piss poor home, if anything," Coffin commented.

Pembroke nodded "I usually ain't around town much. Not with all the highwaymen, claim jumpers and bushwhackers we got around here. Christ, I'm traipsin' all over the goddamn countryside chasin' those lawbreakin' bastards."

"You never was one to do much sittin' around," Coffin said with a smile.

"That's for sure. As I recall, you weren't much different."

"A failin' we're both stuck with, I figure."

Pembroke nodded. He drained his whiskey glass and poured another. "What're you up to? You lookin' for work?"

"Hadn't thought much on it. I've only been in town a few days."

"You got enough money to live on?" Pembroke asked, somewhat surprised.

"For a while." Coffin grinned tightly. "Got me a few bounties back in Missouri."

"Bounty man?" Pembroke asked. It was obvious he did not like the breed.

Coffin shrugged. "More a case of protectin' myself and others and havin' the money fall into my lap. I've got no real desire to take up such a thing for a livin'."

"That's good," Pembroke said firmly. He hesitated, not sure he should say anything, but then he decided he had to. "I got a job for you, if you want it."

"Doin' what?" Coffin was surprised this time.

Pembroke fished around in his shirt pocket for a moment, pulled something out and placed it on the table. He slowly pushed it across the table toward Coffin.

Coffin looked at the small, glittering star in a half circle. "You are joshin' me, ain't you, Major?"

Pembroke shook his head slowly. "Nope."

"I've got no experience in bein' a lawman, and I ain't so sure it'd be somethin' I'd want to do."

"I could use the help, Joe."

"I still don't see why you'd want me," Coffin said quietly.

"Look, Joe, there's a heap of ground to cover, and I can't do it all myself. I need men I know, men who ain't afraid of goin' against long odds. Christ, just tryin' to track down the road agents who hit between here and Virginia City's damn near a full-time job."

"There's no others you can trust?"

"Only Beryl. If he wasn't marshal here, I'd never leave town to hunt outlaws." He paused. "I can trust you, Joe. It's been a few years since we saw each other, but I don't see no signs in you that you've given up what you was back in the war."

"And what's that?" Coffin asked somewhat wryly.

"A straight-shootin', tough-ass, no-give-up son of a bitch. An honest man and one who lives by his word."

"Such praise is likely to make my head swell," Coffin said modestly.

"Bullshit."

Coffin laughed. "Can't get nothin' by you, can I?"

"Nope." Pembroke grinned. "Besides, you don't take this job, I can't go pullin' your nuts out of the fire all the time like I did tonight. And knowin' how easy you get into scraps, you'll likely to be in some deep shit more often than not."

"You always this full of compliments for folks you're tryin' to hire?" Coffin asked with another laugh.

"Hey, some of us just have the gift." Pembroke could no longer contain his laughter. When it wound down, he said earnestly, "Me and Beryl could really use the help, Joe."

Coffin sat there looking at the scrap of metal. Slowly, hesitantly, he reached out and touched it with a forefinger. He felt odd even considering such a thing. He had always thought he was a reasonable man, one who wanted to see justice done no matter what the odds. But to think of becoming a lawman—a U.S. deputy marshal, no less!—was utterly foreign to him. He supposed it shouldn't be such a surprise, but he couldn't help being baffled—and worried—by the possibility.

"You allowed to hire people just like this?" Coffin finally asked, still uncertain about it all.

"Officially, I'm supposed to clear it with the U.S. marshal for the territory. He's appointed by the president and doesn't have to really do anything except to show up at church of a Sunday and at public functions now and again. Since it's me got to do all the work out here, I figure I'm entitled to hire my own deputies." He grinned. "Actually, the old buzzard give me permission to hire who I want."

"How come you were carryin' this"—he tapped the badge—"in your pocket?"

"Just in case."

"Just in case what?" Coffin asked roughly. "Just in case you found some poor sucker like me to stick it on?"

Pembroke laughed and refilled their glasses. "Hell, that's a good idea," he offered. "To be serious about it, Joe, I took it off one of my deputies yesterday. He was in cahoots with a few highwaymen. I found out about it and confronted him yesterday. I took the badge, and then 'encouraged' him to leave these parts."

"You have any other deputies?"

"Nope. Had a couple, includin' the one who went bad. The other three . . . well, none of 'em lasted too long before I had to plant 'em over in the boneyard."

"Such a cheery future you're offerin' me," Coffin said.

Pembroke laughed again. "Jesus, Joe, you gone soft in your 'old age'? Damn, I remember durin' the war, you were one of the craziest bastards ever to fight at my side. That's the kind of man I want with me out here. Unless you've gone yellow."

"It's a good thing you're a friend—and a former commander of mine."

Pembroke grinned. "And that's the kind of man I want. Jesus, Joe, you weren't afraid of nothin' before. You're about the coolest man under fire that I've ever seen. Such qualities don't come along that often, and when they do, it's wise to avail yourself of them."

"Good God, Marshal, you gonna set here and whine until I take the damn job?" Coffin asked in mock exasperation.

"If that'll firm your mind to the task, sure," Pembroke said with another laugh.

"And you'll promise to quit the damn whinin' if I take it?" Coffin was grinning hugely.

"I promise."

Coffin sat a few more moments staring at the badge. It was still an eerie feeling to contemplate wearing a badge. He had never done so; never had even given it a thought. Still, Enoch Pembroke was a former commanding officer, and a fair and compassionate one. Coffin would have no problem working with him. Or with Beryl Pembroke either.

Finally Coffin picked up the badge, holding it as if it were a red-hot piece of iron.

Pembroke poured them each another glass of whiskey. "To a safe and long life," he said, holding up his glass.

Coffin smiled a little and tapped his glass on Pembroke's. They drank.

Pembroke put his glass down. "Raise your right hand," he ordered.

Coffin did so, but skeptically.

"You promise to uphold all the laws no matter how stupid they are?" he asked.

"Sure." Coffin felt like an idiot.

"Good. Now you're a deputy U.S. marshal."

"Gee, thanks."

"First rule of deputy-dom: Don't piss off your new boss."

"Hell, Major, if I had to work around somethin' like that, I would've never gotten through your command in the war."

"You're right on that one, Joe." Pembroke stuffed the cork into the bottle and stood. Coffin followed suit. Both put their hats on. Pembroke grabbed the scattergun in his right hand and the bottle in his left. "Let's go on and see if we can find Beryl."

They did. It took more than an hour, and the search had wandered through a plethora of saloons. Then they found

Beryl Pembroke in a brothel, of all places.

"Hey, Beryl," Enoch shouted, "look who showed up."

Beryl looked at Coffin, taking no more than a second or two to place the face. "Joe Coffin, right?" he asked.

"Yessir." Coffin was a little surprised to see that neither man had changed very much since the war. Both were a bit over medium height and had barrel chests. Stark blue eyes shone out of the two faces. Big, round heads sat on bull necks. The main difference—physically—between the brothers was Enoch's big, thick brushy mustache. The adornment was so thick and long that it covered the entire bottom portion of his face below the nose except for the long, pointy chin. Beryl was clean-shaven.

"I hired him," Enoch said. "That all right by you?"

Beryl nodded. "As I recall, he was one of our finest soldiers, despite his tender age."

"That he was," Enoch agreed.

"Well," Enoch said, "I'd best get Joe here to the office so he can get to know things a little. You need any help here?"

"Nah. Big Sophie had a complaint about one of the customers. I came right over and pitched him out, nearly buck naked, too," he said with a laugh.

Coffin did not think that very funny, but he grinned vacuously so he did not have to explain himself.

"Anyway, I just got that done, and I thought I'd collect the fine," he said stiffly.

Pembroke laughed again. "We'll see you later over to the office. Come on, Joe."

As he and Pembroke walked outside, Coffin asked, "Collect the fine?"

"The job of town marshal doesn't pay all that well, of course, so we sometimes collect our own little 'fines'. In the case of Big Sophie's place, we generally take our fines out in trade."

Coffin gazed at Pembroke a moment, not sure if he

should laugh or be outraged. He decided, though, that it was not the worst thing in the world. He nodded, thinking that perhaps this job would be a better deal than he had thought. It did strike him as odd that Beryl Pembroke would take such a "fine." Coffin had remembered Beryl as somewhat of a prig. That would explain Beryl's stiff embarrassment, though.

Chapter Twenty-one

As Coffin and Enoch Pembroke walked toward the office the Pembroke brothers shared, Coffin mentioned some of his concerns. "How the hell do you know I ain't been an outlaw since the war ended?" he asked.

Pembroke gazed levelly at him. "You've always been an honest man, Joe."

"Lots of men're honest but go bad somewhere along the way."

"True enough, I guess," Pembroke said easily. "But I doubt it. I've been a pretty good judge of men most of my life, Joe. I ain't infallible—no one is—but I can generally figure out who's on the up and up and what fellas ain't. I'll bet on you."

Coffin smiled, enjoying the praise but quite uncertain that he deserved it. He had always been that way, especially with men he believed in. Men like Pembroke. "I just hope I can live up to your trust, Marshal. I . . ."

"Joe, I might be your boss, but I ain't your commander no more. Call me Enoch."

"Yessir."

"And don't you worry about livin' up to my trust. You did so durin' the war, and, by God, if you could come through that all right, this here'll be a piece of cake."

"Now I'm *really* worried!" Coffin said with a laugh.

They arrived at the jail, and Pembroke showed Coffin around. It was larger than Coffin had expected it would be, but when he thought about it, it made sense. Madison was a fairly big city with a lot of tough men, which meant more than a little crime. It also was shared by two lawmen.

There wasn't much to the place, really—four thick log walls, with a door and two glass windows in the false front. There were two rickety desks, a potbellied stove and several chairs in the office part. A log wall with a plank door separated the cells from the office. The door had a small window in it, with three vertical iron bars. A bunch of wanted posters were held onto a log wall with a stiletto next to the gun rack. A chain and lock prevented the theft of the weapons in the rack.

The rear of the office held seven cells in a horseshoe shape with the "opening" toward the office door—two to the left, two to the right, one dead center from the plank door, and then two slightly larger cells in the far corners. There was little to the cells: simply vertical iron bars planted in the ground at bottom and imbedded in the log ceiling. Bars also separated the cells from each other. The cells had no windows and no furnishings except for a hard iron cot bolted to the logs. They did not even have blankets.

Six of the cells were occupied by nine men, and Coffin asked why the seventh cell was not being used.

Pembroke shrugged. "We always like to keep one of 'em open if possible. We bring in a particularly nasty bastard, it's easier to deal with him that way. Besides, most of these boys ain't in here for anything major. Most of 'em's just sleeping off a drunk or somethin'. Except that one." Pembroke pointed to the left rear cell.

"What's he here for?"

"Robbin' stagecoaches. Asshole got himself caught. He's goddamn lucky he ain't been hanged yet."

"Why ain't he?" Coffin asked. The prisoner was fairly

nondescript. He was about medium height and thin, about Coffin's age. His clothes were filled with holes and patches. His thin, sallow face had locked onto the two lawmen when they had come through the door and had never left them.

"Vigilance committees in these parts've been idle of late. I'd like to think it's 'cause Beryl and me've been doin' a good enough job so they ain't needed. It might even be true. Besides, we're tryin' to get him to talk. We figure he's one of Cady Merkle's bunch."

"Who's this Merkle feller?"

"Head of a band of outlaws. We ain't sure how many men ride with him, but it's a fair number. He only takes a few on each job, so it's not like he's got an army with him. It does make it a little hard, though, to get much information about how many men he does have."

"What's this oaf's name?" Coffin asked, pointing to the man in the cell.

"Alvin Pendergast, a useless little shit if ever one was born."

"Lookin' at him," Coffin said with a smirk, "I don't think he's got the brains to tell you—us—about Merkle's gang."

"He does seem a mite slow, don't he," Pembroke commented.

The two went back out into the office. Pembroke reached into a desk drawer and pulled out a key. He tossed it to Coffin, who snared it. "For the weapons rack," Pembroke announced. "Keys for the cell are over there." He pointed. Another knife was stuck into the log wall next to the door to the cells. On it hung an iron ring with what looked to be about a dozen keys.

"I think that's about enough for one night, Joe," Pembroke said. "Especially when you've been clobbered about some."

Coffin nodded. His jaw still hurt, and he was sure that

by morning his face would be as colorful as the sunset.

"Come on over first thing. We'll all go have us a breakfast over to Terwilliger's. Second best place for eats in Madison."

"See you then." Coffin left, wondering why Terwilliger's was only the second best restaurant in town as he walked tiredly to his hotel.

Coffin stepped out of his hotel into the bright, warm morning sunshine. He still felt very self-conscious about the gleaming bit of metal pinned to his shirt. The brightly mottled purplish-yellow bruises on his face did little to help his self-consciousness, but there was nothing he could do about those.

He was tired, too, having lain awake much of the night wondering about what he might have gotten himself into as well as how foolish this all seemed.

The Pembroke brothers were in the office and rose as soon as Coffin walked in. "Well, good goddamn," Enoch said with a laugh, "you sure are one colorful fella."

"He's gonna blind us for sure as soon as we walk into that sunshine out there," Beryl added.

"Hell," Coffin growled, his self-consciousness trying to assert itself. "Even all thumped-up like I am, I'm still handsomer of countenance than you two." Once more he felt odd. After all, this was Maj. Enoch Pembroke and his brother Lt. Beryl Pembroke he was making fun of. He, a lowly corporal.

The Pembrokes did not mind. Both laughed heartily. "Pugnacious little pup," Enoch offered.

"Enough of all this banterin'," Beryl said, still chuckling. "I'm hungry. You boys want to stand here throwin' insultin' words at each other, you can do so. I aim to fill my belly."

"Crab ass," Enoch joked.

An hour later, Coffin had to admit that Enoch had been right—Terwilliger's was a fine eatery, as least as far as the food went. Little good could be said about the decor, or even the service, but that was all secondary to eating for Joe Coffin. He chowed down on eggs from Mrs. Terwilliger's hen house, bacon from the Terwilligers' hogs, plump, hot biscuits slathered with fresh butter or creamy gravy. All of it was topped off by hot, thick coffee.

The three lawmen walked back toward their office a couple blocks from Terwilliger's. It was a well-laid-out town, with neat streets and clean-looking businesses. Most of the stores and such had false fronts, giving the town a homey atmosphere. President Street was the main street through Madison. It came in from the east and ended at the town square, which abutted a low, barren hill. A brick city hall was straight across from the street on the opposite side of the square. Next to city hall was the courthouse on one side and the offices of the *Madison Tribune* on the other. The marshals' office was a little east of Fifth Street, set back a little from President Street between Rosencrantz's Dry-Goods Store and a two story building that housed Dr. Hyrum Smith on the upper floor and Crenshaw's Pharmacy on the lower floor.

When they entered the office, Beryl put the big pot of coffee he had carried from Terwilliger's on the stovetop and then stoked up the fire. Enoch went straight into the back to check on the prisoners. Coffin felt rather useless.

Those chores done, all three men filled coffee cups and then pulled up chairs around Enoch's desk. Coffin rolled a cigarette, Enoch lit a pipe and Beryl picked at his teeth with a dirty fingernail.

"Well, Joe," Enoch said, "I'd like to officially welcome you to the ranks of the Madison Lawmen's Association." He laughed. "Hell, me and Beryl're just glad to have some help."

"Can't you call on anyone else?" Coffin asked.

"There's enough willin' bodies for posses and such. But nobody wants to be a full-time deputy. We can usually deputize a couple of men when we need 'em for somethin' special."

"Maybe I shouldn't have taken the job either," Coffin said with a regretful smile. "With just three of us, we're gonna be spread mighty thin."

"That we are," Enoch responded. "It's one of the reasons Beryl and I're glad to have you along."

"There's other reasons?" Coffin laughed.

Enoch nodded and smiled, but when he spoke, it was solemnly. "Hell, you handled yourself real well against Gilmore and those other peckerwoods last night. Ain't many fellas can take on four men at once and come out the better of it. There's more, though." He paused for a sip of coffee.

"I remember back to the war how you handled yourself with upclose fightin', as well as long, over the sights of a rifle," Enoch finally continued. "And I recall that time at Seven Pines. Them goddamn Rebs would've overrun our position for sure, if it hadn't been for you and them goddamn pistols of yours."

"Hell, Major," Coffin said, slipping back in time, too, "we got our asses whupped but damn good at Seven Pines."

"That's a fact. But your pistol work kept our militia from gettin' ground into sausage that day. We only lost twenty percent of our men; damn near all the others had far more casualties than that."

Coffin was uncomfortable again. He was proud of his abilities but it somehow seemed wrong to be praised so highly and openly for them, especially since it involved wholesale killing.

"You're gonna need all those things in this job, Joe," Enoch said earnestly. "The boys we hunt out here are tough bastards. Most were in the war and ain't fazed the least by blood, guts and destruction. A number of 'em're goddamn former Rebs, and're as nasty as they can be, especially once they find out we're damn Yankees—and proud goddamn Yankees to boot."

"What Enoch says is true," Beryl said. "A goodly number of the outlaws out here're experienced killers. Have no other real talents, many of them."

"Just like us three," Coffin said softly.

Enoch nodded. "Yessir, just like us. That don't change the situation none, though. We chose the right path—the path of law and justice. Them, well, they went the other way. And now it's our job to bring 'em all to heel."

"And just remember one thing about it all, Joe," Beryl threw in. "There's a whole lot more of them than there are of us. We're outnumbered, outgunned, outrun half the time."

Coffin nodded and then grinned lopsidedly. "I get it now," he said, still smiling. "This is the talk that gets me fired up about doin' a good job, ain't it?" he added sarcastically.

"You know, Beryl," Enoch said, "I think Joe here's gonna do all right for himself.

They all laughed.

"Seriously, Joe, this is a dangerous job," Enoch said. "But, I ain't ever seen anybody handle danger and trouble as well as you. You are one cool-headed son of a bitch when the fight's on."

"Comes natural," Coffin said quietly. "All I know is that's the way I am. Can't figure out why I'm that way. Just that I am."

Enoch nodded. "Now, let me tell you a little about the job." He leaned his bulky body back in his chair and laced his fingers behind his head. "Beryl here, being the marshal of Madison handles most of what comes up in town here.

He can usually get some help on the spot, if he needs it. Our job – me and you, Joe – is to handle everything outside of town."

Coffin whistled. "That's a handful, I expect," he commented.

"It is that. I try'n help Beryl when I'm around, which ain't too often these days. Maybe that'll change with you around, though. I might be able to stick around Madison more."

Coffin nodded.

"Any questions, Joe?" Enoch asked.

"Supplies?"

"Get 'em at Rosencrantz's next door. Or at Williams' over on Fourth Street. Just have 'em put on our tab. Pay's three dollars a day – ninety a month."

Coffin nodded again.

"Anything else?" Enoch asked.

"Why don't you work out of Virginia City? It's a much bigger place."

"I hate that festerin' sinkhole. Marshal McAllister don't give a damn where I operate from, just as long as I do my job. And, this way, Beryl and I can help each other when the need arises."

"I was just wonderin'."

Chapter Twenty-two

"Where're you stayin', Joe?" Enoch Pembroke asked as they walked down President Street.

Coffin pointed. "Blake's. Why?"

"Well, we got us enough room in the house, if you want to light and tie there."

"I don't want to put you out none."

"You won't. And it seems foolish to be payin' rent on a place that you ain't gonna be in half the time."

"You did say I was gonna have to spend a lot of time huntin' down outlaws, didn't you?"

"I did."

"You sure it won't put you out?"

"Not at all." Pembroke paused. "Tell you what. Come over for supper tonight. You can see how things are goin'."

Coffin nodded.

They continued on their tour of town, with Pembroke pointing out places, including his house. They stopped in a store now and then, where Coffin would be introduced to the store owner. It took a good portion of the day.

Then Coffin and Pembroke went back to the office, where they went over what maps they had of the surrounding countryside. Coffin would need a good working knowledge of the area if he was to hunt outlaws like Cady Merkle.

"When do I leave?" Coffin asked as he folded up the

maps.

"Tomorrow mornin's good enough, I suppose. Go on and have yourself a nap or somethin'," Pembroke ordered politely. "You're lookin' mighty beat."

Coffin nodded, agreeing not only with the suggestion but the reasoning behind it.

"Be at the house about five."

Coffin felt considerably better when he woke from his nap. He checked his pocket watch. He still had a half-hour. He washed up in the small basin and changed his shirt. He even shaved. At fifteen to five, he left the hotel and took his time getting to the Pembrokes' home, enjoying the sunny warmth of the day. He arrived at one minute to five, by his pocket watch. He rapped on the door.

When the door opened, Coffin was certain he had taken one too many blows to the head in all the fights he had had over the years. Nothing else would seem to explain this vision of loveliness standing before him, holding the door open. She was also saying something, he finally realized. He blinked a couple of times. The vision did not disappear, but at least he could hear now, too.

"Sorry, ma'am," he said quietly. "I was some taken aback by your appearance."

"Why?" the woman asked, a little baffled.

"I didn't know Enoch or Beryl was married. They never said anything about it, except that Enoch said he lost his Netty a while back."

The woman laughed, a deep, merry sound that struck right at Coffin's vitals. "I'm Amy Pembroke," she said with the laughter still bubbling around the words. "Enoch and Beryl are my brothers."

"Ah," Coffin said with a nod. "That would explain it, wouldn't it?"

"It better had explain it," Amy said, her voice endlessly cheery. "Now, come on in, Mr. Coffin. Please. Supper is almost ready."

Still suffering a severe case of befuddlement, Coffin entered the foyer and stopped. Amy shut the door behind him and then said, "Follow me, Mr. Coffin."

Coffin was happy to do so.

Amy led him to a sitting room. "Mr. Coffin's here." She stepped out of Coffin's way as he walked into the room. Then she left.

Coffin sat, still trying to get over his amazement. Enoch brought him a glass of whiskey. "Looks like you could use this, boy," Enoch said with a laugh.

Coffin nodded dumbly, took the glass and drained it. He held it out. "More," he said flatly. Enoch filled the request, and once more Coffin downed it straight and fast. "One more time."

"Hell, boy, you're gonna get drunk on another," a highly amused Enoch said.

"I must be drunk already," Coffin said solemnly.

"Why?" Enoch asked in surprise.

Coffin pointed vaguely over his shoulder.

"Amy?" Enoch asked, still surprised.

Coffin nodded.

"Why?"

"You never said . . . never told me . . ." Coffin squawked.

Both Pembrokes laughed heartily. "Reckon we didn't," Enoch said. "I guess we just sort of expected you to know about her, though there was no way you could know, now that I think about it. My apologies."

"Nothin' to really apologize for," Coffin said in a more normal tone of voice. "Nothin' that is except trying to make my heart give out on me from the shock and surprise."

"Well, in that case, I reckon you do need another drink," Enoch said laughingly.

Coffin sipped the shot of whiskey and then set it down. He began rolling a cigarette. "What's she doin' here?" Coffin asked when the smoke was going.

"Our parents died, I guess it's been about a year ago now. Within a month of each other. Me and Beryl went out there for Pa's funeral, and we was still there when Ma went, too. Beryl come back straight after that, while I stayed back there to see to everything. Amy didn't have no place to go really except with some relatives none of us was particularly fond of, so I brought her out here to keep house for us, at least until she marries."

Coffin nodded. "She got anyone lined up?"

"For what?"

"Marryin'."

"Not that I know of," Pembroke chuckled. "You, Beryl?"

"Nope."

Coffin's mind was racing, thoughts of the lovely Amy Pembroke going round and round. Then the vision was in the doorway and announcing that supper was served.

The three men filed into the small dining room and took seats. Enoch sat at the head of the table, as was his right, being the oldest. Beryl had the foot of the table. Coffin and Amy were directly across from each other. Amy said grace, and then the plates and bowls and platters of food went around the table.

Coffin didn't want to seem like a hog, but he was hungry. He was that way a lot, and rarely, if ever, apologized for it. So he piled his plate high with elk steak, white potatoes and fresh green beans. He also grabbed three thick buttermilk biscuits when they came around, and slathered them in butter.

"Where'n the hell're you gonna put all that, Joe?"

Enoch asked with a laugh.

"Watch your language at the dining table, Enoch," Amy scolded mildly.

"Yes'm." Enoch looked a little sheepish. "Well, Joe?" he said. "You never did answer."

Coffin just glowered at him. The two Pembroke men laughed. Coffin took a bite of everything on the plate and chewed appreciatively. "Whoa, now I know why you said Terwilliger's was the second best place to eat in Madison."

"It's all Amy's doing," Enoch said.

Amy beamed in pride, but lowered her eyes lest she be considered vain.

"Well, ma'am, I can say in all honesty that this's the best meal I've ever eaten."

Once more Amy's face pinked up in happy pride. Knowing that everyone was looking at her, she knew she had to say something. While she liked the comments about her abilities as a cook, she did not want them to get out of hand. She brought her eyes up and looked at Coffin. "What happened to you, Mr. Coffin?" she asked quietly. "Your face, I mean."

"Please, ma'am, call me Joe." When Amy nodded, Coffin said, "My face got in the way of somebody's fist a couple of times."

"You men," Amy chided, though she did not really sound angry. "All you do is fight." Then she smiled at Coffin, who suddenly found he couldn't breathe all that easily.

Coffin did get more accustomed to Amy's presence as the meal progressed. After the main course was done, Amy brought out an apple pie. She cut it into four pieces, giving the three men very large slices. She took the small piece for her own.

Finally they all were done. Coffin rolled a cigarette and puffed on it while sipping another cup of coffee.

"Well, Joe, now that you've seen our humble home," Enoch said, "what do you think about stayin' here instead of at a hotel or boardinghouse?"

Coffin studied his thoughts a little. Finally, he said cautiously, hoping he was not overstepping any bounds, "I ain't sure." He paused, and then decided to just say it and see what the consequences were. "It's probably mighty presumptuous of me, but I'd . . . well, I'd like to court Amy." Figuring that he would get a lot of argument, he hastened to add, "I know I just met her and only seen her this one time, but I am powerful attracted to her . . ."

"Whoa, boy," Enoch said with a laugh. "Slow down, boy and give a body room to speak." When Coffin had clapped his mouth shut and sat there feeling a trickle of worry in his midsection, Enoch said seriously, "I know you to be an honorable man, Joe. Unless you've gone and changed a hell of . . ."

"Your language," Amy warned.

". . . hell of a lot in the past few years," Pembroke went on just for spite. "And as such, I have no problem with you courtin' Amy." He glared at Coffin. "Unless you're just tryin' to take advantage of . . ."

"I've killed men for such insults," Coffin said evenly.

Enoch stared at Coffin, and liked what he saw in those hard blue eyes. He smiled just a bit. "No, you wouldn't do somethin' like that," Enoch said. "My apologies, Joe, for havin' said such a thing to an old and trusted friend."

Coffin nodded, accepting the apologies.

"As I said, I ain't put out by you courtin' Amy. How about you, Beryl?"

"Amy could do a lot worse for a suitor," Beryl said.

Coffin could feel the excitement rushing through him. It had been only three months or so since he had lost Edna Yarnell, but it seemed a lifetime ago. He thought he would never get over that, but Amy Pembroke, just by being here, was enough to make him almost forget Edna. If he hadn't forgotten her yet, she was very far back in his mind.

"I guess the real question," Enoch said, "is whether Amy wants your attentions. She don't and you come around to bother her . . ."

"That's twice, Enoch," Coffin said flatly. "Don't do it a third time."

Enoch nodded. He looked at his sister. "Well, Amy, what do you think of all this?"

Her smile fairly lit up the room—at least for Coffin. "I'd be mighty proud to have you call on me, Mr. Coffin. Joe."

Coffin's heart felt like it would burst right out of his chest. Then reality hit him, and he sobered. "That might put a hitch on plans for me to stay here, Enoch," he said.

"It will?" Enoch was surprised, but mostly because he was watching his sister's reaction to Joe Coffin. He looked at Coffin.

"Are folks gonna talk poorly of Miss Amy if I'm courtin' her *and* livin' in the same house while I'm doin' it?"

"That they might," Enoch said. He was of a mind to blast anyone who made a fuss over such a thing, but he knew that was totally foolish. People were bound to talk about it, and Enoch Pembroke did not want any of that dirt to touch his sister.

Finally Enoch sighed. "I expect it's an imposition on you, Joe, but it might be best if you was to stay elsewhere. At least for the time bein'."

"No!" Amy objected vehemently. "I don't care what others say."

"You should," Enoch said. "Such talk'll drive a wedge between you and Joe. Maybe even between you and the two of us. People're like that. It ain't right, maybe, but it's a fact."

"I agree with Enoch, Amy," Coffin said. "I'd not want

anyone to go around soilin' your name or your reputation. Besides, I'd be in a fight every ten minutes tryin' to protect you."

"I still don't like it," Amy pouted.

"Tell you what, Amy," Coffin said slowly. "Let me stay at the hotel, or maybe even at a boardinghouse, at least for a while. Enoch says I'll be on the trail a lot anyway. We'll see how things go that way for a spell."

Amy didn't like the idea, but she acquiesced.

Chapter Twenty-three

Coffin was just a tad annoyed as he rode out of Madison the next morning with a pack mule in tow. He figured it ridiculous that he had just last night asked to court Amy Pembroke, all the while knowing that he would be gone this morning. He should've known better than to have opened his mouth.

Still, he had had much of last evening with Amy. Granted, they were in the sitting room with Amy's two brothers right in the next room, but they were alone together. That was all he could ask, at least at this point. They were, of course, uncomfortable since neither knew the other, but they had talked a lot.

Coffin also knew now that Amy would be waiting for him when he returned, however long that would be. Worrying about it now wouldn't do him any good anyway, and might even do some harm. If he allowed his mind to rest too comfortably on thoughts of Amy, and on his regrets of having to leave her just as he met her, he could become easy prey for the many outlaws in the land.

Helping him, though, was the picture of Amy in his mind's eye. He could conjure it up easily enough; it was harder to put that mental picture away.

He sighed as he hit the trail leading east out of Madison and then northwest toward some of the other mining towns. He didn't expect to find much about the outlaws this soon, but he would have to be alert.

Late in the afternoon, he pulled into Busted Shovel, a mining camp with no amenities and a lot of paranoia brought on by gold fever. A man named Lemuel Partridge seemed to be the closest thing to a leader in Busted Shovel, and Coffin sought him out.

Partridge quit shaking the sifter box and looked at Coffin. Over the roar of the Beaverhead River, he asked, "Where's Marshal Pembroke?"

"Back in Madison. I'm his new deputy."

Partridge shrugged. "You're awfully small for a lawman, ain't you, boy?" He stared evenly at Coffin.

"Nobody told me I had to have big feet—or a big mouth—to wear this badge," Coffin said.

Partridge shrugged again. He pointed to Coffin's bruised face. "Looks like you ain't a very good lawman."

Coffin grinned tightly. "Took four of 'em, all of 'em big, ugly fellers like you, too."

Partridge stared at Coffin a few more moments. Then he nodded and laughed. "I just bet it did," he said firmly. "Now, Marshal, what can I do for you?"

It took Coffin a moment to realize that Partridge was addressing him as marshal. "You have any trouble hereabout lately?" he finally asked.

"A couple claim jumpers come through the other day."

"Where'd they go?" Coffin asked.

Partridge pointed. Coffin followed the man's finger until his eyes lit on two wood crosses.

Coffin nodded and smiled. "That'll keep 'em from jumpin' any more claims, won't it?" Coffin commented.

"That was the idea," Partridge bellowed.

"Anything else?" Coffin asked. "Somethin' you might need me to look into?"

Partridge stroked his hard, square jaw. He was unsure

whether he should say anything, seeing as how he didn't know Coffin at all. Then he shrugged. If Coffin wasn't a marshal like he claimed to be, it wouldn't cause much more trouble than a man had any right to expect in a place like Busted Shovel.

"Some folks caught Jasper Daniels headin' for Madison a few days ago. Killed him and took his poke—our poke. He was comin' on down to get some supplies."

"You know who done it?"

"Cady Merkle."

"You sure?"

Partridge nodded.

"You or someone else see him?"

"Didn't need to. Marty Hardings found the body. There was a note stuck to Jasper's chest with a knife."

"A note?"

"Yeah." Partridge pulled a piece of paper from his shirt pocket and held it out.

Coffin took it and opened it. The paper, coated with dried blood, crackled. "Obliged for the stake, pilgrim. Cady Merkle," Coffin read. Coffin looked up at Partridge. "This happened before?" he asked, holding out the paper.

"At least once I know of. Around other camps . . ." He shrugged.

"Mind if I keep this?" Coffin asked.

"I got no use for it."

Coffin nodded. "You got a place I can spend the night?"

"Jasper's tent"—he pointed to a sagging canvas tent a few yards from the river—"ain't bein' used but for some storage. I expect you can find a little bit of room in there."

"Obliged." Coffin turned and walked off. He unsaddled his horse and unloaded the mule and tended to both animals. Still tired, he picked up firewood and started a small blaze near the front of Daniels' tent. By the time dark covered the camp, he was chawing down on bacon and beans. Not his favorite meal, but it filled the hole in his belly, which was all that mattered.

After eating, Coffin relaxed with a cigarette and another cup of coffee. He let his thoughts drift to Amy. She was a little shorter than he and not very heavy, though she was curvaceous where she should be. Her hair was a deep, shimmering chestnut color, her lips full and pale pink, her nose and ears small and dainty, her throat long and graceful. Coffin loved her voice from the first time he had heard it. It was soft and melodious and seemed to reach right down into his innards.

He found it hard to believe that he had been so overwhelmed by Amy Pembroke, especially since it had not been all that long since he had been hurt by Edna Yarnell. That made him wonder, too. He considered it quite possible that the pain he felt from his separation from Edna might be part of the problem. He thought he might have been so overwhelmed *because* of that heartbreak, and that he really didn't feel this strongly toward Amy.

Still puzzling it over, he spread out his bedroll and went to sleep. In the morning, he ate and then looked up Partridge. "Where's this Marty Hardings feller?"

Partridge pointed out a tall, fat miner panning along a slow spot in the river. Coffin walked over to him. "You Marty Hardings?" he asked. When the man nodded, Coffin said, "I'm Marshal Joe Coffin."

"So?"

"I'd like to talk to you about Jasper."

"Jasper's dead."

"I know. That's why I wanted to talk to you about him."

"I'm not interested in talkin' wit' you. I'm interested in findin' me some goddamn color."

Coffin's hand snaked out and snatched Hardings' pistol

from the holster. Then he whacked Hardings a good shot on the side of the head with the revolver. "Now listen to me, you fat tub of shit, I want some information from you, and I'll get it if I have to beat you to death in the doin'." He paused. "Now, what's it gonna be?"

"I don't know much," Hardings whined.

"Then why make a goddamn fuss over it, you stupid bastard? Christ, if you had talked to me in the first place, I'd have been gone by now. Dumb shit." He paused a moment to control his anger. "Where'd you find Jasper?"

Hardings half turned on his fat, stumpy legs and then pointed to a thin track moving out through the trees along the base of a stony hill southeast of the camp. "About three miles that way."

"What were you doin' up there?"

"We'd heard some gunshots that way, and we figured it was trouble. But when Jasper didn't come back, and nobody else showed himself, we didn't know what to think. We drew straws, and I got the short one, so I rode out. Then I found Jasper and brought his body back here."

"He have any money on him when you found the body?"

"Nope. Only thing he had on him when I found him was the note stuck in his chest. And the knife holdin' the note."

"You able to tell anything about which way the killers went?"

Hardings shook his head. "I found Jasper, and I got his body and my ass back here with the utmost dispatch," Hardings said with what little dignity he could muster.

"There any side trails or anything up that way?"

"Not that I know of. I reckon there's a bunch of 'em, though. Either that or Merkle and his men appear and vanish by magic."

Coffin squatted there a little longer, mulling things over.

"Why was he on that trail?" he asked. "I come up from Madison on a more direct route, comin' into camp here from the southwest."

"Yeah, ain't that a ball buster?" Hardings said quietly. "Jasper decides to go by a side way. It's a little longer, but not hardly known, so he figures he'll be safer than on the track that sees a heap of folks traveling. A heap of folks for this area, anyway. And he gets himself killed. Damn if that don't beat all."

"You were good friends with him then?" Coffin prodded.

Hardings nodded. "We're all friends here. Small camp like this, you'd best be able to get along with everybody. But, well, me and Jasper go back a little ways. He was a good man."

Coffin nodded and dropped Hardings' pistol back into the battered old holster. As Coffin rose, he slapped Hardings on the shoulder. "Thanks, Mr. Hardings," he said.

Hardings appeared not to hear Coffin. He was already back to his panning.

Coffin saddled his horse, loaded the mule and rode out. There was nothing more he needed here, though something nagged at him. He could not place it, though, and he tried to put it out of his mind. He figured that if he left it alone in there to percolate in his brain, the answer would come sooner or later.

He tried to guess at the distance he traveled, and eventually found the spot where Daniels had been killed. Looking around there told Coffin nothing, so he pressed on, moving with deliberate slowness, trying to spot any indication of a trail cutting off this one. He had no luck, though, and because of it he was frustrated and annoyed when he decided to call it a day.

He pulled into a clump of trees near a trickle of water and went about his chores. They did not take long, and soon he was spooning in a poor stew he had made for himself. It was nearly tasteless, and he was grateful to at least have coffee to wash it down with.

After eating, he puffed on a cigarette. On a whim, mostly to keep his mind off Amy, he pulled out the wanted posters Pembroke had given him and started looking at them in the firelight.

Suddenly he started. He was looking at the face of one of the men in Busted Shovel. "Damn," he snapped. Now he knew what had tugged at his brain when he left the mining camp. It was too late to head back there now, but he knew he would be riding back to Busted Shovel sometime tomorrow.

With that plan firmly in mind, he went to sleep. It took a little while as he was torn between thoughts of Amy and thoughts of regret at having not recognized Dick Swafford when he was in Busted Shovel. Finally, though, he drifted off.

In the morning, he wanted to be on the go, so he hurried through breakfast and the rest of his chores. Less than an hour after dawn, he was on the trail.

He wanted to race down the trail, to get to Busted Shovel as fast as possible. But that, he knew, was foolish. If Swafford had been worried, he would've slipped away from Busted Shovel already. But since Coffin had seen Swafford when he had ridden out of the mining camp, he figured Swafford was still there. So he beat back his sense of urgency, and rode at a reasonable pace. There was no need to punish the horse and the mule just because he wanted to go arrest somebody.

By midafternoon, he was on the edge of the ramshackle mining camp. He stopped and watched over things for a while. Everything seemed the same as it had the day before. Some of the men squatted by the side of the river and panned. A few more worked sifter boxes, and several more were building a sluice box. Coffin spotted Swafford. The man was one of those working on the sluice.

Coffin had no experience in such things. His first thought was to just ride on into the mining camp and blast Swafford a couple times. However, that would not be a good way to get information on the rest of the outlaws. It also was not the way a United States deputy marshal should act. What he needed to do was arrest Swafford. He'd never done that before, and he wondered how he should go about it.

Then he shrugged. He would just go down there and tell Swafford he was under arrest. He would react then to whatever happened, rather than sit here all day wondering what he should do.

"Come on, horse," he said quietly, brushing his spurs on the horse's sides.

Chapter Twenty-four

None of the men looked up at his approach. Not only were they dedicated to their work—obsessed as they were with finding gold—but they also had the roar of the river in their ears.

Coffin pulled up near Partridge and dismounted, tying the horse and mule to a wind-blasted tree.

Partridge looked up as Coffin approached. "Christ, you back already?" Partridge asked, irritated.

"You always this friendly?" Coffin countered.

"Eat shit, Marshal. What do you want now?"

"A question first."

"Well, out with it, dammit. I ain't got all day to jawbone with you."

"Tell me, are you in cahoots with Merkle?"

"What the hell kind of question is that?" Partridge snapped. "Why in hell would I be in cahoots with a bloodthirsty son of a bitch like that?"

"Because, you parsimonious bastard, one of your men is one of Merkle's men."

"Bullshit," Partridge growled. "Who?"

"Dick Swafford."

"We don't have nobody named Swafford here. Now get

the hell out of here, you bastard, or I'll drop you where you stand."

"Now I'm terrified," Coffin said scornfully. He pulled out the papers and peeled the top one off. "Take a look."

Partridge's face contorted in anger. "That son of a bitch!"

"What name did he give you?"

"Russ Elgin. Not that it matters now." Partridge was steaming. He turned his hard-looking face on Coffin. "You want some help arrestin' him?"

"Wouldn't put me out none to have some help." He looked a little sheepish. "Hell, I'm still new at this marshaling shit."

"It don't show," Partridge said honestly. "Let's go."

They walked up to their quarry, who had his back to them. "Dick?" Partridge said.

The man almost jumped, but then he continued working as if he had heard nothing. Partridge and Coffin looked at each other and nodded.

"Russ?" Partridge tried again.

Swafford turned around. "You want somethin', Lem?" he asked, wiping a sleeve across his forehead. He was a short, pudgy man with a sweaty face and a mouthful of buck teeth. His face was covered with stubble, and one ear was deformed.

"Marshal Coffin here wants to chat with you a bit," Partridge said tightly. He wanted to pound Swafford—or Elgin or whatever he wanted to call himself.

"What about?" Swafford seemed more tense.

"About this." Coffin held out the paper with the sketched likeness of Swafford on it.

"Piss on you both," Swafford snapped. He kicked Partridge in the leg and tried to jerk out his pistol at the same time.

Coffin's right hand flew to the butt of one of his

Remingtons and hesitated there just a second, then moved away. Coffin's left arm knocked Swafford's gun away, and then Coffin pounded him a sharp shot to the face with his right hand.

Swafford fell backward, but caught himself on the partially built sluice. He was dazed.

Coffin took advantage and popped Swafford in the face twice more. Then he grabbed Swafford's shirt and jerked him forward, bringing his own knee up. The knee thudded into Swafford's stomach. Coffin let him fall to the ground.

Coffin knelt next to him. "There's a few things I'd like to discuss with you," Coffin said quietly. "When you get your breath back." Coffin rose, turned and picked up Swafford's fallen pistol. He tossed it into the river. "You packin' another piece, Swafford?" Coffin asked, looming over him, placing a boot on his back.

"No," Swafford squawked.

"I find out you're lyin', asshole, I'll carve off your ears."

"You let me up, you bastard, and I'll stomp your little ass into the ground."

"You had your chance, boy." He moved his boot. "Get up."

Swafford rose and brushed off his worn, dirty clothes. He turned to face Coffin, looking for a chance to pelt the lawman.

"Mr. Partridge," Coffin said, "would you see if he's packin' another piece, please?" It was an order, not a question.

Partridge patted Swafford much harder than really was necessary, but Coffin did not mention it. All Partridge came up with was a pocketknife. He pitched that in the river. "He's all yours, Marshal."

Coffin nodded. "He got a horse?"

"Rides a mule," Partridge said.

Coffin nodded. "Would you mind havin' someone saddle the mule? I'm gonna truss this bastard up, and then we can head out."

"Right away," Partridge said, turning and leaving.

"Where you gonna take me?" Swafford asked, worried.

"Madison. Me and Marshal Pembroke have a few questions we'd like you to answer."

"I ain't gonna tell you shit," Swafford snapped.

"No skin off my ass," Coffin said almost gleefully. "I'm sure there'll be a few folks who'd be plenty willin' to encourage you to reveal your secrets." He shoved Swafford's shoulder to spin him around. Then he pushed Swafford on the back. "Move out."

When they got into the heart of the camp a few minutes later, Partridge came up. "You want some grub before you pull out, Marshal?" he asked.

"Might not hurt."

"It wouldn't put us out none was you to stay another night here. That'd let you get a fresh start in the morning."

Coffin thought about that for a few moments, then nodded. "That'll be good. You want me to stay in Jasper's tent again?"

"Yep."

"What about Swafford?"

"John, Sam!" Partridge roared. Two men hastened up. "Tie Elgin—Swafford, whatever the hell his name is—to that big oak. Make sure he's good and snug."

The two men pushed Swafford along, and within minutes he was tied to the tree.

Coffin ate with Partridge and several other men. After the meal, he passed around the posters he had, since he wanted the others to know about Swafford. He also hoped that the miners might be able to give him some clue as to where he might find the other men in Merkle's gang. He had no luck in that, though, and he turned in soon afterward.

Coffin was up first in the morning. Or so he thought. When he stepped out of the noisily flapping tent, the eastern sky was ablaze with red. It spread a faint, bloody glow over the whole camp. As Coffin headed toward the river, he glanced over at the tree. And he stopped.

Swafford was gone.

Coffin ran to the tree, thinking that perhaps someone had gotten up early and had freed Swafford to tend to personal needs. He skidded to a stop and picked up the pieces of rope. They had obviously been cut. "Goddamn son of a bitch," he snapped quietly. He headed for his tent, fast. But then he had a change of heart. He went to where the men kept their horses and mules. Coffin's chestnut and mule were there. Swafford's mule was not.

By the time the others were stirring, Coffin had his horse saddled, and he was putting the last of his supplies on the mule.

"Leavin' so soon?" Partridge asked, rubbing the sleep from his eyes.

"Swafford's gone," Coffin growled.

"Where? How?"

"I don't goddamn know, but I goddamn aim to find out."

"How'd he get loose?"

"Somebody cut the ropes."

"Who?"

"If I knew that, the son of a bitch'd be dead now. I'm not fond of being made to look the fool. And when I find out which one of your cohorts here helped Swafford, he's gonna pay and pay hard."

"You don't think one of my men did it, do you?" Partridge asked, affronted.

"Who the hell else would it be? A goddamn ghost?"

"Could've been another of Merkle's men come in here after dark," Partridge offered.

"Could've been, I suppose. Could've been you, too."

"Me?" Partridge exploded. "Why you badge-wearin' little bastard, I ought to . . ." Partridge shut up when one of Coffin's Remingtons suddenly bloomed an inch from his nose.

"What should you do, Lem? Huh?"

Partridge looked as if he wanted to chew the muzzle off Coffin's revolver, but he neither said nor did anything.

"It could've been you since you got the run of the place here," Coffin said, not moving the pistol. "But more importantly, you were the one who urged us to spend the night."

Partridge nodded—carefully. "That's all true," he admitted. "But I'll tell you somethin', Marshal. It wasn't me. I find out it was one of the men here, and I'll string him up with my own hands. I know you ain't got much reason to believe me, but I'm tellin' you the truth."

Coffin uncocked the pistol and holstered it. "On the other hand, Lem, I ain't got too much reason to not believe you either. So I'll take you at your word—for now."

"Fair enough, Marshal."

Coffin swung into the saddle. He looked down at Partridge. "You find out who it is, you hold him here and get word to me."

"If I'm of a mind to at the time."

Coffin nodded. Then he spurred his horse and trotted out of Busted Shovel, heading north on a hunch. He figured Swafford would not want to head toward Madison or Virginia City.

Coffin did not bother trying to track Swafford. He just

pushed up the well-marked trail at a steady pace. He rode until almost dark without seeing any sign of Swafford. He angrily pulled off the trail and made his camp. He was in a sour mood, and his humor was not lifted any by the meal of salted beef and beans.

He was feeling no better as he ate his breakfast the next morning. He had begun to doubt himself, thinking that he was not cut out for being a lawman. He wondered if perhaps he hadn't missed a turn that Swafford had taken. He had not seen anything that resembled a real trail all along his ride yesterday, but if his anger was getting the better of him, he might've easily missed something. He cursed himself for not being a tracker, and he cursed himself for letting Enoch Pembroke rope him into wearing the badge.

For one brief moment, Coffin considered tearing the badge off and tossing it away. But he was not that kind of man. He might not be much at reading sign on a trail, but he was tireless and pugnacious. He would not quit until he had accomplished what he set out to do. And right now, that meant finding Dick Swafford.

Determined, he broke camp and hit the trail again, pushing a little harder than yesterday. His hope was that Swafford had moved fast yesterday and would be moving slower today, not thinking there would be much pursuit. Of course, Coffin realized he could be spitting into the wind here. There was as good—maybe even a better—chance that Swafford had gone south. It would be easy enough for him to ride around Virginia City, or even ride right through it at night. Nobody would see him, or most likely would know him.

The longer Coffin rode, the more certain he became that he was on the wrong trail. He decided sometime in the afternoon that he would give it till nightfall. If by then he had no proof that Swafford was on this trail, he would turn back.

The day began winding down, and Coffin was about ready to call it quits for now, when a faint aroma of wood smoke slid into his nostrils. He stopped, sniffing, trying to catch another scent of the smoke. He did, and nodded. He thought he had it pegged now.

Coffin pulled off the trail amidst trees and large boulders. Quickly he unloaded the mule and unsaddled the horse. He figured they could wait a while for their tending. He checked his pistols. Then he pulled off his spurs and tossed them on the ground next to his saddle. Finally he moved out on foot, edging through, over or around tangled brush, fallen logs, trees and rocks.

He slowed as he neared where he thought the fire smoke was coming from. He proceeded carefully until he suddenly stopped behind a large cottonwood and peered out from behind it. He felt a great deal of relief when he saw that it was Swafford.

Chapter Twenty-five

Swafford was leaning back against his saddle, sipping coffee from a battered tin cup. He seemed at ease, but there was no easy way for Coffin to sneak up on him. The outlaw was in a clearing with an arc of trees and brush about. Directly behind where Swafford was sitting, a rocky outcropping bulged out from the mountainside.

Coffin's instincts told him to just put a bullet into Swafford from here. But his head told him that he had taken on the duties of a United States marshal. Those duties did not include killing people in cold blood. Not when he hoped to get information from the man. He sighed. There was only one way to do it.

Coffin eased out a Remington and swiftly checked it. Keeping it uncocked alongside his leg, Coffin moved through the trees to his left. Once more he stopped and scanned the outlaw's camp. Then he stepped out of the brush, pistol leveled but not cocked.

"Evenin'," he said quietly.

Swafford looked like he would jump right out of his skin. "You!" he hissed angrily.

Coffin nodded. "Yep. And I am one unhappy son of a bitch, too."

"Well, you got the son of a bitch part right," Swafford said with a smirk.

"That very well might be, boy. But when I'm unhappy, I get real mean."

"You think you're a tough one, don't you?" Swafford said with a nasty tone. "Think 'cause you walloped me when I wasn't lookin' that you're a tough man. You put that gun down and give me an even chance without weapons, I'll clean your goddamn plow for you."

"You must think I'm as goddamn stupid as you are," Coffin said evenly.

Swafford grinned without humor.

"Who helped you back at Busted Shovel?"

"I told you back there, I ain't gonna tell you shit. You're gonna shoot me, go on and get it over with." He was feeling mighty confident. A United States marshal wouldn't shoot somebody like this. No, they preferred legal niceties and such.

Coffin shot Swafford in the right leg.

"Holy shit!" Swafford screeched in shock and surprise.

"Now," Coffin said, voiced unchanged, "who helped you get away?"

"I can't tell you that, Marshal," Swafford said nervously. He was sure now that he was in deep trouble here. "Merkle and his boys'll kill me sure soon's they find out I said anything."

"And I'll kill you here and now if you don't tell me. That leaves you with a choice. Tell me and take your chances that the law'll find Merkle first. Or keep your mouth shut now and die."

Swafford looked down at the blood welling out of his leg. There was relatively little pain, but Swafford knew from experience that it would get worse, and soon. "That ain't a very good choice, is it?"

"Nope. But it's the only one you're gonna get."

"Can I cogitate on it a spell?" Swafford asked.

"Sure. I'm in no hurry. Well, not too much of a

hurry." He figured Swafford was trying to figure out a way to get out of this predicament, maybe distract Coffin for a moment or two. Coffin would not, however, give Swafford any false sense of security and then kill him. Coffin tried to be evenhanded in such things.

Time ticked on, until Coffin started to get bored. That, he knew, would leave him vulnerable. "You gonna think on this forever?" he asked.

"If I had my druthers, I would," Swafford answered honestly.

"Well, I might not be in a real hurry, but I think forever's askin' a bit too much." His voice hardened. "Now, who helped you? I won't ask again."

Swafford sighed. "Floyd Biggs. He cut me loose, gave me a gun and some grub and I skedaddled."

"I ain't got a paper on him," Coffin said, a little baffled.

"Hell, there's a lot of Merkle's boys you don't have paper on."

Coffin nodded. "Why didn't you come on and blow my brains out while you had the chance?"

Swafford shrugged. "That would've got me killed sure as anything. Hell, that parsimonious bastard Partridge would've made sure of that."

Coffin nodded in agreement. "Anybody else in Busted Shovel belong to Merkle's band of cutthroats?"

"No." He paused, but when he got no response from Coffin, he asked, "So, what next?"

"Depends on you, boy."

"How's that?"

"You give over your gun and promise not to be a nuisance, I'll take you back to Madison. Marshal Pembroke and I'll ask you some questions. You cooperate there, we'll speak up for you when you go on trial."

"Don't sound like there's much good in that for me."

Coffin shrugged, unconcerned. "Think of the alternative."

"Yes, most unpleasant, I'd venture to say." Swafford had seen enough of Marshal Joe Coffin in just two short encounters to know what kind of stuff the lawman was made of. He had no doubts whatsoever that Coffin would put a bullet in his head at the first hint of resistance. Swafford sucked in a deep breath and then let it out slowly. His leg was beginning to hurt a lot. "Reckon I ain't got much choice, do I?"

"I suppose not."

Swafford nodded. "All right, then. But you'll have to help me out some once we hit the trail." He pointed to his leg.

"I could whack it off for you," Coffin said coldly. "I saw it done enough during the war to figure I could do it in a pinch."

"I'll get along all right," Swafford said, sweating. He figured Coffin was crazy enough to do it. Still, he really had no plan to be dragged back to first Busted Shovel and then Madison. Not if he could prevent it.

"Good. Now, let's . . ."

Swafford threw his coffee cup at Coffin, who ducked reflexively. It gave Swafford two or three heartbeats of time, in which he managed to jerk out the belly gun he was carrying. He had barely gotten it out and cocked when two balls from Coffin's Remington punched holes in his heart.

Coffin didn't regret for a moment killing Swafford. Not with the record the outlaw had amassed. What he couldn't figure out, though, was why Swafford had been tin panning in a place like Busted Shovel. Not that it mattered now.

Coffin holstered his pistol and walked back to where he had figured to make his camp. He tossed his saddle loosely over the horse's back and led it and the mule to Swafford's camp. Then he made another trip to get his supplies and such. Finally he tended his horse and mule, after which he had a cup of coffee from Swafford's pot.

He checked through Swafford's supplies but found little that he could—or would—use. His supply of food was better, so he cooked some of that. He ate quietly, sitting two feet to the side of Swafford's corpse. In the war, he had eaten a great many of his meals within spitting distance of bodies.

When he was done, he tossed a good pile of wood on the fire. It was not that cold, but he was hoping the man scent as well as the fire would keep the scavengers away from the body, which he covered with a piece of canvas.

In the morning, Coffin uncovered Swafford's body. Going through the man's pockets, he found a penknife. Pulling the wanted poster on Swafford out of his pocket, he scribbled on it in pencil: "Your days are numbered, Merkle." He signed it "U.S. Deputy Marshal Joe Coffin." He placed the paper on Swafford's chest. Then he stabbed the penknife through the paper and into the body to hold the note in place.

He loaded his mule and saddled his horse. Trailing Swafford's mule behind him, he pushed as hard as he dared. He didn't want to be on the trail forever. He finally stopped just before dark.

He reached Busted Shovel shortly before noon the next day. He stopped where he had the last time and tied the horse and mules off to the tree.

Partridge looked at him. "Where's Elgin? Or is it Swafford?"

Coffin shrugged. "Either way, he's worm food now."

"Why didn't you bring the body back? Hell, he had a price on his head."

Coffin grinned viciously. "I left him back there with a

note pegged to his chest. I used his poster for it, and left it as a warning for Merkle."

"He tell you who helped him?" Partridge asked harshly.

"Floyd Biggs. Which one is he?"

Partridge pointed to a big, lumpy looking man. Coffin remembered from the last time he was in the mining camp that the man had a scarred face and dead eyes.

"Thanks," Coffin said curtly. He headed toward Biggs.

Partridge caught up to him in a moment. "This is *my* camp, Marshal," Partridge snapped. "I'll deal with him."

"Like hell you will."

"Now, Marshal . . ."

"You get in my way, goddammit," Coffin growled, "I'll put a slug in you as fast as I will him."

Partridge saw the anger and determination on Coffin's face, and he nodded. "Mind if I walk along?"

"As long as you keep out of my way."

Biggs was kneeling at the edge of the river, where the water eddied around a large rock. He swept his pan round and round, dipping and shaking.

When Coffin was ten feet from Biggs, he drew a pistol and calmly shot Biggs through the right arm. The big man dropped his pan and screeched. He pushed to his feet and turned while reaching for his own pistol. It was an awkward maneuver since his right arm hung uselessly at his side.

"You got one goddamn chance to stay alive, Biggs," Coffin snapped. "You pull that pistol on me, and I'll shove it up your ass and blow your brains out."

"What the hell's wrong wid you, lawman?" Biggs asked, voice gravelly and uncultured.

"You're under arrest."

"For what?" He did not seem in the least surprised.

"Well, for now, just helpin' a known criminal to escape. I reckon I'll be glad to find a heap of other charges given some time to think on it."

"You're *loco,*" Biggs said.

"That's funny," Coffin said easily. "Dick Swafford said the same thing just before I put two slugs in his heart."

Biggs's eyes narrowed a little. It was the only sign of recognition of the name or deed.

"Now, I'm gonna make you the same offer I made him. You ride back to Madison with me, nice and peaceable, and answer the questions we'll be askin' of you, and we'll speak up in your defense at your trial."

Biggs laughed loud and hard.

"That's not very polite," Coffin said.

"Oho, did I make the little lawman mad at me?" Biggs said with a sneer.

Coffin shrugged and shot Biggs in the other arm.

Biggs looked like an enraged bull, his eyes popping, and snuffling grunts popping out of his nose.

"Naw, I ain't mad at you, boy," Coffin said lightheartedly. "You still havin' a good time?"

"You little bastard," Biggs snarled. "You goddamn, backshootin', busybody son of a bitch."

"I ain't backshot nobody," Coffin said. "You want to try it, though, I'll be glad to oblige you if you turn around."

Without warning, Biggs charged, snarling and snorting.

Coffin calmly moved back a few steps and to his left a little. Then he emptied the Remington into Biggs. The big man had so much momentum that he continued on for a yard or two before he fell facedown in the dirt.

"Have some of your boys get him up on Swafford's mule," Coffin said coldly to Partridge. "Tie him down good and cover him over with canvas."

"I take it you're not going to enjoy our hospitality one

more night?" Partridge asked dryly.

Coffin smiled just a bit. "Reckon not."

"Want some grub?"

"If you got somethin' ready, I'll bolt down a bit."

"We do." Partridge walked off, shouting orders.

Coffin followed more slowly. Stopping at his horse, he got his materials and quickly cleaned, oiled and reloaded his pistol. Then he sat at the fire and hungrily downed several large hunks of venison, a half-dozen biscuits and three cups of coffee.

Lethargically, he rose. He felt like doing nothing more than climbing into his bedroll and sleeping for a couple of days. But he could not afford that luxury. He wanted to get back to Madison to see Amy. He also wanted to get back there before Biggs's body really started to ripen.

"Well, Mr. Partridge," Coffin said, holding out his hand, "I hope I don't see you for a while."

Partridge shook Coffin's hand. "I know what you mean, Marshal."

Coffin mounted and rode off without looking back. His opinion of Lemuel Partridge was not all that good, but it had risen a little since he had first met the man.

Chapter Twenty-six

Coffin rode into Madison just before noon the next day after traveling all night. He stopped at his office and tied his horse and the two mules to the hitching rail. He ignored the small crowd that quickly gathered, talking and gesticulating at the canvas-wrapped corpse.

Inside, Beryl Pembroke had heard the noise growing, and he was about to step outside to see what all the commotion was about, when Coffin walked into the office. "Joe," Pembroke said with a small smile. "Glad to have you back."

"Glad to be back," Coffin said wearily.

"What's going on outside?"

"I brought a body in." When Pembroke's eyebrows raised in question, Coffin said, "One of Merkle's boys."

Pembroke nodded. "Let's go take a look."

Coffin nodded and turned slowly.

"You look bushed, Joe. You all right?"

"Just tired. Had a few hectic days out there, and I rode through the night to get here."

"Somethin' chasin' you?" Pembroke asked warily.

Coffin offered up a wan smile. "Yeah. Scavengers looking for fresh meat." He indicated that corpse outside.

"I reckon he is gettin' a mite aromatic in this heat,"

Pembroke said with a shake of his head.

The two men went outside and stopped. "Get away from here now," Pembroke bellowed at the crowd. "None of this is your affair. Go on now, get going."

Grumbling, the crowd began breaking up, and the people wandered off, somewhat angry at having been denied an opportunity to see who it was under the canvas.

Pembroke peeled back the covering from the body and lifted the head by the hair. "Never saw him before," he noted. "You got paper on him I'm not aware of, Joe?"

Coffin shook his head. "Let's go on back inside and set."

"You got a bad story to tell?" Pembroke asked, a little worried.

"Nah. I just need to rest my bones," Coffin said with a small grin.

Pembroke nodded. "Go on inside. I'll be in directly, soon's I can get this fella taken care of."

Coffin walked inside and sat heavily. He thought about rolling a cigarette and decided he didn't have the energy. He felt the same about a cup of coffee. He felt himself drifting off and unsuccessfully tried to fight off sleep. He jerked awake, hand streaking to a revolver when he heard the door rattle.

Pembroke froze in the doorway and shouted, "Joe! It's me, Beryl!"

Coffin shook his head, which did little to clear away the clinging fog of sleep. "Sorry, Beryl," he apologized sheepishly.

Pembroke let out his breath. With his relief came a little smile. "Damn, I forgot that about you."

"Forgot what?"

"The way you come awake if disturbed. It's rather amazing you haven't killed more people—friends."

"Maybe I have, and don't remember it," Coffin said. He holstered his revolver, and then rubbed his face with both hands.

"Hogwash." Pembroke poured two tin mugs of coffee, handed one to Coffin and then sat at his desk. "So, what happened? And who is that guy out there?"

Coffin explained it quickly, though he was not sure it all was coherent. He couldn't remember ever having been this tired, and it worried him a little. When he was done, he rose wearily. "You got any more questions, they'll wait till tomorrow. I need to get me some shuteye."

Coffin was the one with questions the next day. He had slept the rest of the day before and most of the night. He rose an hour or so before dawn, dressed and found that Terwilliger's was open. He was famished, and so packed away a huge breakfast. His appetite amused even Terwilliger himself, who generally had a sour disposition.

When he got to the office, Beryl Pembroke was there. Coffin poured himself some coffee and took a seat. "Where's Enoch?" he asked.

"Gone, as usual," Pembroke said with a smile.

"Somethin' in particular?"

"Sort of. The day you left three stages were hit."

"Makes me a suspect, don't it?" Coffin said in mock suspiciousness.

"There's some that'd think that way," Pembroke said. "But unless you've got a gang—and a large one—it couldn't have been you. One was hit between here and Virginia City, one between Flat Busted and Bannock and another—one from here—northeast of Virginia City."

"Merkle's gang?" Coffin asked.

"Ain't sure about the first two. He usually has enough men at his beck and call that he could hit three, four places at once. He's sent out three or four bands at one time to hit stagecoaches and such, while he sat in a Virginia City saloon playin' stud poker. Every lawman in the territory knew it was Merkle callin' the shots, but without him bein' there, we couldn't do a thing. However, on the latter one, someone identified Merkle as well as Kurt Ochs, one of Merkle's top two men."

Pembroke sat quietly for a few moments drinking coffee. Coffin thought it strange that Beryl and Enoch Pembroke could be so similar in looks but so different in some of the ways they acted. Beryl did not smoke, rarely drank. He never used coarse language either. His only real vice was in his occasional sessions with a prostitute. Beryl never talked about it, and Coffin wondered how Beryl reconciled such sins of the flesh with his deep faith. Coffin knew that Beryl had had a wife during the war, but he didn't know what had happened to her, and Beryl would never mention it. Coffin had heard that Beryl was courting a respectable widow in town, but he was not sure that was true. Beryl was not so much closed-mouthed as he was quiet and unassuming. He was also soft-spoken, and many a man took that as a sign of weakness. It was a mistake to do that. Beryl Pembroke was as hard a man as Coffin had ever seen. He came across to many as a pompous, self-righteous prig, but he believed strongly in God, justice and his own abilities. He was not a man to take lightly.

"Anyway," Pembroke continued, "nobody in the first two holdups recognized any of the men as Merkle's. It don't mean they weren't, but we've got precious little to go on. I suspect Merkle is behind those robberies—and the others."

"Others?"

"There were two more stages hit the day after you left, four two days ago, and two more yesterday."

Coffin whistled. "Active little bastards, ain't they," he commented.

"Yes, they're scoundrels, indeed," Pembroke said quietly. "The two worst were the two got stopped northeast of Virginia City. Both were headin' to Denver with eight passengers, several mail pouches, and two strongboxes of gold."

"Well, they ain't gonna hold up a stage just for pickin' the pockets of a bunch of passengers or so."

"True enough. But how did they know to hit the ones carryin' the most gold?" Pembroke mused.

"Do you send shipments that way often?" Coffin asked.

"Fairly regular. The strongboxes hold the gold paid to the merchants for their goods. The merchants and workmen toss their gold into a pot, such as it is, for takin' back to Denver. It goes to pay what they owe for supplies, or for new supplies they need to bring in."

"Do those stages run regularly to Denver without the gold sometimes?"

"I suppose." He paused. "What I mean is they don't too often have big shipments of gold like these. They almost always carry a small amount. Miners sending it back to families in the East. A miner or merchant wanting some personal items. The big shipments generally go about once a month. Every once in a while, though, it works out like it did this time—two big shipments within a few days."

"Could the robbers just have gotten lucky? You know, hitting all those stages within a week or less in the hopes they might hit a mother lode?"

"Possible," Pembroke said. "But mighty unlikely." He fiddled a few moments, then said, "I think Merkle and his men are responsible for all of them. I also think that he has somebody in Madison—or maybe even in Virginia City—who's alerting Merkle and his men when the big shipments are being made."

"Sounds reasonable, in an odd sort of way, Beryl," Coffin said. "But what about the other ones?"

"I think they were done to throw suspicion off Merkle and his men. And to divert attention away from the two big robberies."

Coffin thought about that for a bit, then nodded. "I think you're on to somethin', Beryl."

"It's certainly plausible," Pembroke said. "But I have no proof. No proof at all. Makin' it all the worse is that I've heard that vigilance committees are going back into action. That's somethin' we really don't need. I've not ever seen a vigilance committee who hasn't hanged at least one innocent man."

"Anything we can do to stop 'em?"

Pembroke shook his head. "No. The only way would be to catch 'em in the act of hangin' somebody and arrest 'em. Trouble with that, though, is there's usually a passel of vigilantes and only one or two lawmen. Those odds aren't very favorable. It's possible you could arrest 'em later, but you'd have to be able to identify 'em positively. And that's nearly impossible."

"They caused any trouble yet?"

"None that I know of, Joe. But if the rumors are true that they're back in operation, it won't be too long before someone's found with his neck stretched."

"Damn," Coffin muttered. "Enoch's headed east, then?"

"No," Pembroke said flatly. "We heard about the two

local holdups almost right away since they were so close. Enoch rode out the next morning. It wasn't till the next day that we heard about the other. It took about two days to hear about the second big one. I just found out about that one last night." He shook his head. "There's a road ranch—a way station for the stages, where the folks can get a meal and spend the night while traveling—not far from where the two robberies took place. One of the men there galloped to Virginia City—and then here—with the news. He no sooner got back to his road station when he had to do it all over again."

"Damn," Coffin snapped. "Well, I best get myself back on the trail again. I'll stop by Virginia City first and see if there's anything I can learn there. Then I'll head northeast." He paused, thinking about that for a moment. "Northeast? To get to Denver?"

Pembroke laughed just a bit. "Does seem odd—until you take a look at the countryside. Out past Virginia City is a big valley running north and south. You go south there's a heap of mountains. So the stages head north a ways before turning east. Once they get through Bozeman Pass, they're almost on the prairie. Travelin's easier then."

Coffin nodded, already considering what he might need. "You trust the boys at that road station?"

Pembroke nodded. "For the most part. We've never had any trouble from them. I guess there's always a chance they're in cahoots with Merkle, but it doesn't seem likely."

Coffin nodded and stood. "Well, I'll get my supplies and such. I should be on the trail before noon."

"Tomorrow's soon enough," Pembroke said. When Coffin looked at him in surprise, Pembroke said, "You've had a full couple of days, Joe. You deserve a little rest, and maybe some time for a little spree." His distaste for such things was evident on his face. "And I know Amy'd be real glad to see you." He glared at Coffin. "You are planning to do the right thing by my sister, aren't you?"

"That doesn't deserve an answer, Beryl," Coffin said stiffly.

Pembroke nodded. "Sorry, Joe. I just have Amy's best interests in mind"

"So do I."

Pembroke looked up at him and nodded. He was smiling a little.

Coffin spent virtually the entire day with Amy. He had first stopped at the general store and made arrangements for picking up his supplies in the morning. Then he hurried to the Pembrokes' house. As he had hoped, Amy was very glad to see him.

They strolled around town, happy just to be together. Coffin had never been so joyous. He had thought at the time that he had loved Edna Yarnell, but he knew now that wasn't the case. He was infatuated then, maybe even had loved Edna a little. But now he knew what real love was. In just a few meetings, he was absolutely sure that Amy was the woman he wanted to marry and settle down with. He thought she felt the same about him, but he was a little afraid of asking her about it; afraid that she would respond negatively.

After supper, Beryl went off to make his rounds around Madison, leaving Coffin and Amy on the front porch alone. They sat next to each other on the porch itself, their feet on the next step down.

Finally Coffin screwed up his courage. "May I ask you somethin', Amy?" he asked quietly.

She looked up, worry seaming her perfect face.

"I know we ain't known each other long, Amy," Coffin said earnestly. "But I've come to care for you more than any other woman I've ever met. I know I ain't much to look at or anything, and I don't have any trade. Despite all that, I'd be the happiest man in all God's kingdom if you were to consent to become Mrs. Joe Coffin."

Amy smiled, and to Coffin it was as bright, warm and welcome as the sun itself. "Oh, Joe," she said softly, "I've thought about just that—and almost nothing else—since the moment we met."

Coffin thought he was sitting on a cloud.

Chapter Twenty-seven

Coffin rode out the next morning feeling as if he were split in two. On one side, he wanted to do his job and do it well. He was always proud of himself when he was able to accomplish some goal he had set out for himself. On the other side, he did not want to be away from Amy for even a minute.

He learned little of any use in Virginia City and he pressed on the following morning. He arrived at the road station just before dark, and introduced himself to Claiborne and Thelma Simpson, and their two sons, Will and Augie. Coffin gladly accepted their invitation to supper.

While eating, Coffin pumped Simpson for information. Simpson seemed willing enough to talk, but he seemed agitated for some reason. Finally Coffin asked him about it.

"You're askin' all these questions about some old robberies just 'cause they were carryin' a heap of gold, from what I hear. More damn worried about those rich fellas out there and their damn gold than you are about regular goddamn people."

"What in the hell're you talkin' about, Clay?" Coffin asked, perplexed.

"Why aren't you checkin' out the holdup north of here, up near the Three Forks? The one where they left poor Louise Robbins dead on the ground."

Coffin looked at him, eyebrows arched. "When was this?" he asked.

"Early yesterday. A stage comin' down from Helena."

"What else you know about it?" Coffin demanded, forgetting his supper at least for the moment.

"Not much," Simpson said defensively. "Besides, it don't matter none. You'll sit here and take down what we know and then go right on back to trying to find that gold."

"You listen to me, you skinny sack of pond scum," Coffin hissed. "I've been on the trail since first thing yesterday. Before that I was on the trail near a week. All I stayed in Madison was for two good nights' sleep. Now, unless you want me to gut you with this goddamn dull-tined fork, tell me what the hell you know."

"Not much more'n I already told you," Simpson said nervously. "The stage was comin' down the valley from Helena. Along about the Three Forks area, some highwaymen held it up. From what we heard, Miss Robbins, who'd only been married a month—she was comin' out to be with her husband—tried to stop the robbers from takin' her ring. From what we heard, she tried to claw the eyes out of one of those bastards, so he shot her down."

"There a road station up there somewhere?"

Simpson nodded. "The stage had just left there when it was hit, maybe a mile or two from Henry Wintermeyer's road ranch."

"I just head straight north from here to get there?"

"Yep."

Coffin rose and patted his mouth with a dirty napkin. "I'm obliged for the meal, folks." He dropped a dollar on the table. "But I best get movin'."

Simpson was surprised, but he accepted it. "Sit, Marshal," he said. "Finish your supper. Augie, go saddle the marshal's horse."

"Yessir."

"The horse and mule get enough grain and water?"

"Yessir."

Fifteen minutes later, Coffin was gone, pushing cautiously north. It was a cool night, made more so by a chilling northern wind that shepherded dark, thick clouds before it. Before Coffin had gone two miles, the skies opened up. Thunder grumbled from the Jefferson Range on the west to the Madison Range to the east, back and forth, it seemed, as if God were playing some odd game.

Anticipating the storm, Coffin had pulled on his slicker, but he could not keep all the water out. It hardly let up at all, as Coffin rode slowly through the pitch dark night. It was early in the morning when he finally stopped at the road station. Wearily he slid out of the saddle. A burly, dark-bearded man opened the door but stayed inside under cover. It was still raining hard.

"You Henry Wintermeyer?" Coffin asked as he walked to the building.

"I might be. Might not. Depends on who's askin'."

Coffin pulled his slicker open a little—just enough to give Wintermeyer a glance at the badge.

Wintermeyer nodded and stepped back, allowing Coffin to enter. "That there's my missus, Gertrude, and our boy, Junior."

Junior did not look much like a junior to Coffin. He was taller than Coffin, but only about fourteen. Coffin figured the youth was going to be one big fellow by the time he was full grown. Mrs. Wintermeyer was an attractive, slim woman, though she looked weary from a life of hard work and drudgery.

"Marshal Joe Coffin." He nodded at everyone. "You

mind if I set a spell and dry off some?"

"No, no, of course not," Wintermeyer said. "You hungry?"

Coffin nodded as he peeled his slicker off and hung it on a peg next to the door. "My horse and mule could use some tendin' to."

Wintermeyer nodded. "Junior, go on and see to the marshal's animals."

"But, Pa," Junior said, almost not whining, "he ain't offered to pay."

Wintermeyer chuckled in embarrassment. "Sorry, Marshal."

"Nothin' to be sorry for, Mr. Wintermeyer. A man deserves to be paid for the work he does." Coffin flipped the young man a half dollar. "Of course, most folks wait till after the work's done before they go stickin' their hands out," he added pointedly.

Junior Wintermeyer looked stricken. He wasn't sure why. This short lawman was just standing there, tracing small circles on his abdomen with the palm of his hand.

"All right, go on, Junior," Wintermeyer said.

The young man left, and Coffin took a seat at the table. Gertrude ladled him up a big bowl of stew. "Buffalo," she said, voice just a wispy thing. "Fresh yesterday."

"Thank you."

"You want anything else?"

"Coffee. Biscuits if you got any."

In moments they were provided. Wintermeyer sat next to his wife across the table from Coffin. "What brings you to these parts, Marshal?" Wintermeyer asked.

"I was on the trail of some road agents. Then Clay Simpson told me a woman got killed up here durin' a holdup a day or so ago?"

"That's true, Marshal," Wintermeyer said.

"The unfortunate little thing," Gertrude interjected. "Such a sweet young girl. New married, too, she was."

"So I heard." Coffin looked at Wintermeyer. "You know who done it?"

Wintermeyer shook his head. "From what those passengers said when they come back here afterward, all the robbers had sacking over their faces as masks."

"You have any guesses as to who did it?"

"No, sir," Wintermeyer said firmly. "Even if I did, I'd keep such names to myself."

Coffin nodded. He could understand the man's fear. He was out here in the middle of nowhere with a wife and a son, and no one around to protect them. "You know where—or even which way—they went?"

"I ain't sure. We never saw 'em before or after. Folks on the stage, though, they said the robbers went west. But since they didn't come past here, there ain't no tellin' where they went."

Coffin nodded. It was going to be impossible to find those men. It would take an army to cover every square foot of the vast and overpowering land. "You mind if I stay the rest of the day and overnight? I'm bushed."

"We'd be glad to have you, Marshal," Wintermeyer said. He did not seem totally sincere.

"How much?" Coffin asked with a small smile.

"A dollar'd be just about right, I guess. With the fifty cents you give Junior, it ought to cover a night's lodging, a couple meals and the care for your animals."

"Sounds fair enough to me." He handed Wintermeyer a silver dollar.

Wintermeyer stood and pointed to the back. "That's our best bunk. It's near the stove so you don't catch a chill at night, and it's a bit more spacious than the others."

Coffin nodded. He spent the rest of the day cleaning

his weapons, checking over gear and just generally wasting time. He didn't want to get to bed too early, or he'd be kept awake by the noises of life.

It was not quite dark, though, when he finally lay down on the dirty straw mattress. He was asleep almost instantly.

Junior Wintermeyer watched intently as Coffin undid his gunbelt and hung it on the high corner of an old chair right near to the head of the bed. He wanted to see one of the weapons worse than anything. He wanted to get the feel of a big pistol, one that had been used to kill all sorts of men, he figured.

Junior went to bed but not to sleep. His mind still burned with the desire to see if one of Coffin's pistols made him think he was a big man. It surprised Junior that such a little man could be a deputy marshal. It didn't seem right. Maybe the magic was in Coffin's pistols, he thought.

He waited until he was sure everyone was asleep. Then Junior climbed quietly down from his loft bed and crept on tiptoe toward Coffin. He stopped right next to the bed and reached out a shaking hand for the glossy walnut butt of a Remington. And he suddenly found the muzzle of a pistol brushing the crevasse between his eyes.

"You want to live to see the dawn, boy, you'll get your ass back to bed and stay there," Coffin growled quietly.

Junior looked angry and sheepish in the morning. Coffin paid him no mind. Coffin simply ate a filling breakfast, while Wintermeyer had Junior go saddle Coffin's horse. It was still raining when Coffin left, but not nearly as much or as hard as it had yesterday.

He headed north, figuring that was as good a direction as any to go. Two days later, he pulled into Helena. He asked around at the stage station and elsewhere, but he learned nothing. Disgusted and dispirited, he stopped in a saloon for a couple of drinks before heading out again.

He had just downed a shot of bourbon and was working at a mug of beer when a nondescript man clomped up beside him. “Hey, Shorty,” the man said. He paused to belch. “I hear you been askin’ a bunch of questions around here about Cady Merkle. That right?”

Coffin ignored him, since it was obvious that the man was not going to offer any information about Merkle. Instead, Coffin just sipped his beer and stared straight ahead. He kept an eye on the man in the mirror set in the back bar.

“Hey, goddammit, I’m talkin’ to you, Shorty,” the man snapped.

Coffin set his mug softly on the bar. Then he whirled and slammed his right fist into the man’s midsection.

The man’s face contorted and reddened while his mouth flapped ineffectually.

“I could arrest you for botherin’ a federal marshal, but I don’t think that’ll be necessary, will it?”

The man shook his head, still unable to breathe, let alone speak.

Coffin nodded. “I’ll be right back,” he said over his shoulder to the bartender. He turned to the man and then grabbed a handful of his shirt and another by the seat of his pants. He frog-marched the man across the saloon and out the door. Then he gave the man a good shove. He landed in the muddy street, still trying to breathe. Coffin brushed off his hands and went back to his drink.

Half an hour later, Coffin saw in the mirror that the man had come back into the saloon, this time with two other men. They spotted him and moved forward, stopping about eight feet from Coffin, who turned to face them.

“I come to make you pay for what you done,” the man

said.

"All I did was to throw out the trash," Coffin said easily. His right hand moved up, as if it had a will of its own, and began the little circular pattern on his stomach.

"You shouldn't have insulted Stony here," another man said. "He's a good . . ."

"Stony?" Coffin said with an insulting laugh. "That his name? Stony? I guess it fits, come to think of it, since he's got nothin' but rocks in his head."

Stony seethed and went for his revolver. The man who had spoken stopped him.

"I'm gonna say this only once. Get your asses out of here, and stay the hell out till I'm done and gone from here."

"We can't do that," Stony said angrily.

"Then you're gonna die today. You think about that for a while."

"The hell I will." Stony and his two friends went for their guns.

Coffin wasted no time in grabbing a Remington, but he was far slower than these three. Stony had fired two shots, and the talker one by the time Coffin got his pistol out. Bullets were still flying at Coffin, but the closest one only clipped his left sleeve.

Coffin calmly fired, emptying his one Remington. He had learned long ago that accuracy and steadiness were generally a heap better than sheer speed in a gunbattle. It proved true here, as all three men went down, dead before they even hit.

Coffin turned and drained his beer mug. He tossed a twenty-dollar gold piece on the bar. "That's for buryin' those three assholes." He put on his hat, turned and walked out.

Chapter Twenty-eight

Coffin left Helena the next morning. Ted Whitmore, Helena's town marshal, had come by the hotel and started giving Coffin a hard time about the three killings.

Coffin took it for a bit, but then said, "Shut your yap, or I'll shut it for you."

Whitmore looked at him in angry surprise.

"It was evident that those three assholes were either members of Cady Merkle's gang, or they wanted to be. I just rid your town of some vermin is all."

"But . . ."

"You keep on pesterin' me with this, and I'll throw your ass in your own jail for obstructin' justice." Coffin paused, then nodded. "Now I know what this is all about," he said with more nodding. "You figure there's bounty on those three, and you're figurin' I'm gonna take it. Well, I reckon I deserve it, seein' as how I was the one who sent 'em across the divide." He could tell he was right by the sudden spark of greed in Whitmore's eyes. "I got no use for that bounty. Nor do I have the time to sit around here and wait for it. It's yours."

"That's not what I wanted, Marshal, no, not at all."

"Not only are you a poor lawman, you're also a poor liar. Now get the hell out and let me get some shuteye."

Coffin headed west out of Helena through MacDonald

Pass across the Continental Divide. In the vast north-south valley to the west, he rode north a little way to Goldcreek. He spent a day or two there, but learned nothing more than the people there had reactivated their vigilance committee in the wake of several stage robberies, in which two people had been killed.

He pushed on, heading south through Deer Lodge and then east to Butte, where he spent a few more days learning that he once again was too late to be of any use, and that the good citizens of Butte would take care of the problem themselves. Coffin knew better than to argue with a mob. He just nodded, told them not to hang any innocent men, and rode out again.

He rode south, stopping to question anyone he happened to see, as he had since he left Helena. His frustration was increasing each day. Leaving Butte, he worked his way through Pipestone Pass and down into another big valley. He generally followed the Jefferson Fork south and then southeast.

Five weeks after he had left Madison, he rode back into town. He had nothing to show for all his time on the trail other than a scruffy beard and a sour disposition. Coffin stopped in front of the office and dismounted. He rubbed his rear end and went inside.

A drawn, haggard Enoch Pembroke sat at his desk. His eyes were ringed with black and red, and he looked like he hadn't slept in a week. "Joe," he said quietly, his voice sounding small and far away.

"Jesus, Enoch," Coffin said as he poured himself some coffee, "you look terrible." When he got no response, Coffin turned, looking at Pembroke curiously. "Where's Beryl?" he asked, suddenly feeling a chill of anxiety.

"Dead," Pembroke croaked.

"Dead?" Coffin echoed in a faint voice. "How? When?"

"Sit," Pembroke said. "And bring me some coffee while you're over there."

Coffin grabbed another tin cup from the nail on the wall and filled it. He carried both cups to Pembroke's desk and set them down, and then slumped into a chair in front of the desk. "What happened?" he said.

"Beryl doesn't usually go chasin' outlaws—alone or with a posse—out of town if I ain't here. Too risky. But a couple boys we think are new recruits by Merkle tried robbin' the stage to Virginia City almost within sight of town. Some poor miner was headin' the same way, saw what was happening and raced back here to tell Beryl. He didn't really have any time to throw together a posse, so he just jumped on the nearest horse and rode like hell." He stopped, choking back some tears.

"And he found them?" Coffin said softly.

Pembroke nodded. "Yes. After an hour or so, when Beryl didn't come back, a couple boys rode out to look around. They found him shot several times."

"I'm sorry, Enoch. I really am."

"I know. But sorry doesn't mean shit right now."

"If you weren't here, how do you know all this?"

"Folks told me. Damn, Joe, I rode in here that goddamn afternoon. Shit."

"How long ago, Major?"

"Five, no, six days ago now." He dragged a listless hand over his sagging face. "I looked in on Beryl, who was already being worked on by Horst. Christ, Joe, he looked like they used him for target practice. He was shot full of holes."

Coffin could see that Pembroke was getting angry, and he figured that was a good thing. Pembroke would be able to deal with his loss more easily if he was enraged and looking to make someone pay for his brother's death.

"But I swear, that ain't what killed him."

Coffin almost choked on a mouthful of coffee. "What the hell's that mean?" he asked, drying off his face with his sleeve.

"Joe," Pembroke said with deadly earnestness, "I think he was hanged."

"Hanged?"

"Hanged."

"What makes you think that?"

"I looked the body over pretty well. I think Doc Smith just saw a heap of bullet holes and decided that was what killed him."

"But you don't think so?"

"Well, sort of." He lit a pipe, trying to keep his composure. "I ain't sure the hangin' killed him, but I'll swear on Ma's gravestone that he was hanged."

"You don't want to talk about this no more, you don't have to," Coffin said sympathetically.

"No, no, I'm all right." Smoked poured out of Pembroke's pipe as he puffed furiously. He finally pulled the pipe away from his mouth. "You know what I think they did, Joe?"

Coffin only shook his head.

"I think they pulled that job to lure Beryl out of town. I think Merkle and his men were waitin' out there and then . . . then . . ." Pembroke looked stricken and suddenly the pipe was pouring out billowing clouds of smoke.

Coffin got up and walked around Pembroke's desk. In the bottom drawer, as he knew there would be, was a quart bottle of rye whiskey. He pulled it out, opened it, and poured a heaping dose into Pembroke's coffee cup. Coffin took a good swig straight from the bottle and then set it on the desk. "Drink it," he ordered.

Pembroke did, and it seemed to settle him. "Sorry,

Joe."

"No need to be sorry, Enoch. I know what you're goin' through." He sat back down and had another swig of rye. "You feel like stoppin', I ain't gonna argue."

"No, it's best gettin' it out and done." He paused, ordering his thoughts. "I think they hung him in a tree and then used him as a target," Pembroke got out before he gulped down half his cup of rye in one prodigious swallow.

"Jesus," Coffin said.

"Yeah. Jesus."

"Why would anyone do that?" Coffin asked, baffled by the horror of something so heartless.

It took a little before Pembroke spoke. He had thought of almost nothing else than the reasons for such inhumanity. He thought he had an answer, but he was not sure. "I think maybe Merkle and his gang are trying to pay back in kind," Pembroke said.

"What?"

"With all the stage robberies goin' on these days, the vigilantes have been busy. Not only in Madison, but Virginia City, Butte, Helena, Bannock. All over. I think Merkle was tryin' to send us a message."

"But why didn't they leave him hangin' then? There would've been no question then that they were warning us."

"I don't know," Pembroke admitted. "I can't figure it out, but I'm as sure of it as I am of anything." He paused, looking up at Coffin. "I want their heads, Joe," he said, voice cracking. "I was just waitin' for you to come back so there'd be someone to watch things."

"You stay here and do that," Coffin said. "I'll dog those bastards to Kingdom Come if need be."

"No," Pembroke said flatly, harshly. "I'm goin' after 'em."

"No you ain't. The people here in Madison need you. To these folks, I'm only a newcomer, and not to be fully trusted. But you, you've been here for quite a spell. Somebody's got to act as town marshal. That's you. Not me. The people here wouldn't accept me as their marshal. Not yet anyway."

Pembroke was about to argue, but Coffin cut him off. "No, Enoch, your place is here. Besides, you have to think of Amy."

"I ain't the one courtin' her," Pembroke said.

"True. But she still needs her brother, especially when she's just lost her only other brother. You're about the only family she's got left." He smiled tightly. "Soon's I get those bastards, I'll come on back here and marry Amy, take her off your hands."

"I still don't like the idea, Joe," Pembroke growled. "But I expect you're right." He smiled wanly. "I reckon I am gettin' a mite old for such runnin' around. I figure you're a hell of a lot better than me these days at living on the trail."

Coffin was ready to just up and leave, but he realized that he had no idea of where to go chasing Merkle's men. "You still got that feller Pendergast locked up?" he suddenly asked.

Pembroke nodded. "Yeah. He was sentenced to six months for bein' drunk in public. It was all we could get him on. Why?"

"I'm gonna go talk to him."

Pembroke looked shocked, but bit back a retort. As soon as he thought about it, he changed his mind. The idea sounded fine to him. He nodded in agreement and started to rise.

"Just stay where you are, Enoch," Coffin said quietly but firmly. "I'll handle this."

Pembroke sat back down. He smiled weakly at Coffin.

"Ain't it somethin'," he said, "with a corporal givin' the major orders."

"You ain't a major no more. You told me that yourself. And I ain't givin' you orders. I'm just tryin' to pound some sense into you. And I'm tryin' to help a friend."

Coffin grabbed the keys to the cells and went into the back room, shutting the door tightly behind him. Two smoky lanterns attached to the wall on each side of the door spread a sickly light. Coffin stopped to remove his gunbelt and hang it on a peg next to the door.

Several of the prisoners looked at Coffin with hope in their eyes; hope that he might be coming to let them go. All of them but Alvin Pendergast lost interest when Coffin went to the cell in the left rear corner.

"Comin' to set me free, eh, Marshal?" Pendergast said with a sneer.

Coffin said nothing. He opened the barred door, stepped inside and smashed Pendergast in the face. Pendergast staggered back until the back of his legs hit the iron cot, and he sat involuntarily.

Coffin calmly locked the door behind him, and left the keys in the lock. He turned back toward Pendergast. "I'm gonna ask you a few questions, Alvin," he said coldly. "If you give me a hard time instead of answers, I will pound you until you beg me to kill you."

"You made a big goddamn mistake comin' in here like this," Pendergast said with a blood-coated grin. He pushed himself up, and Coffin hammered him again, knocking him right back down on his seat.

"I don't have the time or the patience to play games with you, Alvin."

"Eat shit," Pendergast grumbled.

"I sense some rebelliousness on your part, Alvin," Coffin said derisively. "You want a little more softenin' up before I start askin' my questions?"

"You ain't gonna get nothin' out of me, dammit."

Coffin shrugged. "I don't mind kickin' the shit out of you for a while."

Pendergast suddenly bolted off the cot, charging Coffin. The lawman deftly shifted a little and then shoved Pendergast's back, adding to his impetus. Pendergast slammed into the cell's iron bars.

Coffin grabbed the back of Pendergast's shirt and pulled him a foot or so away from the bars. Then he shoved forward, slamming Pendergast's face into the bars again. He repeated the maneuver, then asked, "Feel like talkin' yet, Alvin?"

"No," Pendergast mumbled.

"Oh, well." Coffin smashed Pendergast's face into the bars twice more, then pulled him away, turned him and shoved him away. Pendergast groaned as he hit the cot and fell on it.

Coffin knelt beside the cot. "I'll start breakin' other parts of you, Alvin, unless you answer me. Now, where can I find Merkle?" Coffin asked.

Pendergast groaned again.

"Not much of an answer." Coffin grabbed Pendergast's bloody, broken nose with two fingers. Then he squeezed and twisted it.

Pendergast sucked in a breath and let it whistle out. "I'll talk, dammit," he said. The words were distorted some, but still understandable.

Coffin released Pendergast's nose. "Where's Merkle?" he asked.

"I don't know." His eyes widened in horror when he saw Coffin's hand heading toward his nose again. "Wait!" he screeched. "Wait!" When Coffin hesitated, hand an inch from Coffin's mangled proboscis, Pendergast said, "I don't know. I really don't. I been in here a couple of months now. I can't know where he is."

"Any idea of where he holes up?"

"Several places. Nearest one's in Virginia City."

"You expect me to believe that? The most notorious outlaw between Denver and San Francisco, and you tell me he's hidin' in Virginia City. I'm afraid you'll have to do better than that."

"Wait! It makes sense!" He breathed heavily, trying to control the pain in his battered face. "He's got somebody in Virginia City helpin' him. Somebody respectable. Only Cady, Kurt, and Hugh know who he is. But what better place to hide than right under the noses of folks lookin' for him?"

"Where else?"

"A cave in the mountains outside Helena. Another one overlooking the valley from the Madison Rage. There might be others, but that's all I know of. Cady's a close-mouthed fella most times."

"You know about Beryl Pembroke?" Coffin asked.

"He's dead. I suppose Cady had it done."

"You know how or where?"

"No. I ain't seen none of Cady's boys since I been in here."

Coffin nodded and rose. "Well, it ain't much of a payment, but it's somethin'." Coffin took Pendergast's throat in his hands and squeezed the life out of him.

Chapter Twenty-nine

It was two days before Coffin could head out after Cady Merkle's band of cutthroats. He had needed some sleep, and so had Enoch Pembroke. The two had gone to Pembroke's house, where Amy kissed Coffin and then ordered her brother to bed. She came back downstairs after seeing her brother into his room, and she sat next to Coffin on the couch.

"You hungry, Joe?"

"Some."

She bounced up off the couch and held out a hand. "Come with me to the kitchen. We can talk while I fix you up something. Or not talk, if you'd rather."

He took her hand and let her tug him up. "We'll see."

In the kitchen, Coffin sat at the table and watched Amy. She had been delighted to see him, but he could see the remnants of tears in her red-tinged eyes. He knew she must be torn by happiness at his return and grief over her brother's death.

"What's going to happen now, Joe?" Amy asked as she set a cup of coffee in front of him.

"I'm going after Merkle," Coffin said flatly.

Amy, who had gone back to the stove, looked over her shoulder at Coffin. "Do you have to?"

"Yes."

"But it'll be dangerous."

"Life's always dangerous."

"But you don't have to go. You don't," she insisted.

"Of course I do," Coffin said evenly as he rolled a cigarette. "What would Beryl think of me if I didn't. What would *you* think of me if I didn't go?"

"I'd have you here, and that'd make me happy."

"Maybe, but when I put on this badge, I agreed to do the hard things as well as the easy." He grimaced. "Besides," he added flatly, "I've offered him a challenge. I've got to see that justice is done. Nobody ever said it was going to be pleasant."

Amy nodded. She didn't like it, but she understood. Having had two brothers who were lawmen made it easier for her to understand. No easier to like, but easier to understand.

Coffin ate listlessly, almost numbed from what had happened today. Still, Amy was a fine cook, and he did not want to insult her by not seeming to enjoy the meal. Afterward, they went back to the sitting room. Amy was of a mood to chat, but Coffin wasn't. Then he realized that she wanted to talk as a way of getting her mind off all that had happened—and all that might happen yet. So he made an effort to be more social.

Amy sensed after a while that Coffin's heart was not in chatter, but by then she was feeling considerably better. It had been almost a week since they had buried her brother, and she had never let that thought out of her mind. But she knew she had to go on, and her love of and fear for Joe Coffin would help her get through. She also thought that since she and Coffin were planning to marry, that she should begin putting his interests before her brother's. It helped her a little that she was closer to Enoch than she had been to Beryl. She often had thought Beryl too prim.

"Why don't you go on down to Duncan's, Joe, and get yourself cleaned up. A haircut, shave, and bath'd do you a lot of good, I suspect."

"You tryin' to tell me I'm a dirty, smelly old coot?" Coffin joked, though there was little heart in it.

"Well, not old," Amy responded in kind.

"And I asked you to be my bride?" Coffin said, warming a little to the lightheartedness. "Lord, what was I thinkin' at the time?"

"You were thinking that you were getting the most desirable woman in all of Madison," Amy said, breaking into a small giggle.

"I must've been talkin' to a different woman then."

"I ever catch you even talkin' to another woman, I'll . . ."

"You'll what?" Coffin was actually smiling a little.

So was Amy. "I'll lock you up in your own jail and keep you there just for me."

"Oh you would, would you?" Coffin said with a little laugh. He grabbed her and pulled her close, then kissed her hard.

She responded willingly, even a little desperately, and she was rather breathless when their lips separated.

"Maybe you're right," Coffin finally said. "A sprucin' up'd probably do me good. I'll be back directly. You'll be all right?"

Amy nodded. She looked a lot more confident than she felt.

Coffin was only a little surprised when he got back to Amy's house that he felt so much better. The ablutions refreshed him more than he had anticipated.

Pembroke had not stirred when Coffin had returned, and showed no signs of waking anytime soon.

"You want to take a stroll, Amy?" Coffin asked. He was edgy, anxious to move on, to be doing something.

Sitting around would not lessen his tension.

"Oh, I don't know." Amy's eyes looked up the stairs toward Pembroke's bedroom, and her eyes grew a little misty.

"It'll do you a lot of good. A dose of your own medicine."

Amy nodded. She looked in a mirror to make sure she looked presentable. The walk was not long, but it seemed to brighten both Amy and Coffin. When they returned to the house, though, Coffin was still on edge.

"I've got to do somethin', Amy," he said.

"What?"

"I don't know. All I know is I can't just sit here twiddlin' my thumbs. Maybe I'll head to the office and see if I can find somethin' to do there."

"I'd rather you stayed here, Joe."

"Me, too. But if I stay here much longer, I might do somethin' to insult you." What he figured to do was head over to Big Sophie's place and work off some of his tensions with one of Big Sophie's girls. But he certainly was not about to tell Amy that.

"I trust you not to do anything that'd shame me."

Coffin had no answer for that, but he said, "Well, I'd still like to be doin' somethin'. Maybe I can make the rounds for Enoch. Let him sleep some more."

"He'll sleep all right. And he hired on two men to act as temporary town marshals. They'll make do for most things. If there's a big problem, they'll come get Enoch. He told me he doesn't think anything'll happen. Not for a while."

Coffin nodded, more or less glumly. He decided he would humor her, at least for a little while, and then argue it out again. Maybe an hour or so of his grumping around would serve to change her mind. "All right," he said quietly. "I could do with some more coffee and another piece of that peach pie you made."

Amy smiled proudly. "Here or in the kitchen?"

"Kitchen'd be better, I reckon, sloppy as I am."

When he was eating, Amy said, "I'll be back in a minute." When she returned, Coffin was done with the pie and was smoking a cigarette while sipping coffee. "Can you come help me for a minute, Joe?" Amy asked.

He looked up at her sharply. Her voice had not sounded right to him, and he thought she looked more than a little nervous. He wondered why, but all he said was, "Sure."

She led him to a former pantry that had been converted into a spare bedroom for guests. Inside the room, Amy shut the door and then leaned back against it.

"What's this all about?" he asked, both hoping and worrying that it was what he thought it was.

"I . . . I . . ." She paused to lick her dry lips. "I'm eighteen, Joe, and have never been with a man. Never even wanted to till you come along."

"We'll be married soon enough," Coffin said, finding it a little hard to talk. "Then we can . . ."

Amy moved forward and into the welcome warmth of Coffin's embrace. She kissed him, then said, "Joe, ever since Beryl was killed, I've had a feeling that something else bad was going to happen. I'm afraid for you, Joe. Scared right down to my toes."

"But that's . . ."

"Hush," Amy said, placing a soft, dainty finger against his lips. She let it linger there for a few moments. "I know you're going out after those outlaws, and I know there's nothing I can do to stop you. I tried earlier today to stop you, because I'm so afraid for you. But even then I knew deep down I couldn't stop you."

"So why this? Here, now?"

"Joe, I'm scared to death you're going to get killed out

there. And if that comes to pass, well, I want to know the intimate touches of the man I love just once."

"What happens if I come back alive?" Coffin asked seriously.

"Then I'll have had my wedding night a little early," she said practically.

"What about Enoch?"

"He's not slept more than a few hours since Beryl . . . Well, anyway, he won't be waking up anytime soon."

Still Coffin hesitated. That was unlike him, but then again he had never been so deeply in love with a woman. Not even Edna Yarnell.

"Joe," Amy said in a tiny voice, "Joe, don't reject me. I couldn't bear it if you didn't want me."

"Oh, I want you all right," Coffin said with a low growl. "But I don't want you doin' somethin' you don't want to do because you think you should, or because of some premonition."

"Joe, I love you, and I've made up my mind to do this," Amy said, almost as if she were scolding him. "If you don't want to, say so and we'll forget all about it. If you want to, then hush up and let's go on."

"You ain't worried about your name bein' sullied in town?"

"No one's going to know except you and me."

"Well, ma'am," Coffin said with a small smile, "it seems you leave me no choice."

"That's right, sir," Amy breathed. She leaned her head back some, waiting for his kiss. It was not long in coming.

Coffin looked at Amy's sleek form lying naked beside him. He felt fulfilled, whole, and far more pleased than he had any right to be. Amy stirred a little beside him, and he returned her happy smile.

Despite his enjoyment in just lying here and enjoying looking at Amy, he said, "I reckon we'd best get movin'."

Amy stretched, self-conscious of her nudity. "Do we have to?"

"Yes, ma'am, much as I hate to say it."

Amy rolled out of the bed, then stopped and turned back to face him. She bent and kissed his lips gently, just a mere hint of a buss. "Thank you, Joe Coffin," she breathed into his mouth.

"My pleasure, Miss Amy."

Twenty minutes or so later, they were eating a supper of fried beefsteaks, yams and broccoli. After the meal, Coffin stood. "I really should go take a look around town, maybe make sure the prisoners have been fed."

Amy nodded. "I'll clean up here. Don't be gone long."

He wasn't. The two acting deputies—Russ Chapman and Casey Baldwin—were at the office and had made sure the prisoners were fed. They had even cleaned up the jail cell in which Coffin had killed Pendergast. The two men had nothing amiss to report and were planning to make the rounds about town.

"I'm obliged to you both for helpin' out like this."

Both nodded, and Baldwin said, "It was the least we could do after Marshal Pembroke was done in. Is Enoch goin' after the killers?"

Coffin shook his head. "I am," he said flatly.

The two temporary lawmen were quite sure they would not want Marshal Joe Coffin on their trail. Not when he had that cold, deadly gleam in his eyes.

"Goodnight, boys."

When Coffin got back to the house, he found Enoch up and eating hungrily. He looked considerably better than he had when Coffin had first seen him that morning.

Pembroke looked up and nodded. "How's everything?"

"Fine. Russ and Casey have things under control."

"Good." Pembroke paused to swallow. "I'm obliged for you letting me get some sleep, Joe. Damn . . . Sorry, Amy . . . I needed it."

Coffin shrugged. "Looks like you can use some more, once you pack away those groceries."

"You'll need it more than me now."

"No reason we can't both get some sleep. It's night already. I'm just wonderin' how to arrange it."

"What do you mean?"

"By rights, I ought to go back to the hotel for the night. But with the way things are, I'd feel a little better about stayin' here."

"So would I," Pembroke said.

"What about . . . ?"

"To hell with the people," Pembroke said vehemently. A fierce glance at Amy cut off any protests she might be thinking up about his language. "Those bastards didn't do a damn thing to help Beryl. Let 'em think what the hell they want. This is all over, I'm pullin' up stakes. You and Amy get married then, you'd be wise to leave here, too. You're stayin' here tonight, Joe, and that's all there is to it. You can use the spare room."

At that, Coffin and Amy glanced knowingly at each other.

Chapter Thirty

"You sure you got everything you need, Joe?" Pembroke asked. He was nervy, skittish. He had lost a brother already. He didn't want to lose a friend and soon-to-be brother-in-law.

"Yes, dammit," Coffin snapped more peevishly than he wanted. He was anxious to be on the way now that he was prepared.

"Bye, Joe," Amy said, interjecting herself between the two testy men who meant so much to her.

"Bye, Amy. Enoch." Coffin smiled tightly as he climbed on his horse. "Enoch, you best keep a good eye on Amy, you hear?"

"I will," Pembroke promised.

"And, Amy, keep that brother of yours out of trouble."

"I'll try."

Then Coffin trotted out of Madison. As he rode, his anger simmered just below the surface. When it was time to release it, it would be at a full boil and would push him on as hard as was necessary, through any hardship and any pain.

He rode straight for Virginia City. Since Pendergast had told him that Merkle had an insider in Virginia City, he figured it was the logical place to start. He tied his horse and his mule to the hitching rail in front of the town marshal's office, and he went inside.

Marshal Jud Wilson looked up, spotted Coffin's badge and stood. "You must be that new deputy marshal Enoch Pembroke hired," he said, holding out his hand.

"I am. Name's Joe Coffin." He shook hands, then tossed his hat on the desk and sat.

"Make yourself at home, why don't you," Wilson said sarcastically.

"Just sit down and skip the smart-ass remarks," Coffin ordered.

Something in Coffin's eyes made Wilson obey. "What can I do for you, Marshal?" Wilson asked stiffly.

"We had a prisoner over in the jail in Madison. A whinin' little puke named Alvin Pendergast. He was a known confederate of Cady Merkle."

"What's that got to do with me?"

"Under some persuasion, he was encouraged to spill what he knew about Merkle. One of the interesting things he told me was that Merkle had a man—a respectable one—here in Virginia City helpin' out."

"Who?"

"Pendergast claimed he didn't know. Since he was just a gun to Merkle, I figure he really didn't know. I was hopin' you'd be able to enlighten me."

"Me? How would I know that?"

"You're the town marshal. You're supposed to know what goes on in your town."

"I do know most things," Wilson said stiffly. "But if what you say is true, he's well hidden here. I couldn't think of a single respectable townsman who might be involved with Cady Merkle."

"I suspect it's more likely you can't think at all," Coffin snapped.

"There's no call for such talk," Wilson said, offended.

Then he sneered. "After all, you're the important, hot-shit deputy United States marshal," he said, drawing the words out. "And you come lookin' for help from little ol' me."

"You best hope that you ain't lyin' to me about this, boy," Coffin said harshly. His face was like stone, and his words cold as old ice. "Because if I find out you've hidden information from me, I'll pay you another visit, and I won't be so friendly."

Wilson tried to brave it out. "Hell, them boys're scattered all over hell and creation, I suspect, what with the great Marshal Joe Coffin on their trail." There was another sneer in the words.

Coffin grinned a little, and Wilson began to sweat. There was the hint of death in Coffin's chilling smile. "Just remember," Coffin said. "Those boys killed Beryl Pembroke, and neither me nor his brother Enoch is likely to forget that." He paused. "You got anything useful to me?"

Wilson shook his head. As Coffin stood and put his hat on, Wilson said, "I hope you get the bastards, Marshal." There was a note of respect in his voice this time.

Coffin nodded and stalked out. He spent the rest of the day poking around Virginia City, talking to people, trying to pry loose any scrap of information that might help him hunt down Cady Merkle. He kept coming up dry. He gave it one more day, but still nothing.

That night, as he was eating, Wilson showed up and sat down uninvited. "Pardon my takin' liberties, Marshal Coffin, but I got some information that might help you."

Coffin nodded and wiped his mouth on a napkin.

A waiter came along and set an empty cup down. "You want somethin', Marshal?" he asked, looking at Wilson. The waiter was just to the good side of surly.

"No."

"You want some coffee?" Coffin asked. When Wilson nodded, Coffin filled Wilson's cup and replenished his own. "Now, what've you got to tell me?"

"Well, nothin' definite, but a few of the men who frequent a festerin' den of iniquity called the Bull's Blood are the kind who stray into criminal deeds on occasion." He paused, as if waiting for something.

"You expect me to be shocked at that?" Coffin asked, annoyed.

"No, but I suspect—though I can't prove, of course—that some of 'em ride with Merkle's bunch now and again. They ain't in his inner circle, you understand. Anyway, two of 'em told me they thought Merkle was headin' down to a place just filled with hot springs and such."

"Down along the Yellowstone?"

"Yep."

Coffin nodded. "I've been through there. Why's Merkle gone there?"

"There's a heap of folks like to partake of such springs, Marshal. Just 'cause a man's an outlaw don't mean he wouldn't enjoy that, too."

"I expect you're right. These friends of yours tell you how long ago this was supposed to have taken place?"

"They ain't no friends of mine," Wilson said stiffly. "They said, though, that they headed down there in just the past week or so."

"Any particular spot?"

"Not that they knew. Or if they knew, they weren't sayin'."

Coffin nodded. "Well, if any of that's true, it might be of a help. At least I got a direction to go in now."

Wilson stood. "You need my help again, don't wait to ask," he said. Then he got out of there. Wilson was not a coward, but something about Coffin got to him, sent little crystalline pieces of iciness into his innards. He was glad Coffin would be leaving town soon.

Coffin finished his meal and went to a saloon. Two hours later, he was back in his room twelve dollars poorer since he had had his usual luck with cards. He was sure at least two of the men were cheating, but he did not have the heart or energy to call them on it. He climbed into bed.

He was on the trail early, his loaded pack mule placidly following the horse's lead. He turned south once he was in the valley and moved on steadily if not too rapidly. Three nights after leaving Virginia City, he came on the small town of Bendersville. It did not appear to offer too many amenities, but Coffin figured it was better than spending another night in the open, especially since it had been raining off and on for the past day and a half.

A tent had a sign saying it was a hotel. Next to it on one side was another tent announcing it had whiskey for sale. On the other side was yet a third tent, this one proclaiming it offered EATS. Coffin stopped in front of the "hotel." Minutes later he was the proud renter of a cot in a room with eight other cots.

Since there seemed to be no real livery, Coffin brought the horse and mule back around the hotel and cared for them. He wondered what he should do about his saddle and other tack. He finally shrugged and carried it inside and dropped it near his cot. Then he went to the proprietor of the grand establishment. "My saddle and other gear's back there by my bunk," he said "Anything happens to it, I'm gonna hold you responsible."

"Sure." The man sounded disinterested.

Coffin felt like clubbing the man on the head, but he didn't figure it would change the man's attitude any. He went to the restaurant next door and managed to swallow something they told him was a beefsteak. Coffin suspected that the charred, gristle-ridden thing had never been part of a steer, or a buffalo. He politely decided it was horsesteak, or maybe even mulesteak. To really try to figure out what it was did not fill him with joy.

After the meal, he went to the saloon on the other side of the hotel. Like the other two places, it was a makeshift affair. Two or three old tables with rickety chairs were scattered about. A few planks on a barrel on one side and a sawhorse on the other comprised the bar.

Coffin ordered a whiskey, hoping it would kill the aftertaste of the meal. Trouble with that was that the whiskey was about as poor as the food was. "Jesus," he complained to the bartender, "which end of the mule did this shit come from?"

The bartender shrugged. He couldn't care less what folks thought. His boss paid his wages, and if the boss wanted goat piss served, then he would do it willingly.

Coffin shrugged and ordered another shot. He had managed to down three of the foul beverages when two familiar-looking men walked in. Coffin stood sideways to the front of the tent. That kept his badge hidden for the time being while allowing him to keep an eye on people who entered the tent.

Coffin turned back to face the bar square. He slid a hand into his short pocket and pulled out the papers he still carried on Merkle's men. He quickly looked through them. With a smile, he put two faces with two names. He shoved the papers back into his pocket and then drained his whiskey glass.

Coffin drew one of his Remingtons and, making sure his slicker was flapped open enough to allow people to see his badge, he turned. He walked to where the two men stood, backs to him, at a table. He tapped the nearest man on the shoulder with the barrel of his pistol. The man started, then turned to stare into the muzzle of Coffin's revolver.

"You're under arrest, Mr. Burke," Coffin said quietly.

"What for?"

"Murder, theft, robbery, rape. There's more, but that ought to do for now."

"You got the wrong man, Marshal," the man said nervously. "My name ain't Burke. It's Stephens."

"I don't give a pile of squirrel shit what your name is. I got paper on you under the name Orval Burke. That's what I'll call you. And I'll let a judge tell me I got the wrong man. He does, I'll apologize to you. But go before a judge you will. Unless you'd rather visit with St. Peter at the pearly gates."

"Whoa, there, Marshal," he said, trying to sound lighthearted. "I ain't in no hurry to die."

Coffin nodded. "Tell your partner there that if he takes another step toward the outside, I'm gonna blast a big, ugly hole in your head."

"Dammit, Hubie," Burke snapped, "stay where you are."

"By the way, Hubie," Coffin said, "you're under arrest, too."

"You ain't takin' me, boy," Hubert Pendergast, Alvin's brother, bolted for the open end of the tent.

Coffin drew his pistol back and then slammed Burke in the face with it. Burke fell, giving Coffin a clear shot. He fired, hitting Pendergast almost in the center of the back. Inertia and the bullet's impact pushed Pendergast ahead. He slid to a stop face down in the mud a few feet outside the tent.

Coffin bent to pull Burke to his feet, and a bullet whizzed past his head. He dropped Burke's shirtfront and dove toward the door. As he came up on one knee, his eyes took in everything in one quick glance, and his brain processed the information. Two heartbeats had passed. He fired twice and hit the pistol-wielding bartender in the throat with one shot. The other missed by half a foot.

Coffin swung toward Burke, who also was on one knee, pistol in hand. Blood dripped down his face, giving him a devilish look. Both men fired at the same time. Coffin felt Burke's shot tear through one of the flapping ends of his yellow slicker.

Coffin's shot shattered Burke's chin, knocking him back a little. Coffin fired once more, and finished Burke off. Slowly he stood, slipping the empty Remington away and pulling the other. He turned in a circle, but no one else was threatening him.

Coffin checked on Burke, who was dead. So was the bartender. Pendergast was alive, though not by much. Coffin knelt in the mud next to Pendergast. "Where's Merkle?" Coffin asked.

"Down along the Yellowstone somewhere," Pendergast gasped.

"Anyplace in particular?"

"There's a place where hot water shoots out into the sky every so often," Pendergast said, his voice growing fainter. "He likes to stay near there." Pendergast wheezed a few times. "Bastard," he muttered and died.

Chapter Thirty-one

Coffin followed the Madison River southward through the long, rugged valley. Three days later, he left the Madison and rode southeast through Raynolds Pass and then the next day, he made it through Targhee Pass. Two days later, sitting in a small saddle of land between two low peaks, he wondered which way he should go. He had no clue as to where Merkle could be. This land was so vast, so filled with canyons, valleys, peaks and strange landscapes that Coffin was afraid it would take an army years to cover the land. How could he do it alone? he wondered.

Not being a man given over to worrying too much about things he could not change, he made his camp, and the next morning he turned north, riding near the bottom of one of the small peaks.

He continued on for days, taking the easiest paths he could find. He moseyed north and then east, later south. Despite a pressing urge to want to find Merkle's men as quickly as possible, he took his time, weaving from side to side trying to find tracks, stopping to check out small canyons, caves and crevasses, scanning far-off ridges and hills with the collapsing telescope he had brought with him.

Time seemed to lose its meaning after awhile. There

were just too many bizarre sights. There were small founts of burping mud; steaming holes in the ground surrounded by odd-colored, circular hillocks of crystalline salts and rock; the stench of sulfur. It was, at times, a nightmarish vision of Hades.

The grotesque scenes made Coffin's horse and mule difficult to handle. That also slowed his progress. And it caused him no end of frustration, annoyance and, finally, anger. Yet he pressed on, stoically doing his chores each morning and evening, patiently searching and probing during the long days on the trail.

He was no longer sure of how much time he had spent in this hellish place, but after he had turned east and later southward, he saw a giant falls, tumbling hundreds of feet. Its roar blocked out all other sounds. This, too, spooked the animals, and Coffin pressed on more quickly.

Soon after, he found frequent meadows, populated by great herds of buffalo and elk. And bears. More than once he had to warily move past a grizzly, going well out of his way. With all the buffalo, though, he did eat well. It was of no consequence that he killed a buffalo every day and took only a couple pounds of meat. There were more buffalo than man could ever kill.

Finally he reached the shores of a great lake. Here, too, animals abounded. He saw buffalo, elk, deer, moose, grizzlies, black bears, and a host of smaller animals and birds. He spent the night there, eating well, and trying to beat back a steadily growing sense of urgency. In the morning, he decided to go eastward, following the lake shore.

The next day he left the lake, since it had headed southward. Soon after, the meadows gave way to low, rugged hills, and his horse struggled on the steep slopes that were more plentiful.

That night he decided to head back to the lake. This trail apparently was going nowhere. He figured that if he did not find Merkle that way, he would try tackling this mountainous route again.

He headed south along the lake, and found himself distracted a few times by long fingers of land that stretched out into the lake. So annoyed was he, that when he found what looked to be a gently swelling pass, he headed that way. He tried to figure out exactly how long he had been gone from Madison. He wasn't sure, but he knew it had to be at least three weeks, maybe closer to four.

As he chewed on fresh buffalo tongue that night, he decided it was time to head home. It was still odd to him that he considered Madison his home now. It became a less-strange thought when he conjured up a vision of Amy Pembroke waiting for him.

Smoking a cigarette, he argued silently with himself about the decision. He sort of half believed that he might want to get back to Madison just to see Amy. His more rational side told him that after this long, it was almost certain that Merkle would be long gone from this area. "Bastard's probably back around Madison holdin' up stages again," he muttered. That was the factor that made up his mind.

He wasn't sure how he felt the next morning as he rode out of his little camp. He was, in some ways, glad. On the other hand, he felt miserable, seeing as how he had failed to catch Beryl Pembroke's killers. That hurt him deeply. He tried to assuage his conscience by telling himself firmly that there was still a chance he would run Merkle to ground on the ride back. He was only partly successful in making himself feel better with such thoughts.

Early the next morning, he started through Craig Pass.

It was tougher than he had anticipated, but still quite a reasonable way to go. On the western side of the pass, he found a nice stand of tall, thin pines along a little narrow, fast-running river. He stopped and dismounted. It was, he concluded, a good place to stay. It was only mid-afternoon, but he needed some rest, and more importantly, the animals needed some rest.

He took care of his horse and mule, then pulled out his Spencer breech-loading rifle. He walked off a little way to the edge of a line of trees. Spread out before him was a marshy meadow. And, as he had thought, game. He fired, and brought down a moose. Taking his time, he butchered out some meat and walked back to camp. A fire was quickly made, coffee was heating, and moose was sizzling.

Coffin found out with one bite that moose meat was not for him. In disgust, he threw away all that he had cooked. With growing annoyance, he again set out with his rifle. He found a bison cow, which he dispatched and butchered.

There was still quite a bit of daylight left after he had eaten his fill of buffalo tongue. After a cigarette, he drowsed. He awoke several hours later, feeling fairly refreshed. He ate again, watching the storm clouds gathering in the north and west. The wind had picked up, and the temperature was swiftly falling.

After eating, Coffin put his canvas tarp over his supplies, cleaned up a little, opened his bedroll a little away from the trees and crawled in. Minutes later the rain started with a roar and a rush. Coffin curled up in his bedroll—made of two thin blankets and a large piece of waterproofed canvas—so his head would be out of the rain. He had his slicker inside the bedroll, too, so that in the morning he could slip it on without getting drenched. As the lightning snapped and crackled, and the thunder boomed, Coffin fell asleep.

It was still raining in the morning, and Coffin had a devil of a time trying to get a fire started. He finally managed, but it was such a puny thing that it was unusable. With a curse, he kicked the feeble blaze into oblivion and ate a cold breakfast. His foul disposition turned worse.

He started loading his small store of supplies on the mule. While doing so, he found the one bottle of whiskey he had allowed himself to take along. He had not touched it, since he had brought it mostly for emergencies. He felt now was an emergency of spirit, so he pulled the cork and drank deeply, smacking his lips as the whiskey warmed his mouth and gullet. He took one more long swallow before reluctantly corking the bottle and putting it away.

At last he pulled himself into the saddle and rode off slowly, winding through widely spaced trees. That helped keep some rain off him. It was a cold, gray day, with a biting wind and periods of hard, driving rain between times of a light, prickly drizzle. Fog and mist shrouded everything beyond a few yards away. With the clinging fog, Coffin had no idea which way he was going. He thought it was north or northwest, but he was not certain. He just let his horse pick its way carefully along. Occasionally he could hear the bubbly rush of the river to his left, and he figured he was all right.

By noon, the fog was even thicker, and Coffin was to a point where he could barely see the mule when he looked behind him. In a fine fit of annoyance, he finally pulled to a stop and made a camp, such as it was. He did find enough dry wood under the trees to manage a small but adequate fire, which lasted long enough to boil coffee and roast some of the buffalo meat he still had.

Then he sat back and tried to relax. There was nothing

to do, really. He had done all the necessary chores, including cleaning his rifle. He was sort of half dozing when he heard a gunshot. He jerked to full awareness and listened alertly.

Finally he shook his head. "Damn fool," he muttered, "gettin' spooked by imaginary gunshots."

Then he heard another, followed by several more. He rose, checked his two pistols and walked off, heading to where he thought the gunshots had come from. Occasionally there were other shots, and that helped him head in the right direction. Still, it took him a while. With the fog, the sounds of the river and the wind, the flat echoes off mountainsides, it was difficult to get a bead on the gunfire.

It was two hours and twenty minutes by his pocket watch before he heard voices. He stopped and then crept quietly forward. He finally stopped behind a tree, watching intently. The scene before him seemed ethereal. The mist shifted and moved, created a world that was somehow not real. It was disconcerting to Coffin. He would think he saw someone or something, and then it would be shrouded, and Coffin was left wondering if he had really seen anything at all.

He carefully made an arc around the camp, stopping every few feet behind a tree to watch the camp. He still occasionally heard gunfire, and each time, he froze, just in case.

It was another hour and forty minutes before he got a good look at one of the men in the camp. His eyes narrowed in anger when he spotted Kurt Ochs, one of Merkle's two lieutenants. That did not mean Merkle was here, but Coffin knew now that at least some of Merkle's men were in the camp.

Coffin mentally debated just attacking the camp. The fog, as well as the rain and the river, would mask him and any sounds he made. That would boost his advantage of surprise. On the other hand, he had no idea how many men were here. There might be only a few, but there might be a dozen or more. Walking into that snake pit would be fatal.

Another problem was that with the moist air, his pistols might not be as surefire as he would like them to be. Even hidden under the slicker, the powder might be dampened by the fog.

He decided to wait. It was too risky to just go charging in there now. He might not have any better chance tomorrow, he knew, but he figured patience would be best now. There was always the chance that the fog might be gone by tomorrow, thus costing him the element of surprise. But it would also let him see more clearly how many men there were and what he was up against.

He stood watching the camp a little while longer, trying to get even a rough count of how many men there were. He spotted several others whose likenesses were on wanted posters he carried, but he still had no good idea of the total number of men in the camp.

It was getting dark already, what with the thick black clouds overhead and the translucent fog. Coffin did not want to get caught out here away from his own camp in the darkness. He'd never find his way back. It was tough enough even in the faint daylight. Coffin had found himself disoriented several times before, and he had taken to marking each tree he passed. He used those marks now to guide him back to his camp. It was a less-than-direct route because earlier he had been going in all directions trying to locate the gunfire he had heard. But it was the easiest way for him to get back to his camp. By the time he did, the gunfire had stopped, and night had closed in.

Chapter Thirty-two

In the morning, Coffin felt a deadly calm inside, as he always did when battle was imminent. He unloaded his guns, made sure they were dry and then reloaded with fresh powder. When he was done with the Remingtons, he hesitated. Then he nodded. Rising, he got his handmade shoulder rigs from his saddlebags. He emptied and then reloaded those, too. He pulled the contraption on, and then put his long yellow slicker back on. He still felt a little foolish wearing the thing, but it was not so bad since the two smaller guns were under his slicker and not readily visible.

The fog had lessened but was still present. It was a little easier for Coffin to see as he pulled out of his camp, but there was still enough fog to hide him a little. He walked holding the reins to his horse and the rope on the mule in his left hand.

He moved more swiftly, with more assurance. Now that he knew what he had to do, and the process was in motion, he had no doubts. He was confident almost to the point of arrogance. He could hear the voices a short way before he reached the enemy camp. He stopped and tied the horse to one tree and the mule to another.

He walked off, stopping again just outside the camp. He stood there for more than an hour, watching, waiting.

A fresh gust of wind finally blew out most of the fog, and for a few minutes, nothing but a lacy curtain of clinging mist blocked Coffin's view.

He saw three large canvas wall tents, their backs at the base of a sharply sloping rocky hill, in a small semicircle. The area in front of the tents was not entirely without trees, though they were sparse and well spaced. What looked like it had been another tent was torn apart and used as a cover for a central fire. The tarp was held up by four pine trees that had been cut or had fallen. The covering was tilted toward the side away from the mountain, so that water would run off away from the tents. Coffin spotted Merkle stepping out of the center tent.

Then the fog whisked back in. It still was not nearly as thick as it had been yesterday, but it was heavy enough to once again give the landscape a look from some demon's world.

All in all, Coffin had counted nine men in the camp. There might be more in the tents, and there might even be more out hunting, but Coffin was certain about nine.

Coffin saw no more need to hesitate. Except for the fog, he was going to get no other help. He considered waiting until dark, using the night's blackness to hide his approach. But that was a long way off, and Coffin was tired of waiting. He pulled his two Remingtons, took a deep breath and let it out slowly, and then left his haven.

He walked swiftly, with certainty, toward the tents, his pistols held down along each leg. No one outside saw him—until he fired two shots, killing one man and wounding another.

Several other men in Merkle's camp looked up in surprise. Cady Merkle and Grady Whitfield rushed out of the center tent. Hugh Vickers, one of Merkle's top lieutenants, came running from behind the tents, holding up his pants with one hand and a pistol in his other. Then

Merkle and his men froze, seemingly suspended in whatever action they had been making when Coffin fired his first shots.

Coffin stopped and bellowed, "I'm United States Deputy Marshal Joe Coffin! You're all under arrest!" That would sort of make it official, he figured. He wasn't planning on actually arresting most, if any, of them. If he arrested them, he would be expected to guard them from vigilantes. And that was something he had little heart for.

Coffin's words broke the spell Merkle's men had been under. Suddenly curses rang in the air as hands reached for pistols. Men appeared and disappeared, though they did not move, as the fog shifted with each gust of wind.

Coffin began walking again, steadily, though slowly. He fired smoothly with both pistols. The fog still shifted constantly, and now Merkle's men began moving in all directions. Powder smoke added to the haze. Coffin heard and sometimes felt bullets whiz by him. He got winged once that he knew of, but it didn't bother him.

Then silence came, swift but uncertain. As if on cue, the fog thinned enough for everyone to get a look around.

Five of Merkle's men were down, including Kurt Ochs, Merkle's other lieutenant. Coffin did not know how many of them were dead and how many only wounded. Merkle, Hugh Vickers, and Grady Whitfield were in front of the center tent, which Coffin figured was Merkle's. Vickers and Whitfield were kneeling, pistols held at arm's length. Merkle was crouched.

The three stood slowly; Whitfield and Vickers reloading their pistols hastily. Merkle just stood there, arrogantly. He was a tall, dashing figure, with long blond hair that curled up at the collar. He wore a thin mustache and small goatee and was clad in a swallowtail coat, wool pants and wool vest. He had no hat.

Coffin stopped just under the tarp protecting the fire. He felt blood trickling down his side, and he risked one quick glance just to make sure the wound was not serious. Then he looked back at Merkle and his two cronies.

"Just who the hell are you?" Merkle asked.

"Marshal Joe Coffin."

"Where in the hell are you from?"

"Madison. Come to get you and these other assholes for the murder of Marshal Beryl Pembroke and a passel of stage robberies and other killings."

"And you're alone?" Merkle asked. When Coffin nodded, Merkle laughed with a warm, deep sound. "You made yourself one hell of a goddamn mistake comin' here, Marshal," Merkle said in a pleasant tone of voice.

"I took out most of your boys already." He slid his two Remingtons away.

"Yeah," Merkle said with a chuckle, "that's true. But new men are easy to get. There's hundreds of 'em all over this country. Your real mistake was running out of bullets." He laughed a little harder.

Vickers and Whitfield also were laughing now, and were nearly finished reloading.

"I expected that would be a problem. That's why I brought these." He tore out the two smaller Colts from the shoulder rig and snapped off a shot from each.

Vickers and Whitfield fired, and then just as quickly as it had gone, the fog returned.

Coffin dropped into a crouch not a moment too soon. A bullet flew out of the clinging fog and slapped his hat off. He fired twice more and thought he heard a grunt of pain.

Suddenly the silence came again. Coffin frog-walked to his right a few yards, then stood and slipped forward. Even with the fog, he could see a few feet, and as he neared the tents he could see one body. Whitfield was dead, but Merkle and Vickers were gone. They could be running like hell, or they could be ten feet away. There was no telling in this fog.

Coffin knelt beside Whitfield's body trying to figure out what to do next. Vickers and Merkle were gone, where he did not know, and he did not want to go stumbling around in the fog. Of the others he had shot, some might still be alive and so a threat to him. He figured that he would have to check on them first, to see who was alive and who wasn't. Then he could worry about Merkle and Vickers, and any other of the outlaws who were still alive.

Moving cautiously, he circled around the back of the tents. He stopped at the first man he found and rolled him on his back. The man was dead. Coffin neither knew nor cared who he was.

Of the five Coffin knew he had shot first off, three were still alive—Kurt Ochs, George Davenport and Doug Koop. The latter looked to be in bad shape, so Coffin left him where he was, figuring the man would not live another quarter-hour. The former two seemed as if they'd live. One was lying where he had been and looked dazed and frightened. Coffin knelt next to him. "Where're you hurt, boy?" he asked.

"My head," Davenport said shakily. "I'm gut shot, too."

Coffin looked at Davenport's head, then ripped his shirt open. "Shit," he muttered. "You barely got winged." He grabbed Davenport's shirt and hauled him up as he rose. "March," he ordered.

Coffin finally found Ochs, who had been crawling away. When Coffin stopped and pulled him up, too, he found that Ochs's right leg had been broken by a gunshot. "Help him, boy," Coffin said to Davenport, shoving him toward Ochs.

As Coffin walked the two men warily toward the tents, he heard horses galloping off. He swore. He had his two captives lie facedown on the ground, limbs spread wide. He backed into the first tent, watching the two captives as best as he could. He found some rope, which is what he had been hunting for. He went out and tied the two wounded men tightly—Davenport hand and foot, Ochs only his arms because of his shattered leg. He left them lying under the tarp.

He poked into the other two tents. In Merkle's he found a woman—young, pretty, naked and dead—on a dirty pile of blankets. "Jesus goddamn Christ," Coffin muttered. He jerked one of the blankets out from under the body, and covered her with it.

Back outside, he scouted the rest of the area as well as he could in the fog. Finally he went and got his horse and mule. He put them with Merkle's animals. He wasn't sure, but he thought four, maybe five horses were gone.

He stoked up the fire. A coffeepot already sat in the flames. He checked it and found it was nearly three-quarters full. He put some of the buffalo meat he had found on sticks and dangled them over the fire.

Minutes later, he heard another horse galloping. "Damn!" he hissed. Coffin jumped up and raced to the small horse herd. He threw himself on his own horse and raced off. Through the sometimes patchy, sometimes thick fog, Coffin spotted a horse and rider. He spurred his own horse to more speed.

Doug Koop looked over his shoulder. He was hurt bad, he knew, but he wanted to—needed to—get away from the demon who appeared and disappeared with the fog.

From his position behind Koop, Coffin could see Koop riding into an area of small fumaroles, their steam wafting up to mingle with the fog a little. Still, in some ways it seemed clearer.

Suddenly Coffin jerked his horse to a halt. The animal whinnied and neighed, unhappy. Coffin could see that Koop's horse felt the same.

Suddenly the crusty ground on which Koop had wandered gave way. Koop and the horse screamed as they fell into the boiling, sulfurous water of the fumarole.

Coffin shook his head as the screams faded fast. He turned and rode back to the tents. He checked the ropes holding his two captives, and saw that they had not been tampered with.

So fast had the episode with Koop started and ended, that the meat Coffin had put on to cook was still not done. Coffin plopped heavily down at the fire. He placed one of his Colts right next to him, within easy reach. Then he began cleaning and reloading the Remingtons.

Ochs kept up a running stream of comments and curses until Coffin could no longer bear it. He cocked a Colt and aimed it at Ochs's nether region. He said nothing, but Ochs shut up fast.

After taking care of his weapons, Coffin ate the buffalo meat and drank coffee, knowing Ochs and Davenport were staring at him with undisguised hatred. When he finished, he stood and stretched. It seemed as if the fog was really beginning to lift now. It was still there, but now it was faint, wispy, like a lady's handkerchief.

Coffin walked around the camp, trying to see if he could spot any sign of Merkle and Vickers. He didn't, but he did idly pick up two pistols from dead outlaws, doing it more as a reflex action than anything else.

He went back and squatted in front of the trussed-up Ochs and Davenport. "Howdy, boys," he said coldly. "I believe we need to talk a little."

"Eat shit, Marshal," Ochs said.

Coffin clobbered Ochs on the side of the head with one of the pistols he had picked up. "Tell me about Cady Merkle," he said.

"Nothing to tell."

Coffin hit Ochs on the other side of the head, the pistol's front sight tearing a jagged line across Ochs's temple.

"You might think that with me bein' a U.S. marshal and all that I'm duty bound to drag your ass back to Madison, or maybe Virginia City, and protect your rotten ass from vigilantes and bounty hunters and all such folk that'd like to see you dead. So I'm advisin' you now that I feel no such pressure. In fact, I'd as soon peel your hide off you inch by inch right here and now. Still, you might get in my good graces if you were to give me a little information."

"What do you want to know?" Davenport asked. He was a young, frail-looking man, who seemed scared out of his wits.

"Shut up, boy!" Ochs growled.

"But . . ."

"But shit, boy. This scum ain't gonna let us go, nor is he gonna take us back to face the law. It's too goddamn dangerous, especially since I'll gut him first chance I get." He looked defiantly at Coffin. "So you don't tell him nothin'! You hear me, boy?"

"I don't want to die, Kurt," the young man said. He was on the verge of tears. "I'm too young to die."

"You weren't too goddamn young to kill some people and terrorize others, you goat-pokin' little snot," Coffin said harshly.

"You see," Ochs said, "he ain't gonna let us live more than two minutes after we tell him what he wants to know."

"That true?" Davenport asked, eyes pleading.

Coffin shrugged. "Could be. The thing you have to remember, though, boy, is that dyin' fast can sometimes be a blessin'. Dyin' slow ain't much fun. And if you and donkey-face over there don't talk to me of your own free will, I'll be forced to encourage you."

Davenport looked like he wanted to cry, urinate, or vomit, or maybe all three. "I don't know all that much about Cady," he whined. "I don't. Kurt knows all about him, though. He's one of Cady's . . ."

"Shut your trap, goddammit," Ochs snapped. He rolled and swung on his buttocks and lashed out with his good foot, hitting Davenport in the side. Davenport winced but said nothing.

"Calm down, Ochs," Coffin said. "I know that you and Vickers are Merkle's right-hand men. Hell, from what I heard, you two even give Merkle a hand when he needs to piss."

Ochs spit at Coffin. He missed, but Coffin would not take even such an attempt. He clouted Ochs again with the gun. But that brought him a little too close to Ochs's good foot. He kicked at Coffin, catching him high on the side and bowling him over.

"Damn," Coffin snapped as he rolled once. He got to his feet, his blood boiling in anger. He picked up the pistol he had dropped and walked over to Ochs. He said nothing. But he did begin pistol whipping the outlaw. Davenport's eyes were wide in fear as he watched the brutal assault.

Chapter Thirty-three

Coffin suddenly stopped beating Ochs to a pulp. He had decided for no real reason that he would take the two captives back with him. Along the way he might be able to coax—or beat—information out of one of them. That would be better than trying to do it in this hellish land. He also figured that if neither Ochs nor Davenport talked during the trip, Coffin could take the two on separately once they were in the jail in Madison. Davenport was certain to spill his guts with a little encouragement.

Coffin also wanted to get back to Madison. He wasn't sure why—beyond wanting to see Amy again. But he felt an unease, a sense that something horrible was about to happen. He assumed a large part of it was brought on by the strange land he was in. It was not a place that was conducive to a warm, homelike atmosphere where one felt protected and secure.

Coffin could see no real reason to delay his departure, so he let Ochs lay there bleeding in the dirt while he went off and saddled horses for Ochs and Davenport. Then he crudely fashioned a splint for Ochs from wood and rope.

Getting Ochs onto the horse was some chore, but Coffin finally managed it with help from Davenport. Then he tied Ochs's feet with a rope under the horse, no longer caring about Ochs's broken leg. Ochs sat there slumped, almost lying on the horse's neck. Coffin tied the horse tightly to a tree in case Ochs was playing possum.

He loaded some of Merkle's supplies on a mule, and then helped Davenport onto his horse, tying him the same way as he had Ochs. Next he grabbed some rope and looped it around the necks of all fifteen of Merkle's animals that were left in the camp.

Finally he mounted his own horse and rode northwest. The other animals, attached to one lead rope, followed. Everything took longer with two captives. At least twice a day he would have to drag them off their horses, let them eat and then help them back on. Each night he had three horses to unsaddle; each morning he had to saddle them again. Two mules had to be loaded and unloaded. Five animals needed tending to. Coffin had to do all the cooking, all the gathering of firewood.

Coffin enlisted Davenport's help right from the start. Anywhere Ochs had to go, Davenport acted as a crutch. That helped Coffin a little.

The small wound along Coffin's left ribs was more annoying than painful, but it limited his movements a little, which he had to take into account.

Ochs gave him little trouble, at least for the first five days, since he had been pretty well battered around. Davenport was no trouble since he was too scared. In the evenings, after supper, Coffin would try pumping Davenport for information. He got little, since Davenport still seemed more afraid of Merkle and Ochs than he did of Coffin. Still, Coffin was sure he would be able to pry information out of Davenport once they got back to Madison. It didn't hurt for Coffin to keep rekindling Davenport's fear. It would make him more pliable later.

Nine days after leaving Merkle's camp, Coffin and his

small procession walked into Bendersville. Coffin was welcomed with all the tenderness he had been accorded the last time, and it irritated him more than it had before.

He stopped outside the tent hotel and dismounted. He hollered for the hotel keeper, whom he could see sitting inside at a makeshift table. He got no response. With a sigh of annoyance, Coffin grabbed the lantern hanging at the entrance to the tent. He lit it. "You got three seconds to get your ass out here, or I'll burn you out."

He counted to three, loud enough for the man inside the tent to hear him. Coffin was aware that a small crowd had gathered. When he reached three, Coffin smashed the lantern on a wood post and then threw it onto the canvas roof. With the spread of the coal oil, the tent leapt into flames.

"What the flyin' hell're you doin', you dumb bastard?" the hotel man screeched. He raced outside and looked up. "Jesus goddamn Christ all-flyin' mighty!" he screamed, bouncing up and down in useless agitation. He turned, glaring at Coffin, but then hollered, "What're all you bastards standin' there for? Goddammit, put this fire out."

No one moved.

Coffin studied the bright flames for a moment, then said, "Looks like it's a little late for help there, friend. Now, since you're not distracted by your elegant hotel there, maybe you'll give me some of your attention."

"Whatcha want?" the man growled.

"There a real hotel around here?"

"No," the man spat.

"There any kind of lawman around? Or a jail?"

"No."

Ochs laughed. "Looks like you ain't got no place to go, Mr. Big Shot Marshal." His face was still a mess, covered with striped red welts, bluish-yellow bruises, dirt, and dried blood.

"You got any real buildings in town?" Coffin asked the hotel owner, ignoring Ochs.

"Not a goddamn single one," he gloated.

"You've been a big help," Coffin said sarcastically. He looked up at the sky and figured he only had another hour or two worth of daylight. He was well aware that Bendersville was little more than a waystop for outlaws in the region. He decided he would leave the town behind and take his chances with a camp out in the wilds. But first he would eat, despite his remembrance of the rotten grub he had gotten last time. At least he would not have to cook it.

He untied Davenport's legs and eased him down onto the ground. Then Coffin did the same for Ochs. As soon as Ochs's good foot hit the ground, though, he balanced and swung his bound-together wrists at Coffin.

The marshal sidestepped the attempted blow and then punched Ochs in the kidney area, Ochs groaned and sagged, then fell. Coffin grabbed a handful of shirt and hauled Ochs up. "Care for another?" Coffin asked.

Ochs spit at him, and missed.

Coffin whacked him a good shot in the solar plexus. "I can stand here all day and pound on you, if that's your wish," Coffin said coolly. "Or you can behave for ten minutes and get some grub I ain't cooked."

"Hard choice," Ochs grumbled, "but I'll take the grub for now."

"Fine." He shoved Ochs toward the restaurant next to the remains of the hotel. Davenport automatically slid under Ochs's arm.

The men in the restaurant had formed a quick bucket brigade and doused their tent-restaurant to keep it from catching fire. It seemed they had succeeded.

Coffin stopped and looked at the small crowd of hard-eyed, heavily armed men. "Any one of you messes with my animals, and I will shoot you dead then and there." He turned and shoved Ochs and Davenport forward again.

The food was every bit as bad as he remembered. Coffin gave the cook two dollars to bring a bottle of whiskey over to help wash down the foul meal. Coffin even took pity on Ochs and Davenport and gave them each a couple of drinks.

Coffin could not even drink the coffee, and settled for a cigarette and sips on the bottle of whiskey to remove the lingering bad effects of the supper.

Finally Coffin rose and stretched. "Time to go, boys."

"I ain't done," Ochs protested.

"Yes you are. Now get up."

Davenport stood first. He had come to think that Coffin was not all that bad, even if he was a lawman. The young man thought that maybe, just maybe, if he behaved himself on the ride to Madison, and if he told Coffin all he could about Merkle and his men, then he might get off fairly easily. It was a hope—the only hope he had.

Ochs remained seated, steadfastly shoveling in food. He would show this young punk of a lawman that he was not a man to be rushed for anything.

Coffin grabbed the back of Ochs's shirt just under the collar and twisted it several times. The front of Ochs's shirt, buttoned all the way to the top, swiftly tightened on his neck. He could neither breathe nor swallow. Coffin bent over close to Ochs's ear. "Are you ready to go now?" he asked politely.

Ochs, whose face was red, nodded vigorously.

Coffin pulled a little on the shirt, getting Ochs started up, then he released the shirt. Ochs stood, sucking in breath, almost choking again, this time on the food. He angrily beckoned Davenport to help him walk.

Just as they stepped outside, a gun fired to Coffin's left, and he grunted as he was struck by a bullet. He started to swing that way, drawing a Remington and crouching as he did. Another gun fired, behind him, and knocked his hat flying.

"Shit," he mumbled. He saw a gun-wielding man in front of him, and he fired twice. Without waiting to see if he had hit the man, he half jumped, half dove to his left. He came to a stop on one knee. A fleeting glance told him that the man he had shot at was hit and down.

Coffin saw the second gunman and fired the three balls left in the Remington. He was certain as soon as he fired that the man was dead.

He stood, sliding away the empty Remington and pulling the other. He surveyed the crowd. All looked threatening, but he figured that was their normal look. No one seemed to be particularly upset that he had just gunned down two men. He glanced down and saw blood on the front of his shirt, and the left shoulder holster was hanging oddly. Carefully he pulled his shirt out a little. He nodded, understanding. The bullet had clipped the metal buckle of the holster, which diverted the ball a fraction of an inch, and it had slid across the width of Coffin's chest.

Warily, Coffin went to the man he had first shot, and he checked the body over. The man was dead. Coffin quickly went through the man's pockets, taking the eighteen dollars and four cents he found.

Coffin walked to the other body and looked down at the twisted face. He had no name for the man, but he remembered that scarred, ugly face as being in Merkle's camp just before the battle had started. Coffin figured the man had cut and run as soon as the first shot was fired. How he came to be here with another man, both trying to kill him, was puzzling to Coffin. He shrugged. There would be no answer to it here, he figured. And until he had an answer, there was nothing to be done about the situation. The men had tried to kill him, but he had killed them instead. That was all he needed to know.

He knelt and rifled that man's pockets, too, and came up with an additional twenty-seven dollars and seventy-eight cents. "Mount up, boys," he said as he rose.

Ochs glared at him in undisguised hate; Davenport looked at him with awe, and fear. But they mounted their horses. Coffin did the same, and they all rode out of town. It was difficult, but Coffin reloaded the one Remington so that it would be ready.

An hour or so after leaving Bendersville, with darkness sweeping down over them, Ochs turned in his saddle and yelled, "When the hell're we gonna stop?"

"Later." After a few minutes, Coffin called a stop. He pointed. "Take that trail," he ordered.

"You're out of your goddamn mind," Ochs argued.

"Might be. Do it anyway." Coffin wasn't sure this was where he wanted to go, but he decided it was his best chance. Enoch Pembroke had showed him this route on a map. It was not a well-known trail, and so the chances of them encountering anyone was small. It also would allow him to avoid Virginia City and go straight to Madison.

Twenty minutes later, Coffin called a halt. While he didn't think they had put enough distance between them and Bendersville, taking this mountain path in the dark was suicide. He found a place where the wind had gouged a shallow impression in the side of a cliff just off the trail. Coffin figured that would be as good a place to stop as any.

After unsaddling the horses, unloading the two mules, tending the five animals, hobbling all the animals, gathering wood, starting a fire, and cooking and eating supper, he finally rested.

He had a cigarette and another cup of coffee before he pulled his shirt off. He poured some of his one bottle of whiskey on the raw, oozing wound. He hissed as the alcohol burned into the open flesh. He got his one extra shirt and tied it around his chest as a primitive bandage. Then he lit another cigarette and relaxed a little. Sipping whiskey helped somewhat.

"How the hell old are you, boy?" Ochs asked suddenly.

"Twenty, twenty-one maybe. I ain't too sure of my birth date. Why?"

"It's a shame," Ochs said with a sad shake of his head, "for you to die at so young an age."

"You'd be a hell of a lot better off if you was to worry about you gettin' killed."

"You'll never make it back to Madison."

"If Merkle sends idiots like those two back in Bendersville, I ain't got a thing to worry about." He paused. "Of course, you do. I still ain't married to the idea of gettin' you back to Madison." He smiled viciously.

Chapter Thirty-four

The trek across the mountains was worse than Coffin had expected. The trail was ribbon thin, at times looking out over sheer cliffs that fell hundreds of feet. At other times, the mountains closed tightly in on the trail. All of it spooked the men and the animals.

After two sleepless nights, they had come down the western side of the mountains, and Coffin set his camp along the Ruby River, even though there was still plenty of daylight left. But the horses needed rest, and so did he.

They put in a long day the next day, and then the one after that, they rode into Madison about noon. Not really stopping much, Coffin turned Merkle's horses into the corral at the livery. "I'll be back later about them animals," he shouted to Ray Hudson, the livery owner. Hudson was working in his barn, and just waved.

Coffin and his two prisoners moved toward the center of town and the jail. Coffin was exhausted as well as filthy, being covered with mud, blood, dust; he smelled of alcohol from the whiskey he had poured on his wounds. His clothes were tattered, and he had several weeks' worth of beard that scratched his neck. Despite all that, he did not think he warranted being watched by everyone in town, all of them seemingly with gloomy faces.

He stopped in front of the office and got Ochs and Davenport down from their horses. He was a little surprised that he did not see Enoch Pembroke, but he figured his friend was off somewhere, or just busy. Coffin locked Ochs and Davenport into separate cells—the two back corner ones. Only one other cell was occupied, by a man snoring off a drunk by the look and smell of him.

"Get comfortable, boys," Coffin said to his two prisoners. "I'll be back after a spell and see you get somethin' to eat."

He left the other two horses and the two mules tied in front of the office as he mounted his horse for the ride to the Pembroke home. Despite his tiredness, he was eager as a young pup to see Amy. He smiled, thinking of how surprised she would be when he walked in, after all her worries about his safety.

Doc Smith's carriage was out front of the house, and as he dismounted, Coffin wondered who was sick. He also hoped it was not Amy. She seemed so small and frail that she could get sick from a little breeze, though he knew she was healthy and robust.

The physician opened the door to exit as Coffin was reaching for the front door knob. Both men were startled, Coffin less so than the doctor.

"Somebody sick, Doc?" Coffin asked.

Smith harrumphed, then said, "Come in, boy. Come on in." He backed inside, giving Coffin some room.

"Is it Amy, Doc?" Coffin asked, fear clutching at him. "She all right?"

"You best talk with Enoch, boy. Come, I'll bring you to him."

"I know where the hell he is, if he's home," Coffin

said vehemently. "Now what's wrong with Amy, dammit."

"Calm yourself down, boy," Smith instructed. "And do as I say. Now, come, let's go see Enoch." He took Coffin's left arm and tugged him along.

Coffin reluctantly let himself be towed toward and then up the stairs. His worry grew with each step he took. At the top of the stairs, he turned toward Amy's room, determined to go see her.

But Smith blocked his path. "Please, Joe," Smith said. "Do what I tell you for right now." He held an aging finger toward Pembroke's room.

Coffin glared at him a moment, and then turned. Numbly he entered Pembroke's room.

Enoch Pembroke was sitting in bed, propped up with pillows against the headboard. He looked pale and worn. He wore no shirt, and his chest was swathed in white bandages. "Sit," he croaked listlessly. He pointed weakly to the chair at the side of the bed.

Coffin ignored it. "Where's Amy?" he asked, voice rough and with a ragged edge of nervousness.

"Sit," Pembroke said again.

"No. Now where the hell's Amy?" he demanded.

Pembroke looked up at Coffin, who was shocked by his old friend's appearance. Pembroke looked as if he had been crying steadily, and all the light seemed to have gone out of his eyes. He was no longer the big, strong, animated Major Pembroke or Marshal Pembroke. He was simply an empty shell of a man.

"What happened to her?" Coffin asked quietly, deadly calm.

"Best go on about your business, Doc," Pembroke said, waving his hand limply toward the door.

"You sure, Enoch?" The physician was very skeptical.

Pembroke nodded. When the doctor left, Pembroke

said, "There's a bottle in the chest of drawers, bottom drawer. Get it." His voice had gained strength.

Coffin stared at Pembroke for a moment, emotions whipped up into a tornado inside of him, yet outwardly he was calm. Then he turned and walked to the chest of drawers.

"Get my pipe and tobacco while you're there, Joe, if you please."

Coffin found the bottle and picked up the pipe and a buckskin pouch of tobacco. He took them all to the bed. He handed Pembroke the pipe and tobacco. Then Coffin pulled the cork on the bottle and tossed it on the small table next to the bed. He took a long, long drink. Then he set the bottle on the night table. "Tell it," he ordered.

Coffin sat and began rolling a cigarette. Pembroke took another moment to get his pipe fired up. Then he sighed and the hurt, pained look came back into his eyes. And when he spoke it was in a dull, flat monotone that had no life or energy.

"Sunday was a fine, fine day. Birds singing in the trees, nice temperature, a little breeze. The kind of day a man wants to go sit out by a pond fishing and just let his cares go for a spell."

He paused, blinking away tears as he spread billowing clouds of pipe smoke careening around the room.

"Well, I walked Amy over to church, like either me or Beryl . . ." He sucked in a breath to try to settle himself. "Like me or Beryl were used to doin'. And, just like always, Amy asked if I wanted to come on in and listen to Preacher Ames. I must admit, I've been right neglectful of going to church and such since the war. I always seemed to find an excuse for not goin'. I was always too busy."

He looked up with those pained eyes, almost pleading with Coffin for understanding. Coffin nodded just a little. Coffin knew what Pembroke was going through.

"I don't know what the hell come over me, Joe. I really don't. Maybe I had some kind of premonition, and I was tryin' to square things with my Maker a little before he took me. I just don't know. But I went in, instead of goin' over to the office like I was used to doing.

"I don't even remember what the sermon was about. I just kind of sat there with the preacher's words dulling my senses. It was peaceful in there, Joe. Lord, was it peaceful."

"Folks like you and me ain't had much peace of any kind since we got into that war," Coffin commented, his voice a strange growl.

"That's a fact." Pembroke stared at his pipe for a few minutes. "And I don't figure we're ever going to know real peace again, unless it's the peace of the grave."

"Men like us, that can't be too far off."

Pembroke nodded. He almost seemed to have fallen asleep, except for the regular sucking on the pipe stem. Finally he pulled the pipe free. "I need a drink, Joe."

Coffin handed him the bottle and helped him take a few swigs. "That's better," Pembroke said. Coffin took another healthy sip before putting the bottle back on the table.

"Anyway," Pembroke continued after what had seemed like a lifetime, "after services, we stood outside talking to folks. Preacher Ames was some astonished to have seen me in church, though he chided me a little for having worn my pistol inside. I didn't feel like explaining that I had had no intention of going into the church, so I let it drop."

He paused to wipe a shaking hand across his face, clearing away a fresh batch of tears. "Amy was more beautiful than I'd ever seen her, her face full of life and energy. It was you who made her so. Since you asked for her hand, she's been beaming like the noonday sun. She was talking to the other ladies after services, telling them of getting married and asking for their advice and such. Happy. She was so happy. So goddamn happy. Just so goddamn, son of a bitching, goddamn happy." He was blubbering now, tears flowing freely. And he was getting crazy.

Coffin stood and leaned over the bed, holding Pembroke down through sheer strength of his hands on his friend's shoulders. "It's all right, Enoch," he said quietly and firmly. "It'll be all right."

Pembroke slowly got control of himself to some degree. Coffin released him and gave him another drink of whiskey. Then he sat back in the chair. "Take your time, Enoch," he said "We ain't in no rush here. Tell it at your own pace."

Pembroke took more time to compose himself. With trembling hands he refilled his pipe and lit it. When it was going well, he lay back against the pillows, and shut his eyes. His breathing was ragged.

Then his eyes reopened. The bloodshot orbs held a lifetime of pain in them. "We started walking back here . . ." His voice cracked, and it took a little time for it to come back. "Just walking down the street, minding our own business when . . . Jesus, Jesus . . . There were three of them, and they just seemed to come out of nowhere. I didn't even get a good look at them. Three horses just appeared. I know it was Merkle, though."

"How do you know that if you never got a good look at him?"

"I got a good look at that prancing, bone-white horse of his." He paused. "Then there were gunshots. I don't know, goddammit, three, four, a dozen. I got no idea . . . no idea."

Pembroke came to a stop again, chest bellowing in and

out. The pain of his loss, coupled with the wounds he had suffered had left him a wilted empty hull.

"I took two slugs in the chest that I know of. Doc says it was three. Don't matter. They all hurt like hell. I managed to get off a couple shots, but I can't even say if I hit any of them. Damn, if we'd only talked a little less with the pastor . . ." He dropped that thought.

Coffin gave Pembroke another dose of whiskey. "Thanks. I was on the ground, bleedin' my life away it seemed. Then people come a running. And those bastards were heading off. Everything gets kind of blurred after that, except for one thing . . ."

"Amy," Coffin said, the word flat and devoid of hope.

"Yeah. I managed to crawl over to her before anyone else really got there, but there was nothing anybody could do for her even then." He visibly tried to keep a grip on his rampaging emotions. "Only thing can be said, Joe, is she died fast, so she didn't suffer none. Not as much as you and me. If only I . . ."

"Stop it," Coffin ordered, torn between rage and grief. "There's all kinds of 'what ifs' we can call on. If you hadn't of gone to church. If you hadn't talked so long afterward. If I hadn't been gone so long. If, if, if. None of that means shit right now. None of it!"

Pembroke nodded and then groaned with new pain in his chest. Since he wanted to get his mind off Amy if he could, he asked, "So how did things go for you?"

"I found Merkle." When he saw the light of wonder in Pembroke's eyes, he added, "Didn't get him though. I killed several of his men and captured two. They're over at the jail now. Merkle and Vickers got away. I figure he either has other men around, or more fled with him. Two of his men tried to gun me down in Bendersville."

"That where you got that?" Pembroke asked, pointing to Coffin's shirt.

"Yep." Coffin took another sip of whiskey, then put the bottle down and rose. "Well, Enoch, I've got some things to see to."

Suddenly a little fire leapt into Pembroke's eyes, and he became more like his old self. "You going to talk to them two you brought in?"

"Yep."

Pembroke looked up at his young friend, and he was suddenly glad he was not Coffin's prisoner.

Chapter Thirty-five

Coffin walked into the office and straight to the back where the cells were. He looked at the only prisoner beside the two he had brought in earlier that day. "What got you in here, boy?" he asked the young man.

"Ah, hell, Marshal, I got likkered up over at the Pittsburgh and slapped one of the girls around."

"That was mighty stupid."

"I know." The youth, only a year or two younger than Coffin, hung his head.

Coffin opened the cell. "Get goin'."

"I'm free?" the youth asked, surprised.

Coffin nodded. "If you got any sense at all, boy, I won't see you in here no more."

"You won't." The young man grabbed his hat and scrambled out the door, still not believing his good fortune.

"It's about goddamn time you come back here, you stupid little bastard," Ochs snarled from his place on the hard iron cot. "Jesus, I got to hit the outhouse."

Coffin said nothing. He just unstrapped his shoulder harness, which he had patched up as best he could, and hung it on the peg by the door. His gunbelt followed.

Ochs watched with growing annoyance; Davenport looked on from his cell wondering just what was going on.

Coffin opened Ochs's cell and stepped inside. "Sit up," he said quietly.

Ochs was about to retort until he looked into Coffin's deep blue eyes and saw something in those orbs that chilled him to his very soul. He struggled, trying not to jostle the broken leg too much, until he was sitting with his back against the wall. His knees bent over the edge of the very narrow cot, and his feet were flat on the floor. He was sweating both from the exertion, as well as a new and very deep wellspring of fear.

"You remember that I was askin' you some questions back at Merkle's camp."

Ochs stared at Coffin. If he had not been watching Coffin, he would have sworn that the voice came from the Grim Reaper, so cold and sparse were the words. Finally he nodded.

"Good," Coffin said flatly. "I don't want to have to go through all the bullshit again, so, you will tell me what you know about Cady Merkle and anybody in Madison or Virginia City who's helpin' him." He paused a moment and stood staring at Ochs with flat, hard eyes. "Since I don't feel like makin' threats every two minutes, I will offer you one blanket threat now. If you answer my questions, you might come out of this alive. If you don't answer, or if you try to sidetrack me, you will encounter pain. Very much pain."

"Why this change of heart?" Ochs asked. He was hoping to distract Coffin just a little so he could build up whatever reserves of strength and fortitude he had in him.

Coffin shrugged. "Merkle killed my wife-to-be and shot Marshal Pembroke full of holes." He waited just long enough for Ochs to digest that. "Now, tell me about Cady Merkle."

Ochs swallowed hard. "Now don't go gettin' too nervous here, Marshal," he said, fear making his voice vibrate. "I don't know all that much about Cady—about his operations, that is. I really don't." Sweat was rolling down his plump, sallow face.

"I expect that from the kid over there," Coffin said, chucking a thumb over his shoulder. He felt a little odd about that. Davenport was about the same age as Coffin. "Not from you."

"But I . . ."

Coffin kicked Ochs's makeshift splint about center on where the leg was broken.

Ochs emitted a low, animal-like moan, and his eyes rolled.

Coffin gave him a few moments to settle back down. "Tell me about Merkle," he said with more insistence.

Ochs's eyelids fluttered as he tried to retain consciousness. He managed but he was still pale. "What . . ." Ochs stopped to wet his lips with his tongue, ". . . What do you want to know?"

"Where is he?"

"I don't know." His eyes got very wide as Coffin moved his foot back for another kick "Wait!" Ochs screamed. "I don't know. I really don't. He could be in a dozen places. Hideouts, friends' houses."

"Where's he likely to go since I kicked the shit out of his little band of assholes?"

"Depends on where he's got supplies or where he plans to meet more of his men. A likely place is up near Busted Shovel. There's a big cave up that way."

Coffin nodded. "Who's helpin' him out here?"

"Nobody." He braced for an assault while holding out his hand, hoping Coffin would not kick him again. Coffin hesitated, and Ochs said urgently, "Nobody in Madison."

"Virginia City?" Coffin asked.

Ochs nodded.

"Who?"

"I can't tell you that."

"Yes you can."

Ochs shook his head. He almost looked defiant.

"You are a fool," Coffin said, almost to himself. "A goddamn fool." He kicked Ochs in the broken leg again. Then he jerked Ochs up by the shirtfront, swung him and slammed him into the bars.

Ochs howled and screeched. He managed to grab the bars, to keep himself from falling.

Coffin grabbed the outstretched arm, pried the arm loose and pulled Ochs away from the bars, snapping his knee up so that it connected with Ochs's stomach. Ochs's breath was knocked out, and he staggered as he tried to keep from putting his damaged leg on the ground. Still, he went down on one knee.

At the same time, Coffin jerked and twisted Ochs's arm up behind the man's back. Almost straddling Ochs, Coffin pushed down on Ochs's back with his left hand and twisted the arm up with the other.

Ochs screamed as ligaments and tendons in his shoulder stretched and then ripped.

Coffin let the arm go and it fell, flapping uselessly at Ochs's side. He grabbed Ochs's greasy hair from behind and pulled the outlaw's head back. "Who's helpin' Merkle?" he asked, voice tight with barely bottled rage.

Ochs gargled and sputtered, so Coffin eased his head down a little. "Giles Crown," he said weakly.

"He the one owns Virginia City Mercantile and Crown Lumber?"

"Yeah. He also owns the Westerly Saloon and a couple other places in Virginia City."

"Why the hell would he deal with Merkle?"

"Old pals."

"You and Vickers, too?"

Ochs tried to nod but couldn't because Coffin was still holding his hair. "Yeah. We was Jayhawkers fightin' for Doc Jennison. When the busybodies from the government took Jennison's commission, we hid out a spell, then we rode as Red Legs for Jennison's friend George Hoyt." He sounded as proud as he could under his circumstances. "Crown was a captain, Cady was a lieutenant. Me and Hugh were sergeants."

"Goddamn murderin' scum," Coffin muttered.

"Soon as the war was over, we all come out here, took a look at how things worked, and then made our plans."

Coffin wanted nothing more than to just pound on Ochs until the outlaw was but jelly, but he knew he could not do that. Not yet anyway. "I heard rumors that Crown was the head of Virginia City's vigilance committee. That true?"

"Can I get up or somethin'?" Ochs asked.

Coffin released the outlaw's head, and Ochs lowered himself down and around. He squiggled on his buttocks a little until he was sitting against the bars. He looked ghastly, all white and sweating.

Coffin rolled a cigarette and fired it up. He handed it to Ochs, who was surprised by the gesture. Then he looked into Coffin's eyes again, and he knew it was not a reflection of Coffin suddenly finding some humanity.

Coffin rolled another cigarette for himself, then asked, "Is it true?"

Ochs nodded, picking a piece of tobacco off his tongue. "Sure is." He tried to chuckle, but that did nothing but jiggle his arm and leg. That hurt too much, so he clamped off the attempt at laughter.

"Why?" Coffin was puzzled. "Hell, if he was that well thought of as a merchant and what not, all he'd have to do is tell the vigilantes he was too old or too fragile to be doing shit like night ridin'. He could've just supplied them with rope and such."

Ochs shrugged cautiously. "I think he just got his jollies by being a vigilante as well as outlaw. It suited him somehow."

"So that's how Merkle and his boys knew when the big shipments were headin' out of here?"

"Yeah." Ochs hawked up some phlegm and spit it in a corner. "He let the drivers know a long time ago to tell him when a big shipment was going through so he could put some of his gold in with it."

Coffin nodded. "Makes sense," he admitted grudgingly. "That's why all the stages with big shipments *didn't* get robbed all the time—people might've linked Crown with the robberies."

"You got it." Ochs was almost enjoying himself.

"And all the other attacks on stages—the smaller ones—were just decoys, then?"

"Most," Ochs agreed. "Sometimes he'd test out some of the new boys, like that peckerless little snot over there," he pointed to Davenport with fingers that still had the smoldering cigarette. "They didn't have the balls for that, we'd get rid of them."

Coffin did not doubt the statement. "Still, the vigilantes were doin' a good job, at least by their lights."

"Yeah," Ochs said, risking another small chuckle. It was no better this time than last. "What better way of gettin' rid of the competition. Besides, then the vigilantes looked like they were doing what they were supposed to be doin'."

It all made morbid sense to Coffin. It did nothing to ease the rage that seethed and rippled inside like a tangle of snakes. "And what about Beryl Pembroke?" Coffin asked.

"He was gettin' too close to us." Ochs seemed to forget for a moment where he was and who he was talking to. "That was a funny one, damn if it wasn't." He started laughing and immediately went into a spate of coughing. When he finished and more or less got his wind back, he said, "We hanged him good and proper. We was supposed to leave him there as a warnin' to others. But then the boys started usin' him for target . . ."

Ochs realized what he was saying and who he was saying it to. He clamped his lips shut.

"What about the attack on Enoch Pembroke? And Amy?"

Ochs shook his head. "I don't know shit about that. I was with you the time that happened, if you'll remember."

"Oh, I remember," Coffin said, words cold and deadly. "I do indeed remember."

Ochs looked up at Coffin, and he shivered. He felt as if his stomach had suddenly frozen as hard and cold as a mountain lake in January. "Wait, Marshal!" Ochs said, panicky. "Whoa. You said you'd let me live if I told ya what ya wanted to know. I did that. And more."

"I said you *might* live. I didn't promise you anything but pain if you lied."

"But I told you the truth."

"I suppose. But you got a long list of things to be taken to account for, boy." Coffin's voice was low, dreadful in its lack of humaneness.

Coffin began to take out all his grief and rage on Kurt Ochs. With each punch or kick he would remember Amy's death, or Beryl's death, Enoch's wounds, or his own troubles. It was a catharsis, purifying his blood and spirit of guilt and anger and loss. Coffin raged and growled, Ochs's screams falling on deaf ears. Coffin was a savage man-beast in his fury, as if possessed by some demon.

Finally he had to slow down as some pinch of sanity began clawing through the curtains of rage inside of him. He stopped then, looking down at Ochs as if seeing him for the first time.

Ochs was a puddle of battered flesh, vomit, blood, tears, feces, urine. There was nothing left in the blob to call it a human being anymore, though it still whimpered now and then.

Coffin absentmindedly wiped his hands on his shirt, and

the stench of the broken pile of flesh and bones began getting to him. He sighed, not feeling any better having done all this, but he assuaged his conscience some by telling himself that Ochs had gotten nothing more than he had deserved. He had raped, robbed, pillaged and murdered from Missouri to Madison, and had done it with impunity for seven or eight years. Coffin might not be feeling very good about himself at the moment for having succumbed to such savagery, but he felt no remorse at the results of that fury.

Slowly, breathing hard, he left the cell and picked up the keys. Then he headed to Davenport's cell. The young man cowered in a corner, blubbering and weeping.

"I ain't gonna do the same to you, boy," Coffin said harshly. "You're free. But if I ever catch you—even get wind of you—committin' crimes again, I'll find you. You understand me, boy?"

Davenport nodded.

Coffin dropped the keys, left the cell and put his guns on. He walked out without looking back. A sizable crowd had gathered outside the office, drawn by the shrieks and screams Ochs had been issuing. Coffin did not look at them either. He simply pulled himself into the saddle and galloped off.

Some minutes later, a nervous George Davenport crept out of the cell and then into the office. He skittered like a rat to the door, saw all the people curiously watching the building, and he bolted, running like Satan was after him.

Some of the people then cautiously edged up and peeked into the office. A few braver ones ventured to the door that separated the cells from the office and peered inside. Then they began moving warily toward the cell in the back left corner. One man vomited, a woman screeched, and all fled out the door to the crisp cleanness of the outside air.

Chapter Thirty-six

Coffin rode all night and arrived in Virginia City around midmorning. He stopped at Marshal Jud Wilson's office. He didn't need Wilson; he just wanted Wilson to know that Coffin was going to kill Giles Crown. Since Crown was an influential man in Virginia City, there would be an outcry if he was shot down. By telling Wilson his plans, Coffin hoped to keep that outcry to a minimum.

Wilson looked up, surprised. "Marshal Coffin," he said. "What brings you here this time?"

"Same as last time."

"Cady Merkle?"

Coffin nodded. "You know anything about Giles Crown?"

"Sure. He's one of the most upstandin' men in Virginia City. He owns several businesses, contributes generously to charities when called on. Why?"

"He's the real head of Merkle's gang and . . ." Coffin stopped, anger almost ready to boil over when Wilson laughed.

"That's the dumbest thing I've ever heard," Wilson said, chuckles still coming regularly.

"Is it?" Coffin said tightly.

Wilson caught the rage in Coffin's eyes and cut off his laughter. "Well, it's gotta be crazy, Marshal. Jesus, Giles is on civic committees, he's thinkin' of running for mayor, he has more money in the bank than just about anyone in Virginia City."

"Think about that for a minute," Coffin said. "If the stages with the big shipments of gold get held up so regularly, where's all Crown's money comin' from?"

Wilson pondered that. "He could be doin' better at his businesses than we're aware of." He didn't seem all that convinced. "Where'd you learn that anyway?" he asked.

"Kurt Ochs."

"One of Merkle's top two men."

"Yep."

"How'd you ever get him to talk?"

"Let's just say I used a little persuasion."

Wilson shivered involuntarily. "You believe him?"

Coffin nodded. "Yeah. He said him, Merkle, and Crown go back to the Jayhawkers under Jennison."

"Well, I still ain't fully convinced, mind you," Wilson said as he stood and grabbed his hat, "but I think we should have a little chat with Mr. Crown."

The two lawmen strode to Crown's Mercantile. As they did, Coffin explained a little more of what went on. By the time they got to the general store, Wilson was worried and agitated. This was going to be no end of trouble no matter how it ended, he figured. He was also more than a little angry at having been played for a fool by Crown.

"Howdy, Chris," Wilson called to the young clerk when he and Coffin had walked into the store. "Tell Mr. Crown I'd like to talk to him."

"He ain't here."

"He's not, huh?" Wilson was a little surprised. "You know where he is?"

Chris Baker shook his head. "All he said was he was goin' out of town a while, and that I should open the store mornin's and close it nights."

"When did he tell you this?"

"Three, four days ago, I guess. I ain't kept much track of it. There a problem, Marshal?"

Coffin and Wilson looked sharply at each other. "No, no problem, Chris. We just needed to talk to him about somethin'. He didn't say where he was goin' though, huh?"

"Nope. Just that he had business to tend to elsewhere."

Wilson nodded. "He comes back, you tell him I need to see him, will you?"

"Yessir."

Outside, the two lawmen stopped. "Well, what do we do now?" Wilson asked.

"Don't he own some other business in town?" Coffin asked.

"Several. You want to try them?"

"Might as well. If that son of a bitch is in town here, I aim to flush him out and then stomp on him." Coffin felt so much older than he had when he had ridden into Madison less than half a year ago. In his reflection in the store window, he could see that he looked older, too. Not so boyish in looks or in wear.

A stop at every store or business that Crown owned produced nothing more than the familiar refrain, "He said he was goin' out of town on business."

At last an exhausted Coffin called an end to the search. It was not an entirely fruitless day, though. For one thing, it seemed certain at this point that Crown was not in Virginia City. For another, Coffin had finally decided that Marshal Jud Wilson was not all that bad a fellow. Under other circumstances, in a different place maybe, they might've been friends.

"You hungry, Jud?" Coffin asked.

"Yeah. You?"

"Almost as hungry as I am tired. How about I buy you supper?"

"Only if I can buy us a bottle to kill afterward."

"It's a deal." Coffin wasn't sure why he had invited Wilson to supper, though he figured that he knew deep down inside that he should not be alone, at least for a little while. He might go off on another rampage. Not that Wilson would be able to stop him if he decided to do it; it was just a lot less likely if Coffin was amid company.

They ate buffalo steaks, potatoes, yams, biscuits, and two kinds of beans. With coffee they ate blueberry pie. Feeling sluggish, they went to a saloon and bought two bottles of rye whiskey.

"Where're we gonna go?" Coffin asked.

"You got a room?"

"Nope."

"Best find you one then, and just set there for the night. I usually just stay at the office, so I don't really have a place to offer for you to stay."

Twenty minutes later, the two lawmen were sitting at a small table in a hotel, drinking whiskey and playing poker for pennies. Coffin did not remember going to bed, and when he awoke in the morning, he felt awful. Too much rage, too much rye, too much hate, and too little sleep.

He dragged himself through the day by sheer will. He slept well that night, though, and in the morning, he headed out early. He just said farewell to Wilson and left Virginia City. He wanted to see how Pembroke was doing, and then load up his mule with supplies. Then he would hunt down Giles Crown, Hugh Vickers and Cady Merkle. No matter where they went, he would find them.

He explained all that to Pembroke when he saw the lawman. He was surprised that Pembroke looked so good. He was still pretty much bedridden, but he could move about some, and he was much hardier. It was almost as if Pembroke had gotten better physically once he was freed of the burden of telling Coffin the bad news. That and knowing that Coffin was back in Madison and ready to take up his duties there. Still, Coffin could see the rage and pain lurking in his friend's eyes.

Pembroke nodded when Coffin was finished. "Soon's I get back on my feet, son, I'm ridin' with you."

Coffin said nothing.

"Don't you get like that with me, son. I can see the thirst for revenge in your eyes. I got every much right – more – as you do to kill those bastards."

Coffin nodded. "I ain't aimin' for it to take that long, but if I can't find 'em by the time you're better, I'd be pleased to have you ride along with me, Major."

"Then it's settled. When're you leaving?"

"Tomorrow, first thing. I ain't of a mind for dawdlin'. Now you get some rest. I got work to do."

First Coffin took his horse to the livery and told Ray Hudson to take especially good care of the chestnut. The horse had done all it was called on to do and then some. He rated top-notch care.

"Sure," Hudson said. "What do you want to do with all those horses and mules you brought in here the other day?"

"Just keep 'em here. If any of 'em needs work, take care of it. Either I'll settle up with you – or the town will."

Hudson wanted to ask Coffin what was going on, but he was not senseless enough to ask such questions when a man like Coffin had that cold look in his eyes.

Then Coffin went to Rosencrantz's Dry-Goods Store and bought new pants, shirt, hat, socks, and bandanna. Then it was off to Duncan's for a shave, haircut, and bath. Dressed in his new clothes, he tossed the old ones on the trash pile out back of Duncan's.

With a sigh, he headed for the office. Someone had come along and dragged Ochs out and cleaned up the cell. He was glad for that. Whoever had done it had also put a new pot of coffee on the stove. Coffin poured some and sat behind Enoch Pembroke's desk with his feet on it. He smoked and sipped coffee, trying to keep the beast of rage caged inside him. He had surprised himself that he had been able to leash the fury when it was needed. He didn't know how much longer he could go on this way, ready to erupt at any moment. He was going to end up shooting someone innocent.

He was still sitting there an hour later, when George Davenport slipped inside the office. He looked furtive and scared, as if he expected to be killed at any moment.

"What the hell you want here, boy?" Coffin asked harshly. He had been getting to a point where he was over the hot fire of rage, and into a state where the hate would stay with him always, simmer slowly below the surface, ready for release when he wanted it released. Now Davenport was jeopardizing that delicate balance of emotions. "I thought I told you to get your ass away from Madison and keep it away."

"You did." Davenport looked like he had just swallowed a horseshoe. "I did. I wanted to. I . . ."

Coffin sighed. "Just tell it, dammit."

"I skedaddled out of here, but I didn't have no money, no nothin'. Only thing I could think of doin' was gettin' to Virginia City. I was hopin' maybe I could get a grubstake there. I took my horse and headed there, but Cady and Hugh stopped me about halfway. They blindfolded me and took me somewhere. Crown was there. They kept me there for a day or two, then took me out, blindfolded again. When they took it off, I wasn't far from here. Crown told me to find you and deliver this." Davenport held out a piece of paper as if it were a skunk.

Coffin took the paper and unfolded it. He read it, tight-lipped. Then he looked up at Davenport. "You got any money, boy?" he asked.

"No. No, sir."

"You still got your horse?"

"Yessir. That, the saddle, and the clothes I'm wearin' are all I got in this world."

Coffin reached into his pockets and pulled out some cash. He counted out several bills and put the rest away. He rolled up the money he had in hand, and tossed it at Davenport.

The young man caught it, counted it, and his eyes got wide. "A hundred dollars?" he said in wonder. "That's more money than I ever seen at one time."

"After all those stages you held up?"

"I didn't hold up that many, and whenever there was big money around, I never got to touch it."

"Take that money and go buy yourself some new duds, get a good meal. No whiskey. Then you get on that horse, and you ride the hell out of Madison. It'd be best if you were to leave Montana Territory. I see you again, I'll kill you."

"Yessir." He spun and went to the door. Then he stopped and looked back. "Thank you, Marshal," he said solemnly.

Coffin nodded, wondering why he wanted to be so helpful toward Davenport. He supposed it was some need in him to prevent someone else young like him getting shoved into a life of guns, blood, and death.

With another sigh, Coffin rose and left the office. He walked to Pembroke's house and let himself in. "Enoch," he called out. "You awake?"

"Come on up, Joe."

Coffin went up the stairs and into Pembroke's room. He dropped the note on Pembroke's lap.

Pembroke glanced at him in surprise, then picked up the paper and read it. "You going to meet them?"

"Of course."

"I doubt they'll stick to what they said."

"What? About just the two of 'em comin'?"

Pembroke nodded.

"Hell, I know Crown, Merkle, and Vickers are together. It might be all that come, but they might hire some other boys."

"This is plain foolish, Joe," Pembroke said, slapping the note against his blankets. "Take off. Get the hell out of here. Those bastards can't do much more to me than's already been done."

"They have to pay."

"Then set an ambush for them. Take one of the girl's rooms over at the Pittsburgh."

Coffin shook his head. "As devious as those bastards are, they might have help in town. Word got to 'em that I was set to bushwhack 'em might cause trouble. Even worse, if I ain't out there, they're liable to set on some innocent people."

"Get some help."

"From who? You're all stove up. Beryl's gone. Hell, there ain't no one else in town I'd trust to go head to head with hard-ass outlaws. No, it's best I meet 'em alone."

"You better get some rest, then." Pembroke sounded done in.

Coffin stopped at the Pittsburgh, had two shots of rye, and two glasses of beer. He fended off curious—well, he considered them plain nosy—people with their questions, and accepted their words welcoming him back into town.

Afterward, he went to Blake's Hotel, which had kept his room open for him. He was asleep almost as soon as he laid down.

Chapter Thirty-seven

Dawn was cracking on what appeared to be a beautiful day. The temperature was just cool enough to make a body feel alive; the light brushing of the wind was refreshing; the eastern sky tinged with a perfect red.

Coffin walked to the office and leaned against the door jamb, waiting. Then he saw them. He counted seven of them, riding in from the east. They stopped at Blake's and tied their horses off, then they marched up President Street as if they owned it.

Coffin flipped his cigarette away and stepped off the boardwalk. He faced east, toward the men and stood. He recognized Merkle, Vickers, and Chris Baker, Crown's store clerk. He assumed the distinguished-looking middle-aged man was Giles Crown. The other three he did not know. Not that it mattered.

The seven finally stopped just past Third Street, maybe seventy-five feet from Coffin. With a shrug, he moved toward them a little. As he passed the corner of Crenshaw's Pharmacy, someone stepped out of the alley. Coffin whirled, hand going for a pistol. Then he realized it was Pembroke.

The two stared at each other for a few moments. "I'm comin' along, Joe," Pembroke said softly. "This's my fight as much as it's yours."

Coffin nodded. Pembroke shifted the scattergun in his hands, and then the two moved slowly down the street, as did the seven other men. They all stopped with about thirty feet separating them.

"You've caused me a lot of trouble, Marshal Coffin," the middle-aged man said.

"You'd be Giles Crown?" Coffin asked.

"I would." He paused, a seemingly reasonable man. "And it's past time that you paid for all the annoyances you've caused me and my fellows."

"Eat shit, Crown," Coffin said flatly. "You're a murderin' bunch of scum and should—goddammit, will—be brought to account for your crimes."

"And I suppose you," Crown laughed, "and the portly old sheriff there are going to administer this justice." His companions picked up the sign from their leader and laughed, too.

Coffin's hand began rotating slowly on his stomach, between his gunbelt and shoulder rig. "Yes," he said flatly.

"That's interesting, Marshal. Yes, very interesting. You law dogs are certainly an interesting breed."

"Joe, I can't stand to hear any more of this bullshit," Pembroke said. "Let's get this over with."

Coffin's hand stopped moving. Then it moved upward until it hit the badge. He pulled it off and threw it in the dirt.

Pembroke, watching him, smiled a little and then did the same. They nodded at each other. Then both turned toward the enemy and began firing. Pembroke's two shotgun blasts opened things up. By the time that was done, Coffin had a Remington in each hand and was firing smoothly.

The scattergun blasts had surprised Crown and the others, and it took them a moment to get into action. By then, Vickers was down, as was one of the unknown gunmen, hit by buckshot.

Coffin fired at Merkle and Crown first. He got Crown, knocking him down. The outlaw leader was not dead, but he was out of commission for a while though. Merkle, however, had flung himself to the side, and ducked behind a water trough.

Pembroke dropped the shotgun and grabbed his pistol. He knew, in a peripheral sort of way, that the outlaws didn't consider him all that dangerous. All of them seemed to be concentrating their fire in Coffin's direction. Pembroke fired slowly and evenly. By the time he had emptied the big Colt, Chris Baker and the two other unidentified outlaws were down.

Pembroke dropped the empty pistol and went for the spare he had tucked into the waistband of his pants. Then a bullet hit him in the right leg. He went down, landing heavily on his shoulder and chest. The pain in his older wounds flared up hot and strong. He groaned, without realizing he was doing it.

Coffin emptied the two Remingtons, hitting Crown several more times, killing him. He had seen the last two unidentified outlaws go down, but they still had some life in them, so he made sure he picked them off.

Then he felt a burning, massive punch low down on the side of the abdomen. It spun him and knocked him down. "Shit," he groaned. He half pushed himself up and fired one more shot, as Merkle poked his head around the trough. The shot missed, but Merkle ducked behind the trough, giving Coffin enough time to get to his feet and stagger toward the side of the street Merkle was on.

He was hit again, as a bullet ripped through the flesh on his left thigh. But he could see, through the pall of gunsmoke, that Merkle was frantically trying to reload.

Coffin grinned viciously and hobbled that way. As he moved he put the Remingtons into the holsters and drew one of the Colts.

He stopped three feet from Merkle. "Your time's up, boy," he said quietly. "Get up."

Merkle complied, figuring that Coffin was planning to arrest him. That almost pleased him. It wasn't good, but at least there might be a chance to break out of jail.

Coffin shot Merkle in the right forearm.

"Jesus," Merkle said, eyes widening. "What the hell's wrong with you, Marshal?"

"I ain't a goddamn marshal no more." He shot Merkle in the other arm.

"Goddamn. Son of a bitch."

In quick succession, Coffin shot Merkle in the abdomen, low down; and then both legs. With the last shot in the Colt, he shot Merkle in the left leg again, this time hitting the femoral artery.

Coffin put the pistol away. He turned and took two steps before he fell.

It took Coffin quite a while to recover. By the time he was able to get around reasonably well, winter was on them, and he knew it would be foolish to leave Madison. So he sat out the winter in the house with Pembroke. Once they started getting better, they spent a fair amount of time in the Pittsburgh Saloon—both downstairs at the bar and upstairs in the fancy rooms.

Both men had ignored the many pleas of town officials to take up badges again.

Spring finally arrived, and Coffin saddled his horse. Pembroke hadn't yet made up his mind what he wanted to do, so he was staying in Madison for the time being.

"Now don't you go pinning on no law badge anytime

soon, my friend," Pembroke told him just after Coffin had climbed into the saddle.

Coffin chuckled a little. "You'll be a grandmother before I ever put a badge on again," Coffin said.

They shook hands, and Coffin rode slowly out of Madison.

FOLLOW THE SEVENTH CARRIER

TRIAL OF THE SEVENTH CARRIER (3213, $3.95)
The enemies of freedom are on the verge of dominating the world with oil blackmail and the threat of poison gas attack. *Yonaga*'s officers lay desperate plans to strike back. Leading a ragtag fleet of revamped destroyers and a single antique WWII submarine, the great carrier must charge into a sea of blood and death in what becomes the greatest trial of the Seventh Carrier.

REVENGE OF THE SEVENTH CARRIER (3631, $3.99)
With the help of an American carrier, *Yonaga* sails vast distances to launch a desperate surprise attack on the enemy's poison gas works. But a spy is at work. The enemy seems to know too much and a bloody battle is fought. Filled with murderous rage, *Yonaga*'s officers exact a terrible revenge.

ORDEAL OF THE SEVENTH CARRIER (3932, $3.99)
Even as the Libyan madman calls for peaceful negotiations, an Arab battle group steams toward the shores of Japan. With good men from all over the world flocking to her colors, *Yonaga* prepares to give battle. The two forces clash off the island of Iwo Jima where it is carrier against carrier in a duel to the death—and *Yonaga,* sustaining severe damage, endures its bloodiest ordeal in the fight for freedom's cause.

*

Other Zebra Books by Peter Albano

THE YOUNG DRAGONS (3904, $4.99)
It is June 25, 1944. American forces attack the island of Saipan. Two young fighting men on opposite sides, Michael Carpelli and Takeo Nakamura, meet in the flaming hell of battle that will inevitably bring them face-to-face in a final fight to the death. Here is the epic battle that decided the war against Japan as told by a man who was there.

THE ONLY ALTERNATIVE IS ANNIHILATION . . .

RICHARD P. HENRICK

BENEATH THE SILENT SEA (3167, $4.50)
The Red Dragon, Communist China's advanced ballistic missile-carrying submarine embarks on the most sinister mission in human history: to attack the U.S. and Soviet Union simultaneously. Soon, the Russian *Barkal,* with its planned attack on a single U.S. submarine is about unwittingly to aid in the destruction of all mankind!

COUNTERFORCE (3025, $4.50)
In the silent deep, the chase is on to save a world from destruction. A single Russian submarine moves on a silent and sinister course for American shores. The men aboard the U.S.S. *Triton* must search for and destroy the Soviet killer submarine as an unsuspecting world races for the apocalypse.

THE GOLDEN U-BOAT (3386, $4.95)
In the closing hours of World War II, a German U-boat sank below the North Sea carrying the Nazis' last hope to win the war. Now, a fugitive SS officer has salvaged the deadly cargo in an attempt to resurrect the Third Reich. As the USS *Cheyenne* passed through, its sonar picked up the hostile presence and another threat in the form of a Russian sub!

THE PHOENIX ODYSSEY (2858, $4.50)
All communications to the USS *Phoenix* suddenly and mysteriously vanish. Even the urgent message from the president cancelling the War Alert is not received and in six short hours the *Phoenix* will unleash its nuclear arsenal against the Russian mainland. . . .

SILENT WARRIORS (3026, $4.50)
The Red Star, Russia's newest, most technologically advanced submarine, outclasses anything in the U.S. fleet. But when the captain opens his sealed orders 24 hours early, he's staggered to read that he's to spearhead a massive nuclear first strike against the Americans!

Available wherever paperbacks are sold, or order direct from the Publisher. Send cover price plus 50¢ per copy for mailing and handling to Zebra Books, Dept. 4228, 475 Park Avenue South, New York, N.Y. 10016. Residents of New York and Tennessee must include sales tax. DO NOT SEND CASH. For a free Zebra/Pinnacle catalog please write to the above address.